# 100 Souls

**Published by Iron & Ink Press** – Kelley, IA www.ironandinkpress.com

Cover design by Iron and Ink Press

**ISBN: 979-8-9943886-0-0**

First Edition: December 2025
Printed in the United States of America

# 100 Souls

Katie Espinoza

*This book is dedicated to my mom, Dalene O'Brien, for always inspiring me to do things for others.*

*And to my son, Eli. Remember that your physical heart may have limitations, but your "heart" has zero.*

*To the rest of my family, for supporting me in my crazy ideas and endeavors.*

# 1.

# Eli

"Whoever dwells in the shelter of the Most High will rest in the shadow of the Almighty. I will say of the LORD, 'He is my refuge and my fortress, my God, in whom I trust.'" read the pastor at my mother's funeral. Her favorite verse; Psalm 91. I looked down at my hands, they were clammy, and I could feel a flash of warmth coming across me as though I had a fever. Looking up towards the altar that was filled with sunflowers, eyes foggy with tears, and a burning lump in the back of my throat as I tried to remain strong. The pastor leading everyone in the 'Lord's Prayer', my voice quivering as I recited the memorized words. A numbness took over as I stood up.

*Move legs.*
*Move.*

My legs shakily began to move as I had directed them as I went to gather the urn of my mother's ashes and walk them back down the aisle. Out the double oak doors with beautiful ornate details that were hand carved into them and to the polished black hearse that awaited them. Outside it was warm for a fall day, but when the breeze swirled around me, I felt a chill rise throughout my body. The soft crackle of fallen leaves brushing across the pavement as they shifted with the wind. I slowly handed my

1

mother's urn to the Funeral Service Coordinator; hands not wanting to open and release the it – a sense of finality that made my hands wrench tighter as he tried to take the urn from me. I stared at the engravings on the silver urn as I grasped tighter. Sunflowers etched the outer rim and below it inscribed into the pewter:

*Dalene Louise Byrne*
*Loving Mother and Wife*
*"I shall fear no evil for Thou*
*art with me"*
*March 10, 1970 – October 20, 2022*

My eyes were like a magnifying glass on the words and etchings. Everything else in my peripherals was a blur. Thinking that if I stared long enough maybe the urn would turn into my mother's sweet, angelic face. That all of this would be a horrible nightmare. The doctors ruled my mother's death as a heart attack. I just couldn't understand it – she always took really good care of herself. She ate right, she tried to exercise, and there was no family history of heart attacks. *This must be a nightmare, right?* I would wake up to find my mother brushing my dirty-blonde bangs out of my face, kissing my forehead; whispering that it would be alright.

*Any minute now.*
*Wake Up.*
*Come on, Eli, wake Up.*

A jerk of reality as the coordinator spoke softly to me, "Mr. Byrnes. Mr. Byrnes, are you alright?"
I blinked my eyes a few times to bring the world around me back into focus. "Sorry," I cleared my throat, "yes." I gently released the tension of my fingers. "I'm sorry."
He glanced up at me as he took over the weight of the urn with both of his hands, "It's quite alright sir. This is a difficult day."
I lifted my head and nodded.

2

My red Toyota Corolla was parked behind the hearse ready to fall into procession. I walked back towards it, opened the driver's door, unbuttoned my suit jacket and slid into the dark leather interior. I sat there for a moment and exhaled, both hands on the steering wheel. I could hear my heart thudding in my chest, the pressure rising within me. The dread coming towards the surface.

*Breathe.*
*Gain control.*
*Relax.*

I started the motor and the burned disc I had made of my mother's favorite songs began to cycle in the disc player. As the hearse in front of me began to pull forward "A Bushel and a Peck" amplified out of the speakers. The pressure I had felt prior fully came to the surface now. Tears streaming down my face, making audible sobs. Ugly crying, as teenagers called it now a days, but I didn't care. The release of pressure was welcomed and the lump in my throat slowly loosened as I let all the sorrow out. This song was my mom and I's favorite. She and I used to spin around our small single-story farmhouse singing at the top of our lungs to this song. At night she would sing it softly in my ear as I would try and fall asleep, pulling me into her soft embrace. My father was on the road a lot as a truck driver. He passed away shortly after I was born in a snowstorm. A Dodge Ram thought they were invincible and were driving much too fast for the weather conditions. They cut my father off and lost control as they made the transition between lanes. My father had no choice but to try and swerve. His trailer sliding around the side of him; jackknifing his truck and eventually turning on to its side. The air bag did not deploy as it should have, and by the time the police and medical staff were able to get through the carnage that ensued behind him and the Dodge, it was too late. It became a sixty-seven-car pile-up on the freeway and took over twelve hours to clear. The driver of the Dodge walked away from the accident unscathed by his poor decisions.

The hearse had moved forward and stopped a little way ahead when it realized I was not following immediately. As I pushed the gas pedal and moved forward it began to creep forward as well almost as if it were a magnet repelling another. We began to move a little quicker as we drove the eight miles from the church to the graveside, cars pulling off as the procession passed by them. Most of them distracted by something on their phones or fiddling with their radios, a few looking towards us as we passed by. I gazed out the open window at the line of trees – the melodic whoosh of each as we passed it. The leaves were beginning to change; prepossessing shades of red, oranges and yellows fluidly creating a sea of fall foliage. As we neared the cemetery the lump that had dispersed in my throat previously quickly regained momentum. A force to be reckoned with. I felt the dried tears on my face begin to burn as my face turned red with the anxiety rising again within me. I could see the blue tent over where my mother would be laid to rest for eternity – a place right next to my father.

The hearse pulled off to the side of the road near the blue tent, and I pulled in line behind them leaving enough of a gap for them to open their back hatch door. I took another moment to regain my composure as my gaze observed the methodical movements of the coordinator. My thoughts, as I watched him, went to wondering why he chose this profession. Was it of his own volition – a calling maybe? Or could it be a family business that he grew up in and was designated to take over as he grew older. Maybe it was the only position available that would give him a job at the time. Either way I knew I would never be capable to do what this man before me did on a daily basis. So much sorrow, anguish, despair filling the air of each day. I then stopped appreciating the fact that there were those in the world who took on these emotionally difficult positions head on, with compassion and sympathy. Presumably it is as sincere as they can be without knowing your loved one personally and without giving so much of themselves to each death that they are overcome by emotion and get burnt out. I continued to watch as he opened the back hatch and, with his white gloves on, slowly and carefully removed my mother's urn from the back of the hearse. He walked slowly over to the blue tent and placed my mother's urn on a lace doily that was already placed on the table underneath; some of the sunflowers from the altar placed on either side. Another coordinator had loaded a couple of the arrangements into another funeral home's vehicle and brought them over ahead of the procession. He now stood next to the table, arms back behind him, hands intertwining. The coordinator who had placed the urn on the table now stood on the opposite side standing in the same position. I slowly gathered myself, opened the car door and slid out into the fresh crisp fall air. The breeze making my hair dance with it as if it were a puppet and the wind a puppeteer. I re-buttoned my jacket, brushed off the front of myself, shut the car door and began walking towards the tent. A 'reserved' seat sat in the very front for me. I saw the small hole dug into the ground behind the slant marker embedded in the ground. My father and mother's names already engraved in the stone, and all their information other than my mother's date of death, which would be engraved in the next few weeks. My mom had her information put on the stone when my father had passed so that when she did pass one day, I wouldn't have to worry about it. We both just didn't realize how soon that truly would be. I unbuttoned my jacket again and sat down on the cloth covered folding chair. I looked down at the stone in the ground again:

*Allen Walker Byrnes*
*November 20, 1969 – December 5, 2002*
*Devoted Husband and Father*
*Always in our Hearts*

*Dalene Louise Byrnes*
*March 10, 1970 –*
*Loving Wife and Mother*
*Always in our Hearts*

I read those words over, and over, again. Someone nearby was burning leaves; I could smell the fragrant aroma as it wafted around me, but it was quickly replaced by the intense smell of lilacs and baby powder: *Aunt Patsy*. She had worn the same perfume for as long as I could remember, more like bathed in it, and was a religious baby powder user. She had one of those industrial sized bottles of baby powder, the kind you find at a Sam's Club or Costco, by her back door so that whenever she returned home, she would douse each shoe – so much so that when she would put them back on powder would 'poof' out of the holes in her shoes and dust the floor around them. Often when you hugged her you wound up with baby powder on your clothes and the smell of lilacs stuck in your nostrils for the next forty-eight hours after one of the dreaded Patsy hugs. Everyone would try and walk in the opposite direction to avoid her hugs. She was my dad's sister but kept involved in my life as I grew up. She was short and plump and had auburn wavy hair that was cut just past shoulder length. Aunt Patsy typically wore it in a ponytail or braid. She had jet green eyes that seemed to be swallowed in her plump face – more so now than I remembered. She was a very kind woman, just intense in personality… and smell. She came and sat down next to me and wrapped her pudgy arms around my shoulders.

"How ya doin' kid?" she asked sorrowfully.
"I'm hanging in there," I tried to make the words sound as truthful as possible, even though I was completely falling apart.
She scrunched up her mouth and raised one eyebrow at me in disapproval. Her eyes were red and puffy probably as much as mine were.
"Boy, I'm no fool," she said in her intense unwavering voice, "it's okay to not be okay."
"I know Aunt Patsy. I'm not doing great, but I'm trying to... be okay...." my voice faltered and trailed off.
She nodded, "you have that Byrnes blood; stubborn Irishman."
I gave her a half smile and nodded in return.

Others filled in around us, some giving their condolences as they were seated, others in silence.

The pastor asked for all of us to bow our heads, "Eternal rest grant unto them, O Lord, and let perpetual light shine upon them. May the souls of all the faithful departed, through the mercy of God, rest in peace." He went on to talk about God's plan for all of us and how my mother was all a part of that plan. The pastor gestured to me and invited me up to help place my mother's urn into the ground. As I grasped the urn it was cold from the brisk wind. *Cold.* Absolutely a word I would never have used for my mother. I held it to my chest and hugged it as I knelt to the ground. The grass brittle under my knees, cold and damp, but it didn't affect me. I sat there by the hole in the ground, fresh earth laid next to the hole. A worm wriggled in the small pile, probably feeling unnerved by his home being destroyed around him. I stared for a while longer as it writhed through the soil until he was buried once more. I continued hugging the urn, hoping that it would turn into my mom's arms around me. I finally gained the courage to slowly bring the urn away from my body and place it gently, slowly into the ground. I grasped a handful of the loose dirt and sprinkled it over the urn. My aunt Patsy had come up behind me and placed her podgy hand on my shoulder. With her other hand she gave me a small bouquet of the sunflowers to place in the vase affixed to my mother's side of the slant marker. As I knelt there arranging the flowers in the vase several bright red leaves danced from the large maple tree behind my parent's stone, twirling and flitting down to the ground around me. I stood up and plucked the dried grass pieces off my suit pants. The pastor continued and finished with a prayer along with a silent prayer. As the service ended some gathered to wait to talk to me while others headed to their cars to return home. Several people, that I didn't know well, came up to me and introduced themselves, said their condolences and then headed on their way.

The last person to come talk to me before I left was a man named Ray Montgomery. He was an Army Veteran. He stood tall, about 6'5" I assumed with me being roughly 6'1", and he was stoic. His face weathered with age and experiences, and scruffy from not shaving in some time, it made him look older than he probably was. Presumably at one time his hair had been jet black but now it was speckled with gray. His hazel eyes glossy with tears. He was wearing a modest suit with a black watch on his wrist – glass cracked, no wedding band, black dress shoes that were cracking around the edges dawning his feet. He reached his callused hand out towards me.

"Ray Montgomery," he shook my hand, "It is really nice to meet you, Sir," he said roughly.
I shook his hand, "you as well. How did you know my mother?"
"You were just a tiny guy when we met, probably about two years old, but your mother... she saved my life." I didn't understand what he meant by "save", but I assumed it had something to do with her work before I was born. She had been a social worker prior to staying home with me and had continued to help occasionally after.

He carried on, "anyway, after she saved my life, I didn't take my second chance for granted. I created a chain of transitional facilities for veterans that provide medical, drug and alcohol rehabilitation, gives basic necessities along with their own room and bathroom, but we have a communal kitchen area to work on cooking skills together, therapy, resume building, etc etc. I teach life skills, coping and resilience classes at these facilities. I wouldn't have been able to do it without your mother."
"Wow... I didn't realize." I stumbled over the words.
"She was an angel here on this Earth," he stated without any hesitation, "I owe her everything." He handed me a business card: *Raymond Montgomery Second Chance 4 Veterans*. His address, email and phone number were also listed and underneath everything was: '*A second chance can give anyone the hope to carry on*'. "If you ever need anything son, please feel free to reach out." He extended his hand once more. I shook it and tears began rolling down his face as he turned to walk to his car.

I assisted the Funeral Coordinators loading the floral arrangements back into the hearse. They were going to deliver them back to the church for their upcoming services. Mom would have wanted it that way. I got back into my car and as I sat there thinking about the interaction with Mr. Montgomery, I couldn't help but wonder more about him. I grabbed my phone, unlocked it and typed into Google 'Raymond Montgomery'. His face immediately populated my screen. A news article dated this summer was the first link and I clicked on it:

*Mr. Raymond Montgomery began his mission of giving Veterans a second chance at life after a mysterious woman gave him a second chance at living. He took his second chance at life and created an ever-growing chain of residential transition homes for Veterans to gain the help they need to get back into society.*

I skimmed through it more and they had asked him about his black watch that I saw him wearing with the cracked glass:

*We asked Mr. Montgomery about why he wears a black watch with a cracked face and his response is that it reminds him of where he came, "I was broken, living on the streets, didn't care about life anymore, but instead of being thrown out I was saved. This watch was in battle with me. It was there when I received my Traumatic Brain Injury and my Post Traumatic Stress. This watch may look a little rough, but it gives its all every day because it was given a second chance; just like me."*

It also talked about his lifestyle:

*We also asked Mr. Montgomery why he chose to dress so modestly when he was so successful in his life. He stated, "I get asked this quite often and I always tell people that money and material items isn't what provides me joy in this world – wearing a nice suit isn't what I want to be remembered for. I live comfortably, but modestly, because I'd rather give the profits from my company back to the company for new programs to assist veterans. Or give the profits to other organizations striving to make a difference in someone's life. Nice clothes, house, car none of that is a legacy that will be carried on, and none of it is helping anyone – to include myself. These facilities, however, they are a legacy, and they are touching so many lives."*

9

He seemed genuine. Not arrogant or greedy like so many others would be in his position, and my mother had a big part in this. She was a small pebble in a pond, and the ripples touched the outer banks.

I headed back to my mother's house. I was in the process of emptying my dormitory and moving back into her home – my childhood home. I only had one more year to get my degree, and I was going to see if I could finish my degree online. I just couldn't sell the house, at least not yet.

As I turned onto the gravel road, I thought back to all the times I rode my bike down this road – several times hitting gravel just right and skidding out. Still have some scars from it, but mom would always run over to me, scoop me up and ask if I was alright. When I would say I was she would lift my bike up and say, 'Good because I don't plan on having any more children so you can't go messing with my perfection.' She would chuckle and I'd roll my eyes and laugh. Mom jokes always and forever with her. I reached the edge of the driveway and stopped to grab the mail before turning in. The gravel driveway was lined with cherry blossoms, one of mom's favorites. It was a long driveway that led up to an attached one stall garage.

My mom's car was still parked inside of it. I parked on the gravel outside of the garage door, grabbed the mail off the passenger seat and got out. The front door was oak. Mom had found it at an antique store. It was a door I imagined would have been on an old Victorian style home. A large vertical oval window from the top to bottom and ornate details around it and the edges of the door. The doorknob was original as well and my mother had a key remade for it. The doorknob itself was brass and had an intricate design in the handle. I went inside the small foyer where my mom and I had sat for hours one day and done a penny floor. Thousands of pennies in rows that we epoxied over when we were done. It held up well over the decades. There was a small closet to the right for coats and such. I walked into the

10

kitchen which was on the right beyond the foyer. The remainder of the home had original hardwood floors that had been sanded down and redone to regain their former glory. In the center of the kitchen was an island – an old grocery counter from a farm store that closed in town. It had twenty some small drawers on one side with the original pull handles, and on the opposite side it had advertisements and different signage for fruits, vegetables, and other items the store sold. My mom had redone the top awhile back with butcher block so she could avoid the dry rot getting into food. She tried to preserve it the best she could before she finally gave in. It looked sleek and a nice focal point of the kitchen now; history of the town, it's past. I set the mail on the counter when something caught my eye. My mother's handwriting. I stopped, moved the letters off the top, and saw a letter addressed to me with my mother's beautiful cursive handwriting. The loops moved effortlessly from word to word. I picked it up and gently opened the flap on the back. Inside was a single sheet of notebook paper:

*My Dearest Elijah – I want you to know first and foremost how much I love you. You are such a gift, and I couldn't be prouder of the man you have become. I will be watching over you always. I want you to know a few things that I didn't feel were appropriate to discuss in our final moments. Simple things really, but important.*

*1.    The lock box key is in the top right drawer of the desk in my office. In there you will find all my ID's, copy of my will (if our lawyer Bert Warner didn't already give you one), and other important documentation for the house, the car, etc.*

*2.    I have a safety deposit box at the bank in town, and the key is in the lock box I mentioned above. Money that I had saved to one day take us on our 'Tour de Overseas', along with the map and plan we had for our trip. Please use this money as you see fit now – I'm sorry that we will never be able to go on this trip together.*

11

*3.   Your Pappy always told me to tell the man of the house where the coupon drawer is – although I think you know exactly where it is – I always thought it was funny that Pappy used to say it. Our coupon drawer is on the top left of the island drawers.*

*4.   There is something I really want you to have, but I didn't know the best time to give it to you. It is on the bookshelf in my office. It is a brown leather-bound journal. It looks a little worn compared to the other books around it, but it just means it has good history. I hope it will help to answer several of the questions that you may have.*

*Lastly, and I know this will come off as a mom Cliche, but there is just no other way to put it. You make me so proud, beyond words. You truly are a gift from God. Continue to be the gentleman you are, kind, compassionate, loving. You will go so far in this world. I love you more than words can ever resonate.*

*I love you baby boy,*
*Mama*

I had to re-read it four or five times before I was able to read it to its entirety. Several tear stains now dot the notebook paper. I set the paper back down onto the island. I wanted to go find the journal she spoke of. I had to know what it was.

*Why didn't she feel comfortable giving it to me before she passed? If it was important enough to put into this letter...*

I went to the other end of the kitchen and out the door on the opposite side. It led into a hallway – if you go right it led to my mother's bedroom and a bathroom next door, left led to a separate hall back to the living room and to the two other bedrooms. The bedroom closest to my mother's room was mine, then the office was at the far end. There was also a built-in linen closet in the hallway. I walked down to the other end of the hall to her office, flipped the light switch on and went over to her bookshelf. It was another antique, which pretty much described

her decorating style. She loved saving things from the past –
bringing their history back to life. *"I'm giving them a second
chance at life"* she always used to say. The bookshelf was from a
one room schoolhouse made from barn wood and square nails. I
always thought that maybe it was made by the older schoolboys
in a shop class or by a local farmer donating it to the school. Next
to the bookshelf hung a coloring that I had always admired. It had
a little tag in the bottom corner that read: *My Future, by Art
McGavin.* I searched the shelves and quickly spotted the brown
leather-bound journal. She was right it was a bit rough around the
edges, but it was gorgeous. It had a gold page marker attached to
the spine. It was tucked inside the front page. My mother had a
Victorian Era chaise lounge in her office with a teal-colored
velvet fabric. I sat down and opened the cover. In my mother's
beautiful script handwriting I read *'100 Souls'*.

# 2.

December 7<sup>th</sup>, 2003: I've woken up several nights over the past three months with the same recurring dream. Normally I don't think much of my dreams, and I rarely dwell on them. I am not one to keep a dream journal or Google 'what does my dream mean'. There is nothing wrong with doing so of course, but that has never been an interest to me. This is one of those dreams that is so realistic when you wake up it seems like it happened. It feels like reality, and you take a few minutes to figure out if it is or not. This dream begins with me sleeping and having a dream. I know that it sounds like a fun house with mirrors all around and when you look in one mirror you see yourself a million times. It begins with me waking up and my back feels raw and sore, so much so that I even selected a sports bra for the day instead of the normal underwire.

For a while I ignored it thinking I slept funny or maybe my back is just dry because of the cold weather. As the morning goes on my back begins to feel as though I am being marked with a branding iron. I go to my bedroom, and the inner part of my closet door houses a full-length mirror that hangs off the back of it. I lift my shirt and look over my shoulder. I stand there staring in disbelief; my body frozen in shock and terror. I have black tick marks all over my back. You know the ones that you score four marks and the fifth goes over the top. My vision was going fuzzy from staring too long. I blinked my eyes a few times to regain focus. I wanted to know how many for sure were there. As if my body was possessed, I ran to the bathroom to grab my handled mirror. My body uncontrollably taking over ran back to the closet mirror. I took my shirt and sports bra off to gain a better look. I held the hand-held mirror in front of me and slightly off to the right. I counted at least six times before I could officially confirm that it was indeed one-hundred tick marks. I sank to my knees in disbelief. My mind went frantic with thoughts.

*How could this happen?*
*How could someone tattoo me in my sleep without me knowing?*
*Had I been drugged somehow?*
*If I were drugged, why would they only tattoo one hundred tick marks... why not steal things as well?*
*What was the goal of this?*

After I regained some composure, I realized that the home phone was ringing. I waited for the answering machine to pick it up as I redressed myself. The phone just kept ringing and ringing uncontrollably, and at this point it seems to be getting louder and louder. *Can a phone ring aggressively?* I walked over to it; nervous to pick up the receiver. My hand shook violently, and I felt a pit in my stomach that made me feel nauseous.

My knees were weak, and I felt as though they wouldn't hold me up any longer. I placed my hand on the receiver but didn't pick it up. It continued to ring violently, getting louder with every ring. My head began to throb. I slowly picked up the receiver. It shook intensely in my hand as I brought it toward my ear. A man's voice began speaking to me, and at this point my knees could no longer hold me and gave way. I fell to them, now grasping the receiver with both hands to keep it steady against my ear. The man's voice was deep, calm, and smooth and had no remarkable accent. He spoke in a 'matter of fact' tone, "Hello Dalene, my name is Azariah. I must speak to you immediately.

Please meet me at the Corner Cafe in one hour. I will have the answers you seek." The phone clicks and the dial tone sound in my ear – and then I awaken. I never get to the point of going to meet Azariah. I have done some research on his name though, as it sounded vaguely familiar. His name means 'Helped by God'. He is present in the Bible.

*I wish I knew what this dream meant.*

December 8, 2003: I think I am going insane. I am trying so hard to wake up, but nothing seems to bring me back to reality. Maybe I'm in a coma? I woke up this morning and instead of coming out of the dream I was living it. My back was raw and sore when I woke up. I didn't even get dressed before running over to the mirror. I raised up my night shirt and sure enough there they were. I grabbed my hand-held mirror from the bathroom and tugged my night shirt over my head clumsily. I went back to the full-length mirror and counted.

*100.*

I felt like vomiting. Eli would be awake soon and I needed to compose myself. I needed to get a grip.
I ran back to the bathroom and jumped into the shower, turning on the cold water.

*Still living this dream.*

I pinched myself.

*Still living this dream.*

I slapped myself across the face (a little harder than I intended).

*Still living this dream.*

I began getting dressed, because regardless of whatever

16

these tick marks meant, if I was actually living in this dream and not waking up two things would happen. 1. the phone will ring and Azariah should instruct me to meet him at the Corner Cafe. 2. Eli would be awake and want breakfast.

I pulled my shirt over my head and tousled my hair up into a bun. I walked quickly to the kitchen where I began preparing breakfast. I shakily cut up a pumpkin muffin I had made the day prior and quartered pieces of a banana for Eli. I went to wake him up. I felt anxiety rush over me, tense, jittery. Eli was standing up in his crib babbling and when he saw me a huge smile lit up his chubby cheeks. His bright blue eyes, and blondish hair shone in the sunlight of the breaking day. His little toddler hands reached up towards me as I approached wanting me to pick him up. I gently raised him out of bed and held him tight and gave him a kiss on his forehead. He laid his head on my shoulder. I walked back towards the living room to change him for the day and he could eat.

As I pulled his Mickey Mouse shirt on over his head the phone rang. I jumped; alarmed. I realized after I shouldn't be, I mean I was expecting this after all. I had distracted myself enough with Eli that I had blanked it from my mind momentarily. I stood up, picked up Eli and put him in his highchair quickly for him to be able to start breakfast. I grabbed the phone off the wall and pressed the answer button.

"Hello," I said with a quiver in my voice.
That same deep, calm, smooth voice that I had heard repeatedly replied, "Hello Dalene, my name is Azariah. I must speak to you immediately. Please meet me at the Corner Cafe in one hour. I will have the answers you seek."
After the initial shock wore off, I stumbled out the words, "I will have my son with me, is that alright?"
"Of course. See you both in one hour."

Next thing I heard was the dial tone in my ear. I stood there for a moment with the phone up to my ear; frozen. The dial tone

17

provided some sort of comfort for me as I collected myself. I slowly put the phone back on its base on the wall and turned around to see Eli grasping a piece of pumpkin muffin in one hand and chasing a slice of banana around his tray with the other. He looked up at me and smiled, "mama," he said. "'nana."
"Is your banana getting the best of you, bud." I replied.

I helped him scoop it up so he could grasp it. He quickly smashed it into his mouth. I looked up at the wall clock: *8:05am.* I went and poured myself a cup of coffee. The aroma wisped up through the air with the steam from the cup, Kona. I sipped the cup while watching Eli eat his breakfast; the coffee warmed my mouth and throat and sent a chill up my spine. I visibly shook with the chill and Eli looked at me with a furrowed brow, pondering in his little mind if I was okay.
"Mama's okay buddy," I said smiling at him. That seemed to suffice because he continued mashing his remaining bananas into his tray.

I set my coffee down and began packing the diaper bag and rounding up things that we needed to go out for an unknown amount of time. It was now 8:30am. I grabbed a wet paper towel and wiped up Eli's tray, hands, face and got most of the banana out of his hair. I put him on the ground, and he toddled over and picked up his blue dump truck, sat down and started rolling it around on the floor. I sat down next to him and slid his boots on. I helped him put his coat, hat, and gloves on. I put my boots and winter gear on, slid the diaper bag over my shoulder and picked Eli up. We walked out the door, got in the car and headed towards the Cozy Cafe.

I opened the door to the Cozy Cafe and the door chime jangled above our heads. I walked in confidently but then realized I had no clue what I was walking in to. The worry, anxiety, fear coursed back through my body. I stood frozen in the doorway a minute, gazing around looking for a middle-aged man. There was an elderly couple in the corner booth drinking coffee, a mother and young daughter peering at the doughnut selection in the glass display, and what appeared to be a businesswoman sitting at the table by the front window drinking a smoothie, typing frantically on a laptop. I grabbed a highchair from the wall, and we sat down at a booth on the opposite wall of the elderly couple. Eli sat in the highchair and played with a toy I had brought on the table. I glanced up at the clock on the wall: *8:55am.*

The time seemed to stand still. Every second seemed to take minutes. A man walked in at 9:00am exactly, but he didn't even look around. He walked straight up to the counter and ordered a coffee and a breakfast sandwich. He paid and then walked to a table in the center of the Cafe and sat down. I studied him for quite some time, watching his movements. He was probably in his late thirties, wavy brown hair, slight bags under his eyes, black square-rimmed glasses, and blue flannel button up under his heavy winter jacket. He pulled a newspaper out from his inner jacket, removed his jacket, and slung it over the back of the chair. He pushed up his glasses on his nose and unfolded his paper to begin reading the front page. The edges of his mouth twitched while he read.

The waitress brought over his coffee and breakfast sandwich, he looked up, smiled, and thanked her. I turned back towards Eli who was busy trying to chase around his toy on the table. I poured out a few Cheerios for him onto a napkin. I looked back up and the man appeared to be frozen. He held his coffee cup midair as if he were about to take a drink but was lost in thought; or about to have a stroke. His eyes looked dull and didn't shine anymore; lifeless. I was about to stand up and go see if he was okay when he suddenly shivered like a chill ran down his spine. His eyes lit up again and he set his coffee cup back on the table, setting his paper down. The man stood up and turned and walked towards Eli and me. He sat down in the booth across from me.

# 3.

I stared at the man across from me. Now that he sat in front of me, he seemed older than his thirties, maybe early forties would be more accurate. Crow's feet around his eyes, and now up close he had speckles of gray across his brown hair. He brought his hand up to his glasses and removed them from his face, rubbing his eyes with the other hand.
"I do not know how this man sees out of these."
I stared at him, mouth agape. There it was, the deep, calm, smooth voice. "Azariah?" I questioned.
"Yes, hello. My apologies as I adjust to this body a moment," he shook his head a bit and rotated his neck. "Alright, I don't have much time in this body, so I need you to listen closely," he said in a very low serious voice.
I nodded my head in agreement. An impulse at that moment.
"None of which I am telling you will be repeated to anyone, and if you don't agree with something I say please let me know and your life will go back to normal immediately and you won't remember any of this."

I sat up in my seat and leaned on the table a little more, "okay."

"The world is in a bad place. It lacks hope, faith, and humanity. God sees this and feels that something needs to be done before the world crumbles. He has chosen twenty people across the world to help restore faith in humanity. These are people who have lost significantly, people that want only the best for others and that will put others first always. People like you. This journey comes with rewards and disadvantages along the way. The 100 marks on your back represent lives of others. God is trusting you to choose who you save, but He will give you suggestions and choices along the way. This journey will take several years to complete. When you find someone that you feel needs a second chance you simply place your hands on them and in your heart and mind pray for them to be cured. You cannot bring anyone back from the dead. The disadvantages of this will be that whatever they were going through..." he paused, "you will too."

"What do you mean?" I asked.

"I mean if someone has cancer, and you decide to cure them you will feel the effects of the cancer. You won't have cancer, but you will feel sick as if you did. This could go on for days depending on the severity of the condition in which the person you save is in. That is why this journey will take you so many years to complete. Your body will need to rest along the way, before saving others. The advantages of this journey are clear. You will be able to help restore humanity and faith to those around you and help others as you so much enjoy doing. You will be taken care of and provided for. You will not have to worry about your home, food, etc. At the very end of your journey, when the last mark on your back is left, we will reward you with something that you have wanted for so long. Something you have dreamed of, prayed for, but it too will come with a cost. Do you have any questions so far?"

"Uh... sorry this is just a lot... I... I don't think so."

"I unfortunately need to know now if you are willing to do this journey or not."

"What if I have questions after you leave?" I asked.

"You pray. You pray about your question, and we will answer."

I stared at him for a moment. I looked at Eli and he looked up at me and smiled. He was so sweet and innocent. What would his mom being sick all the time do to him? Would he understand? Why did God choose me?

"Dalene... I apologize for the shortness of this chat, and my 'to the point' directions, but I really do need an answer," he stated, "I do apologize, I understand this is a monumental decision, but I can't keep this man's body forever, and the longer you think the more time I will need to erase if you choose not to do this journey."
I went with my gut and ended up blurting out, "Yes. Yes, I will do the journey," more loudly than I anticipated.
"That is wonderful news," he smiled. He stood up, "thank you for doing this. You will do wonderful." He walked back towards the table where the man had sat prior, returning the glasses to the man's face that he had removed prior, and sat back down. The man froze again for several moments and then he blinked a few times. He sat there for a moment contemplating, shrugged, and returned to his paper and coffee.

I sat there in a moment of shock myself, also contemplating what had just happened. Unfortunately, I couldn't just shrug and continue. I had so many unanswered questions running through my mind, but none that seemed relevant enough to ask Azariah at the time.

*Will I choose the right people?*
*Will this really bring faith back to humanity?*
*What about the billions of people that would be missed... would changing 2,000 lives over the world really make an impact?*
*How will all this affect Eli?*
*Did I make the right decision?*

I felt deep down that I made the right decision, but my nerves and anxiety rose again. I felt like crying in fear and excitement of the possibility of changing people's lives. For now, I just needed to trust in the Lord and follow his journey.

# 4.

December 24, 2003. Today was the day I saved my first soul. Eli and I were heading out to go to Christmas Eve service. We go to our town's little community church, nothing fancy, but full of love and good people. People that helped take care of Eli and I when my husband passed away. The sanctuary was beautifully decorated with evergreen garland and wreaths; ribbons laced around them and white lights. A Christmas tree decorated with gold and silver ornaments to the right of the altar and an ornate angel topped the tree. White, pink and red poinsettias lined the front of the church's altar.

When we entered, I grabbed a small white candle with a drip base on it. At the end of the Christmas Eve service, we light them as a whole congregation. The service was eloquent and exactly what my soul needed. The sanctuary was dim, and the congregation had their candles all aglow. It was peaceful as we sang 'Silent Night'. There was calm once the song trailed off, and everyone just sat and soaked up the stillness. As the lights slowly came back on the congregation began to calmly gather their items and head towards the aisle to go home. I collected our things and bundled Eli back up ready to head home.

As I walked towards the back of the church, I saw a younger man sitting in the back pew. He looked exhausted, dirty, and malnourished. He was wearing jeans that had tears on the knees, and the bottom cuffs were worn. He wore military grade boots that were coming apart at the seams. His jacket was ripped, and stuffing was hanging out of the tattered edges. He had scruffy brown hair, a long-untrimmed beard, and he wore a black watch with a cracked face. His eyes looked empty, hollow, like he was a shell. My heart hurt for him.

Something, then in that moment, spoke to me. I felt a push from inside, and then as if I didn't have control of my movements my hand rested on the man's shoulder. Before I knew it, I was speaking:
"Come with me. It's Christmas Eve, and I see how tired you are. Come with me and I will make you dinner, a place to sleep, and a place to wash up for the night."
He stared at me; confused, perplexed.
I told him, "It's okay. I promise it will be alright."
"You don't know me at all. How do you know I won't rob you or hurt you?" His voice was gravely and rough, but gentle.
"I guess I don't, but I assume that if you are here that you still have hope and faith within you."
Again, he stared at me.
"Come on. Let's go." I held my hand out, and to my surprise, based on his facial expressions towards me, he stood up and followed me. We got into my car and drove the few miles home.

"Come on in, sir." I held the door open for him. "I'll show you the way to the bathroom if you'd like to get cleaned up, and I will round up some dinner for us." Eli on my hip I walked towards the bathroom. I flicked on the light and showed him where the washcloths and towels were at. I got out the old clippers of my husband's and went to a hall linen closet. I grabbed out a box of old clothes that were my husband's and pulled out a pair of cargo pants, a couple of t-shirts, a pair of socks and an old jacket. I handed the man the clothes and I watched as he slowly took them from me. His hands shook, and

24

his eyes welled up with tears.

"I know it isn't much, but help yourself to the soap, clippers, and anything you need." I indicated to the bathroom. He turned his head towards the bathroom and looked back at me, a slight smile appeared at the edges of his mouth. I walked towards the kitchen and started removing Eli's coat, hat, gloves, and shoes. I placed him in his highchair and got him an applesauce packet so that he could begin eating something while I made spaghetti and meatballs. I poured some milk into his sippy cup and put it on his tray.

I began boiling the water and placed a package of frozen meatballs into a pan on the stove. I was actually a decent cook, but on short notice I wasn't prepared to make a full-fledged meal. I figured at this point the man probably didn't care what he ate. I finished making dinner and had cut up pieces for Eli on his plate. I warmed up some vegetables and scooped some out for Eli.

The man walked out from the bathroom with his clothes in his hands. He had shaved his beard, and his hair was trimmed back. He was wearing cargo pants, and one of the shirts I had given him. He walked to the front door and placed his boots and clothes neatly by the door along with the other shirt I had given him and the jacket. He walked back into the kitchen, and I handed him a plate.

"Please take as much as you'd like," I directed him to the pasta, meatballs, and vegetables, "we also have fruit if you'd like." I pointed towards a bowl that was on the counter.

"Thank you, ma'am. Thank you so much for everything."

"It is my pleasure, sir."

"Ray," he said, "Ray Montgomery." He held his hand out towards me. His fingernails were now trimmed and clean.

I shook his hand and said, "Dalene Byrnes, and this is Elijah, but we call him Eli." Eli looked up at me and smiled.

"May I ask where your husband is at ma'am?" He asked cautiously.

"He passed away about two years ago in a car accident." It still caught me off guard when I talked about it, but I still wore my wedding band. I expected people to ask along the way. It just never gets easier.

I sighed gently, "Enough about me. Tell me about yourself."

"That's a long story ma'am."

"That's okay. We have time."

"Well ma'am I grew up in Guntersville, Alabama. It was a very small town, but everyone was so kind. I was the middle of three boys, and my mother and father were very hard workers. My mother was a schoolteacher and did a lot of charity work at the local church. My father was a welder at the local automotive shop, but also did side carpentry jobs for folks around town. After high school I signed up to be an infantry man in the Army.

Right after I joined, I was sent off to basic training. I was assigned to a unit in California upon completing my training and that unit deployed within a month of me being with them. We were sent to Afghanistan for a year and while I was there several of my buddies died next to me. I've been blown up by IED's and shot a couple of times. I have my demons from that deployment and my aches and pains. We returned home down several good men. I wanted to be closer to my family, so they reassigned me units to be at a base closer to home.

Within two months of me being moved I was deployed again. This time to Iraq. It was supposed to be another year away from my family and friends. Iraq was different. We were one of the first units into the region. We helped set up perimeters and do recons around the area. I remember the day my life changed, it had only been two weeks boots on ground, and it was hotter than normal. It was a dry desert heat, but it was a heat that made you sweat the water you just put in your mouth.

I was the gunner in our tactical vehicle. We came upon a town that had been abandoned, but the higher ups wanted us to clear it to make sure it wasn't being used for other operations. All the gunners remained with the vehicles while the drivers and passengers cleared the town. The other gunners and I kept watching around us for any suspicious activity. The next thing we knew we heard gunfire, as we whipped our weapons around to see where the fire was coming from the building next to my vehicle that had exploded. I, thankfully, was able to react quickly and unsnap my harness and duck down in the truck just enough to protect my head, but the explosion had such tremendous force that it rolled the truck over. I was sent tumbling around the inner carriage of the truck. I was unconscious and I didn't come to until nightfall.

It was so quiet; an eerily quiet. I crawled out through the hatch and began searching for my squad. Sadly, that explosion saved my life. Somehow the enemy found out we were coming to clear the village. They killed my entire squad; fifteen good men. Everyone of my friends, brothers, was gone, and I couldn't do anything about it. At that point I realized that I was injured. My head was bleeding, my leg was probably broken, because the pain set in. I stumbled back to the trucks to see if they had left any in operational order. Thankfully there was one cargo truck. The others were either blown to pieces or had all their components ripped from them.

I went back and forth and carried each of my brothers to the cargo truck. I had to rig up a pulley system to get them onto the back of the truck, because some of them were much taller and, well, more built than me. It took me almost until dawn broke to get them all on the truck. I drove them back to base. I couldn't just leave them there." He paused for a little while, but I knew he wasn't done with his story. He wiped tears from his eyes and hung his head.

After a few minutes he continued, "When I got back, they sent another team out to recover the remaining vehicles and anything else that might have been left behind. They took my squad away in body bags. They took them to be put in caskets with flags over them. They took them to be sent home. The medics determined that due to the explosion I would most likely have a Traumatic Brain Injury and I did have a broken leg and several other wounds that needed mended. I was no longer fit to serve in that deployment, so they sent me home. The military said I would never make a full recovery. The TBI made itself more apparent. I was angry all the time, I was forgetful and then the Post Traumatic Stress set in. I had anxiety, survivor's guilt, blamed myself, nightmares.

Quickly my family and friends left my side. The military

abandoned me, told me to go to the VA for appointments when I needed it, kicked me out and then I couldn't hold a job. At that point it became easier to be homeless. Well, I guess on Christmas Eve you want somewhere to go and want to have faith regardless of how hopeless your situation is. That is when I met you... my Christmas hope. I just really want to say thank you ma'am, again." Now he had me in tears. I stood up and gave him a hug.

Then I asked him a question...
"If you could do anything you wanted, what would you do with your life?"
"Well ma'am, if I could go a day without anxiety and nightmares, anger, and pain I would want to help other soldiers. I'd want to give them hope and give them the help and resources that they deserve. Housing, food, therapies, etc." He said it all with a light in his eyes, sincerity and a deep passion.

At that moment I became one hundred percent sure he would be the first one I saved, but I was scared too. Anger, pain, nightmares, and anxiety among other things I'm sure... how would I cope while I was around Eli? In my dreams the affects didn't happen immediately. Usually, the side effects of saving a soul take place the next day. I had time to plan. My parents will be here tomorrow, and my husband's parents will still come to be with Eli on Christmas day.

*Stop thinking and just do. Don't worry about the pain – it won't last. It is only temporary. Eli will have someone to help watch over him, and maybe I can ask my parents to stay another night to help. Breathe. It's okay. Just do. Help.*

I put my hand on his shoulder, and I prayed with all my heart that this man would be healed of his pain, his suffering. Prayed that he would go on to help so many other veterans who needed someone to believe in them again. To give them hope. To give them a second chance that they so deserved. My whole body started to feel like I had 'pins and needles'. I felt a burning on my back at the base of where the tick marks ended. My body felt like

28

it was expelling all my energy at once. Ray looked at me concerned, "are you okay ma'am?" Then he began to feel it too. He sat frozen in his chair. A few minutes passed by and then as quickly as the momentum picked up in my body it ceased. I fell to my knees, exhausted from the experience. Eli looked towards me and called for me. I slowly stood back up, trying to get my legs balanced again. I walked over to him and placed my hand on his head, brushing his hair back, and gave him a kiss on his forehead. "It's okay Bubba, everything is okay." Ray blinked a few times.

He rubbed the back of his neck with one of his hands, he then rubbed his knees as if making sure they were still attached to his body. He stood up and began walking around the kitchen staring down at his feet as he did.

"I don't understand," he said, "I don't feel pain anymore. What happened? What did you do?"

"It's hard to explain," I did a slight smile out of the side of my mouth, "I was given a gift to give others a second chance. You won't forget what happened to you or where you came from, but the pain will be gone; mentally, physically, and emotionally."

".... but how? How is this possible?" He stammered.

I had been instructed to not give very many details into my gift.

"All you need to know is that you have been given a second chance at life. Don't waste it and fulfill your dream. Save other lives and give them second chances."

He stood there staring at me. "I don't know what to say."

"You can't tell anyone though. You can't tell anyone that I helped you."

"I won't. I promise," he said still astonished.

I paused for a moment. "I need to go and put Eli down to bed, but you are more than welcome to stay the night if you'd like. I can make up the couch for you."

"That would be wonderful ma'am, thank you so much... for everything."

I left to go get Eli ready for bed. I put him into jammies, brushed his teeth and read a book to him. Before bed we sang 'Jesus Loves Me' and said 'The Lord's Prayer'. I laid him in his crib and covered him up. "I love you buddy, more than all the stars in the whole wide world." He smiled and then closed his eyes and rolled over.

I turned on his night light before leaving his room and closed the door behind me. I grabbed a pillow and some blankets from the built-in linen closet in the hallway and brought them back out to the living room. I made up the couch for Ray and said goodnight to him. I went back to my room to get ready for bed. I lifted my shirt and looked in the full-length mirror hanging from my closet – sure enough there was a red mark across a group of four lines at the bottom right of my back. One of the marks had been erased. It felt as if I had just gotten a tattoo, not had one removed.

I had four tattoos before the one-hundred marks on my back. I had one done when my Eli was born – it was his heartbeat with a heart in the middle on my inner left bicep. I got one for my husband once he passed away on my inner right bicep of our anniversary date in roman numerals with a sand dollar next to it. We had a trip to Oregon where we brought back several sand dollars, and they were always our 'thing'. The final one was for me. It slanted over my right collar bone towards my chest. Two lines that read 'I shall fear no evil for Thou art with me. . .' It was my reminder to always have faith in the Lord and to walk through life with no fear. The last was a cross on the back of my neck.

As I lay my head down to go to sleep, I couldn't help but think about what impact Ray would make on the world. I hope that he will take his second chance and truly do what he said. I guess you always need to have faith in people around you, but sometimes it is hard to trust people's true intentions. He didn't know I had the capabilities of healing him though, and he seemed genuine. I was ready to plunge into this more and more. I fell asleep knowing that I had done the right thing; I was at peace.

December 25, 2003. I woke up to a beautiful Christmas day. Snow had fallen and was beautifully untouched on the ground. Sparkling under the rising morning light. I got up, dressed, and got ready for the day. I peaked in at Eli who was still sleeping soundly. I went to the kitchen to begin making my Kona coffee and preparing the icing for the tea rings we would have this Christmas morning. I make it every Christmas morning. It was a tradition that had been passed down through my family's generations.

Ray came into the kitchen smelling the air.

"That smells fantastic ma'am. Good morning."

I smiled, "Good morning, Ray. Come on in and have some."

"Thank you, ma'am." He paused for a moment as I handed him a cup of coffee. "I just want you to know that last night was the first night for as long as I can remember that I didn't have nightmares, anxiety, wake up in night sweats, wake up in pain; I slept peacefully. I …. I can't thank you enough ma'am."

"I'm so glad that I was able to help." I sipped my coffee.

"I promise I won't take it for granted. I promise I will do what I want and help others."

"I know you will." I nodded and smiled.

There was a silence as we sipped our coffee. I finished making the icing for the tea rings and started spreading it on the tops. I sliced a big piece and put it on a plate for Ray. I warmed it up in the microwave for a few seconds and handed it to him. His eyes got wide, and he thanked me again. He sat down and began eating as I continued preparing for the Christmas dinner for my family. When he was finished, he stood up, brought his plate to the sink and said, "well ma'am I know it sounds redundant, but I really can't thank you enough for everything. I should be going now because I know you have family coming."

"Well before you go, I put together a care package for you. It has a few sandwiches, chip bags, snacks, waters, etc in it." I handed him an envelope with some cash from my emergency fund in it. "This should be enough to get you by at a hotel for a little while. I also want to call you a taxi to take you into town at least. I know we don't live that far out of town, but it is a good three miles, and it can take you wherever you want."

He began crying as I picked up the phone to call a cab.

After I hung up and told him they would be here in about ten minutes he came up and asked if he could give me a hug; tears streaming down his face. I gave him a hug, and he whispered 'thank you' over and over. I helped him gather his things into the backpack I gathered for him, and the cab arrived at that time.
"I can't thank you enough ma'am," he said as he waved good-bye to me by the cab door, "Merry Christmas."
"Merry Christmas, Ray."

Christmas continued as any normal Christmas morning would. My parents, Alma and Dale Smith arrived punctually as always. My mother was stoic looking; her hair was always so tidy and neat. Short, shades of gray swirling throughout. 1970's style gold framed glasses bridged her nose, and she wore navy blue slacks with a white sweater. She had a snowman pin attached to her sweater. She was thin, but not in an unhealthy way. She looked like something out of a fashion magazine. My father was balding with a few strings of hair running over the top of his domed head, but he still had a rim of hair around the base of his head too. He wore silver wire-rimmed glasses, and he always wore suspenders. He had gray slacks on and a blue plaid button up. He had gained some weight over the years, but I wouldn't classify him as obese. His hands and face were rough from years of farm work, but he had soft features. My mother swooped in and quickly picked up Eli to give him hugs, kisses and to dote on him.

My in-laws arrived fifteen minutes later – fashionably late per usual, but it didn't bother me. I always knew when to expect them. Larry and Phyllis Byrnes were their names. Larry was the spitting image of my husband. He stood tall at six foot five, but he was wide; strong. He had strong, sharp features; distinct cheek bones, square jaw, piercing green eyes and black wavy hair. Phyllis was petite and honestly, they looked like an odd pair. They were polar opposites when it came to appearance. Phyllis was probably only five foot four at the most, and she had soft delicate features. She had wavy brown hair with twists of gray, hazel eyes and thin, but again, not in an unhealthy way.

I took their coats from them and led everyone into the kitchen for some coffee and tea ring. We sat around the dining room table and chatted. The warmth of having family around me was comforting. We then gathered in the living room around the small Christmas tree Eli, and I had put up earlier in the month. I handed presents to Eli so he could hand them out to his grandparents. We always take turns opening presents; one because it takes longer and the second because then we can see and appreciate what others are given.

As we sat in a pile of boxes, wrapping paper and bows, we watched Eli throwing an array of this combination up in the air over his head, raining down upon all of us. I sat him in one of the bigger boxes and gave him some markers to color inside the box as I went to check on the Christmas ham and creamed corn. I pre-heated the oven and began setting out the green bean casserole that I had prepared the day before to slide into the oven. I added the finishing toppings before sliding them in to cook. As I was in the kitchen finishing the prep work my legs began to tingle.

*It was beginning.*

My mom came out to the kitchen to see if she could help with anything.
"Mom, would you and dad be willing to stay the night or maybe two? I could use some help with Eli tomorrow. I just haven't been feeling the best."
She looked at me with concern and placed her wrist on my forehead and down to my cheek. "Of course, dear, are you okay?"
"I think so... probably just a cold or something." It was so hard not to tell my mother what was going on. I hated to keep things from her.
"Okay, well we can stay as long as you need us to. We always have a bag in the car with some overnight things – you know that." She still had that concerned look on her face. "Well, what can I help with dear?" She shifted her gaze from me to the food on the counter tops.

"I just have to dish things into the serving bowls to put out on the table." I started reaching for the serving dishes and my hands and arms began to tingle as well. It wasn't painful, but a warning.

We finished everything and got it all set out on the table. I filled up Eli's sippy cup and set it on his highchair. We all sat down around the table and held hands to say grace. My father led us in prayer and at the end we all joined in saying "Amen". Food started to be passed around the table and being dished out onto plates. Spiral cut ham with a pineapple brown sugar glaze, creamed corn, green bean casserole, homemade Challah bread with cinnamon butter to accompany it, a fruit salad, homemade cranberry sauce, and pies upon pies for dessert along with multiple Christmas goodies the grandma's brought along with them.

Everything went silent as we began eating, just the gentle clink of forks on plates. As most of the food dissipated, we began conversing again. Discussing the weather, news stories, and sharing old holiday tales. Stories of Allen when he was a child; stories that made us all laugh and others that brought tears to our eyes as we remembered him. Holidays, big moments in the world and in our lives made me miss him even more. Sometimes when I went to bed I would still roll over and put my hand on his side of the bed... hoping... praying that he would be there. To touch my hand, roll over and kiss me goodnight. Instead, the blankets lay in perfect form from lack of disruption; cold.

I stood up brushing away tears and began clearing plates from the table. Mom helped me gather things and began putting things into Tupperware and to-go bins for the Byrnes. I began to rinse off plates and load them into the dishwasher. I filled the sink basin with warm soapy water and washed the few things that could not fit into the dishwasher. Suddenly, I felt my body go rigid, stiff with anguish and despair. I felt a cold flash wrench at the back of my neck and disperse throughout my entire body. My eyes were forced shut with the sensation and then it was as though I was watching a movie behind my eye lids. I was reliving a memory of Ray's... a memory of war, heartache. I watched as he slowly woke up and crawled out of his military vehicle to find all his team members dead; lifeless, motionless... dark surrounding him. I felt anger rising deep within my soul, a hatred that could never be duplicated. Then a sense of remorse and guilt flooded over the hate. I watched as he continued to lie in the sand, screaming and crying out. I felt tears filling my eyes and a burning sensation intensified within my throat; a lump that crept upward until...

...a shaking of my shoulder awoke me from the memory. My eyes shot open, and I saw my mother standing there staring at me with concern. I felt weak and exhausted; lightheaded. "Are you alright?" My mother asked me with a concerned tone. "I think so..." I said much more shakily than I anticipated. "You scared me. Your eyes rolled back in your head, and you were shaking, almost convulsing. Your whole body was flush." "I'm sorry mom, I don't know what just happened." "Why don't you go sit down in the living room and I will finish up here."

I began slowly walking towards the living room still feeling flushed, weak, and tired. The memory kept replaying in my head. Visualizing it... seeing it as if I were there was so incredibly heart wrenching compared to just hearing the story. The story was terrible by itself... kind of like reading a book and then watching the movie after; it is never what your head imagines or pictures. I sat down on the couch and listened to the Byrne's and my father talking about their vacation last year. I felt like I was still in a different world; their words were muffled and distorted. I tried to refocus on Eli who was playing on the floor with his new toys. That seemed to bring me back to this reality a little bit better, but not fully.

A couple of hours passed, and the Byrnes's were getting up to say goodbyes. We hugged and gathered their gifts and leftovers. As they were leaving, I felt shooting pain rising through my spine, and then it radiated back down towards my legs, it rose back up through my shoulders, neck and skull. It felt like needles

puncturing my skin, stabbing, twisting, distorting. It was excruciating, but I tried my best not to let it show. I didn't want to panic my parents or Eli. The moment the door shut I told my mom I needed to go lie down. I gave Eli a big hug and a kiss on the forehead, "be good for grandma and grandpa, okay buddy? Mama is going to go lie down for a little while."
"Okay Mama," he gave me a big squeeze.

I went back to my bedroom and shut the door. I dropped to my knees and curled up on the floor in the fetal position. I couldn't move. My entire body was writhing in pain, numbness, tingling. It felt like I was having a seizure. My neck felt like it was snapping backwards and then it happened again; my eyes wrenched shut and the darkness behind my eyelids flashed into a memory. Yanking, pulling me inward, becoming part of the memory – I was in Ray's perspective. I smelled the stench of gunfire, vehicles on fire, blood, death. I looked down at my hands – they were Ray's hands. Ray looked down just then and saw sand all over his hands, blood dripped down from his face. Ray put his hand up to his brow and realized he had a cut on his forehead, and a couple of large knots. Tears flooded his eyes once more and his hands began to shake, but this time it was because he had realized that his left leg was broken, and the pain was setting in.

Suddenly, his hand rose to his eyes and wiped the tears, and he stood up. He grabbed his rifle from the ground and slung it over him. Stumbling, limping as quickly as possible; with purpose, he began searching for vehicles to find out if any would still operate. He found the one vehicle that was still functional but turned it off to avoid enemies returning too quickly. He began finding his battle buddies and dragging their lifeless bodies through the sand laden ground one by one towards the back of the vehicle, taking care to ensure they were well respected. The sweat and blood trickled down his face. His whole body was soaked in sweat, and the sand adhered to every orifice. After all his battle buddies were placed next to the back of the cargo truck he sat against the tire of the vehicle for a moment. He looked around at the bodies surrounding him, a graveyard. It was the most heart

36

wrenching, desolate, sobering thing he had ever witnessed.

Through the tears he refocused his attention onto his leg. It was swelling, throbbing; he ripped open his pant leg to examine his leg closer. His leg was slit open; bleeding, tendons and bone were showing through the open wound. He cringed at the sight. His face felt flush, his body felt feverish. He feared he would go into shock if he didn't move quickly. He grabbed the tire and shakily stood up. His leg felt warm, rushing with blood from standing up. He felt dizzy, his stomach felt tight – a warmth rose in his throat – he leaned over grasping onto the bumper of the vehicle and vomited. He wiped his mouth with his sleeve. Ray felt the impending doom looming over his head; he needed to move quickly.

He stumbled to the back of the cargo truck. Bracing himself with his left hand he used his right hand to slide the ladder from its storage compartment under the cargo hold and dropped it to the ground. It was attached by two brackets, so it was easy to stow and utilize. He went over to the side of the truck and unlatched the storage box. It was empty. He muttered some curse words under his breath. His chest began to pound; he felt a mix of adrenaline and anxiety racing through his veins. He went to the ladder and clumsily hopped up the rungs with his right leg. In the back there were three remaining ratchet straps. He utilized two of the straps to make a sling and the other to hold them together and use as a pulley system within the cargo hold. Once rigged he carefully went down the ladder with his back to the ladder – hopping/ sliding down the ladder to the ground.

He slung up his first friend; tightening the ratchets to secure his body. He hobbled back into the cargo bed and using the ratchet and his right foot began to pull his friend up. Once close enough to grab hold of he tied off the strap and pulled the body in. Ray slid his first battle buddy towards the back of the cargo bed and rested his hands across his chest in respect. He repeated this act fourteen more times, becoming more proficient by the seventh or eighth time. Once he had all his squad loaded, he finished what little water he had left in his canteen. The warm water rushing against his lips and into his throat helping to remove the sand and grit from the inner cavities of his mouth.

Ray once more slid down the ladder and once at the bottom he used his right leg to lower himself down to lift the base of the ladder back up and slide it back into its compartment. He limped around to the driver's side and used his arms and right leg to climb up into the seat. He started the vehicle and began maneuvering it around the debris that was left. As he left the compound and began driving back towards base, he looked in his side mirrors. He saw lights approaching the compound from behind him. He quickly turned off all the lights on the vehicle. His hands began to sweat; knuckles white from gripping the steering wheel. His stomach churned as if he were going to vomit again. He kept driving, praying that he would stay on the hard-packed sand road versus ending up in a dune or, worse, hit an IED.

His body became even more rigid and tense as he realized two of the lights were approaching him – the remaining seemed to be stationary back at the compound. As the lights grew closer, he began to hear the high-pitched whine of dirt bikes. The lights split off as they approached the tail end of the vehicle. Ray saw one in each side view mirror; panic swelled within him. Then flashing light coming out of the muzzle of an assault rifle lit up his side of the vehicle. His gut reaction was to jerk his wheel to the left – he caught the driver off guard and the dirt bike's headlight illuminated a sand dune. The dirt bike crashed hard into the dune, and the bike went up towards the night sky. The light radiated the night as it fell back towards the sandy earth beneath it.

The bike on Ray's right began to shoot their assault rifle. The flash of the rounds exiting the muzzle lit up the darkness. Ray attempted to jerk his wheel to right, but the driver learned from his not-so-fortunate ally. The biker hit the brakes hard and dipped behind Ray's vehicle. Ray followed suit and hit his brakes hard. The biker was not as lucky this time and crashed into the back of the cargo truck. Ray watched the headlight of the dirt bike fall and spin on the ground. He sped off as fast as the cargo truck would, which wasn't impressive by any means.

Ray kept searching the darkness through his side mirrors expecting to see lights chasing back after him, but nothing ever came. He drove thirty more minutes back to the base; the dawn broke gradually along his journey. As he approached the gate, he could tell the guards were apprehensive. By now Ray was sure that they were aware that his convoy had lost all comms and the standard is to shut down the base until the convoy is recovered.

When only one vehicle from that convoy returns the guards start assuming the enemy has taken over said vehicle. Ray stopped a few hundred feet back from the gate, rolled down his window, and stuck both hands out of it. A guard approached Ray and told him to slowly open the door. Ray complied. He gingerly stepped out of the vehicle and put his hands behind his head. Another guard approached and began patting him down – when he got to his leg he yelled for a medic. Ray gave a quick synopsis to the guard about what had happened. He radioed to the base commander who after a few short minutes sped up in a HMMWV; a cloud of sand swallowing everyone as he came to a halt. Ray went hazy, his eyes becoming blurry – he felt flush, faint. He fell. Fell into blackness.

A rush of heat flashed over me. My body felt as though it was coming out of rigor mortis. I blinked my eyes open and was looking up at my ceiling fan rotating, but it was extremely dark; faded. I blinked a few more times and slowly began realizing that it wasn't just my eyes not coming fully clear, but it was now dark outside. I slowly rolled over; my whole body felt like it was on fire. I looked over at my nightstand and saw the time was just past three in the morning. I couldn't believe that almost nine hours had passed by. I very unsteadily grabbed hold of my dresser and pulled myself back to my feet. I patted my arms and body quickly to make sure I hadn't aged sixty years, because I sure felt like I had. I tenderly walked to my bedroom door, into the hallway, and into the bathroom. I shut the door and began to fill the tub.

*Maybe a good soak will help or at least get me through until this passes.*

The most difficult part of all of this was not knowing how long each stent would last. *Would the effects begin wearing off or would it be like this and one day be over instantly?*

I slowly put my body into the water and sank into the warmth. I was a little afraid to close my eyes again as I didn't know when the next flashback would occur. I attempted to shut my eyes for a moment, against my better judgment. Although no actual memory drug me in, my eyes could not erase the horrific scenes they just witnessed. I snapped my eyes open again hoping that would stop the instant replay from continuing, but my mind continued to wander.

*Was I going to be able to do this every time? Would every time I help someone be this difficult?*

I stopped myself from the negative talking and realized that if the others and I weren't there to help people, Ray and others would continue to feel this suffering and pain constantly... or even die. Saving one hundred lives was worth all my discomfort and pain. I sank into the water deeper and continued to immerse my mind in tranquility.

In between black outs I wrote my first ledger entry: *December 25, 2003, Soul 1, Ray, TBI, PTS, Christ's Birth, Ray's Re-Birth.*

The day was the same as the night. I relapsed into black outs two more times, and I curled up in pain countless times. Baths seemed to help a bit, so I tried soaking after each black out. Thankfully they seemed to have a pattern where there was a couple of hours between each blackout. By day three I was black out free, but the pain lingered; albeit it was tolerable. I was able to release my mom and dad from their Eli duties, and able to begin a semi-normal routine again. Semi-normal meaning we cuddled and watched Christmas movies the next couple of days.

*Soul one was saved...*

# 5.

March 10, 2004. The New Year had come and with it no dreams, no souls to save; nothing. That night before bed I prayed to Azariah and asked him if I was doing the right thing or if I should be putting myself out into the world more to find someone. How long does it take between saving someone? I wanted to make sure I was doing my part.

I dreamt that night of Azariah standing next to a glowing bright light. He looked more like a silhouette, but I knew it was him. His deep, smooth, calm voice spoke to me through the light. "Hello, Dalene, don't worry about anything. You are doing the right thing. The Lord has been pleased so far with everyone's progress in saving lives and changing the world. People may come to you quickly or may take some time between, but you are doing what you need to. They will come to you when it is time or God, and I will point you in the right direction."
"Azariah..." my voice trailed off. I was a little off-put because it felt like a real, normal – well as normal as a conversation like this could be - conversation, as if I were there with him in a room. It startled me a bit. "... uh, sorry, if you and the Lord guide me within a dream how will I find the person in real-life to be able to save them?"

"If the person doesn't present themselves directly to you, like Ray did, the dream we provide you will be filled with all the details you will need to help that person."

"Okay."

"Do you have any other questions for me, before you return to your regularly scheduled programming?" He chuckled, "sorry a little humor."

I laughed, "no I think that is it. Thank you for coming to me."

"You're welcome, Dalene...." his voice trailed off and became almost static as the light dimmed.

I sat straight up in bed breathing heavily even though it wasn't a nightmare it seemed so real. I looked around expecting to see Azariah in my room with me. Nothing but darkness and the moon shining in from the window. I guess now I wait.

May 18, 2004. Miss Annalee Villareal was a beautiful Southern Belle. She had a sweet smile, round features, silver wire-rimmed glasses, and was an amazing cook. She was sweet as can be and loved everyone that came around her. She loved her six grandchildren with all her heart and loved spending as much time as possible with them. She was sixty-four years young, as she liked to say, but had more experiences in life than most. She was African American and had lived twenty-four years of her life prior to the Civil Rights Act passed in 1964. Her family and her had traveled together from Alabama to Washington D.C. to be a part of the March on Washington on August 28, 1963.

While there she met her husband Abel Montgomery who was also from a town in Alabama, about an hour north of where they resided. They were married in July of 1965 and had three wonderful children together: Charlotte, Tallulah, and Beau. In 1970 Abel was awarded a promotion within his company. He was a successful Insurance man, but this promotion would take place in the company's head department in Missouri. The Montgomery family decided to make the move and headed to a small town called Belleville, Illinois just over the border and less than a thirty-minute drive to Abel's office. They moved into a two-story four square, and quickly created an idyllic life and home together, with a fresh start.

Four wonderful years passed, and they thought their lives were perfect, until September 9th, 1974, arrived. Abel didn't arrive home from work, and this was before cell phones, so Miss Annalee had no way of contacting her husband. She tried to call his office, but no one answered. After a couple of hours of worry she called the police. They told her they could do nothing for forty-eight hours and to document anything unusual in the meantime.

She sat awake all night terrified that the worst had happened to him. On September 10th after the bus had picked up her children for school, she took her car that was rarely used other than for grocery runs and such and drove to her husband's office. She asked the receptionist if he had been seen. Everyone began searching in the office for him and no one could find him. The receptionist led her to his office to see if she could find anything.

Abel's office was pristine; family oriented with photos of the children and Miss Annalee on the walls and bookshelves. There were no notes, and everything seemed to be in the proper place. A man by the name of Waylon Thorson stood in the doorway and knocked gently.

"Hello ma'am," he said smoothly, collected. "I don't mean to interrupt, but I left the office with your husband yesterday. He got into his car and left the parking garage; said he was heading home for the evening."

Waylon Thorson was as Caucasian as they came with jet blue eyes, blonde hair, tall and thin with a nice gray suit on. He was in his thirties, a fierce, dark look in his eyes.

Miss Annalee nodded at him, "thank you, sir." She said in her deep southern accent.

"Have you contacted the police at all?" He said it with almost animosity in his voice now.

"Yes, sir, but they won't do anything until he has been missing forty-eight hours."
He sucked his teeth and made a clicking noise with his tongue, "dang shame ma'am."
He continued to lean against the door frame.
"Excuse me, sir, I have children to get home too now."
"Yes, ma'am." He moved off to the side.
She didn't like his aura; he gave her a chill.

After forty-eight hours her husband had not contacted her, no sign of him from anyone at the office or from friends or family. The children and her were heartbroken. Her mind wandered to thinking that maybe he ran off with another woman, but she quickly demolished the idea and felt severe guilt for even thinking such things. Abel loved her and the children so much, there wasn't any way he would leave them. The police arrived at their home and took down a little information, but there wasn't much to give. Miss Annalee gave them a photo of him. They said they would be in contact if they heard anything. She felt hopeless and felt as though they didn't have any hope either. Two days later the newspaper posted a small article about Abel in the local newspaper and one in the St. Louis paper, but to little avail. Months passed; nothing.

January of 1975 arrived, and the St. Louis paper arrived that morning at the Montgomery home. Miss Annalee had it delivered along with local paper ever since her husband's disappearance hopeful that maybe an update would eventually be written. Nothing ever came until January 20th when another article about a man named Jasper Billings appeared. He had gone missing in a small town near St. Louis. He was twenty-nine years old, and his mother, Justine, had reported him missing. He was African American with incredibly distinct features. He looked strong, and she assumed that the paper photo of him didn't do him justice. He had never arrived at his mother's home after work for their weekly supper.

Miss Annalee quickly looked in her St. Louis phone book

45

and searched until she found a listing for: *Billings, Justine.* She fumbled the receiver in her hand, dropping it in her anxiousness. She dialed the number frantically and waited as the line connected and began ringing. A frantic woman answered, "Jasper!" she almost yelled into the phone.

"No, ma'am... I'm so sorry. My name is Miss Annalee Montgomery, and I saw the article in the paper about your son. I was wondering if I could ask you a couple of questions."

"Why would you need to ask me questions? Do you know something about my son's disappearance?" She said sharply, but you could hear her Southern accent coming through.

"No ma'am, but my husband disappeared September of last year and, well, I don't know I guess I just had this feeling that maybe they were related somehow."

The line was quiet for some time. "You mean that man that went missing from work?"

"Yes ma'am. Do you remember it from the papers? Have you heard something? Did you know him?" Miss Annalee said frenziedly.

"No, I'm sorry I just remember it from the paper. An African American gone missing in this town is something you notice being African American too, I suppose. Especially a young family man."

"Yes... I suppose it is."

"Well unfortunately I believe our stories are about the same. My Jasper was supposed to come over to my house the night he went missing for dinner, but he never arrived. I called his office, and they had seen him head to his car... then nothing. He didn't show up to work the next day, and I haven't seen or heard anything since."

"I'm sorry ma'am. I just have this feeling in my gut that this is related."

"It sure seems that way don't it." Her accent really accentuated now.

Miss Annalee gave Justine her phone number in case she heard anything more and they disconnected.

In February another African American went missing and

then again in March. One a month – the police posted that they believed they might have a serial killer on their hands. April arrived and two more were missing. Miss Annalee made it a point to contact each family member that had reported them missing.

May 8th arrived, and another had gone missing. Miss Annalee followed suit and contacted the family member. That night after the children were in bed, she herself got into bed and shut off the light. Around midnight she woke up in a sweat... and then she smelled it.

*Smoke.*

She shot out of bed and ran through the door not caring where the fire originated or where it might be. The hallway was filled with smoke. She ran to her daughters' bedrooms and grabbed them as quickly as possible pushing them onto the ground, "crawl to my bedroom and cover your nose and mouth with your shirt." Miss Annalee ran to her son's room, and he was already up and running to his door. She gave him the same instructions and followed right behind him.

Once in her room she shut the door behind her and opened a window. Her room was positioned above the front porch with a slightly slanted roof. It appeared that the fire was toward the back of the house and so she got out onto the roof first to make sure it wouldn't fall through. She ushered her children out with her, and they crept toward the edge of the porch. Miss Annalee turned to her stomach and scooted over the edge, lowering herself until her toes barely touched the stucco railing below. She let go of the gutter which was bending with her weight. She slowly helped her children one by one down onto the porch and told them to get into the yard. A neighbor rushed out from next door and said they had called the fire department. They offered to take the children inside to keep warm until the situation was under control and Miss Annalee happily accepted. They had been wonderful neighbors over the last few years. A huge support system after Abel disappeared.

47

They brought her a blanket to keep warm until the department arrived. She noticed something flickering in the wind attached to their mailbox on the front porch. Flames began engulfing the home, but she ran quickly to grab the piece of paper. After getting back to the yard she opened the piece of paper to see that it was a scrawled note:

*Miss Annalee, Congratulations! If you are reading this, it means that you have survived. Let this be your warning to stop digging into your husband's disappearance. If you continue searching and inquiring, I will be forced to eliminate you as a threat. You will not tell the police about this letter – I will know, and I will kill you. I would hate to leave your children motherless too. You will put this letter into the fire to demolish along with your home. I am watching you and will know if you complete this task. If you don't, I will kill you right here, right now, before authorities arrive.*

Her palms were sweaty, her breathing shallow and short. She knew her face was flush. She had to think quickly. The fire department would be there any second. What should she do? An idea sparked in her head. She had a grocery list in the pocket of her robe, maybe she could swap the notes out and fool the killer. She walked up to the flames that now inundated her front porch. She held the killers note to her stomach and gently pulled the grocery list from her robe pocket under the blanket. She held it up into the air and tossed it in the flames. She slipped the note into her other robe pocket before returning to the yard. She half expected the killer to be there waiting for her; to kill her. No one came. Lights shown down the road and sirens blared through the crackling of the flames.

Erica Finley was a retired schoolteacher and lived a wonderful sixty-two years on this earth. She was a faithful church goer and loved to do charity work whenever she got the chance.

She was part of countless organizations and had been a Sunday School teacher and assisted at the local orphanage when she could. Erica had been married to a man named James Finley for almost forty years and they had four children: Lily, Lynn, James III, and Henry. They lived in West Peoria, Illinois and enjoyed camping and traveling together. They were an active family and gave back to their community together. Their lives were fairly normal, and their children grew up and moved out of the house.

When Erica turned sixty years old, she got up one morning and began getting dressed to go to work; the only problem was she had been retired for the past two years. James asked where she was off to. She laughed, "you're so silly. Off to work of course." James became panicked, "work? Honey, you haven't worked in two years. Do you have a volunteering opportunity today I wasn't aware of?"
"No, I have my fourth-grade class this morning." She became a bit agitated.
"Erica, you haven't been a fourth-grade teacher in two years. We had a retirement party for you. You've been home and we have been doing charity work and traveling, seeing our grandchildren." She shook her head and stood there confused; defeated.
"I think we should get you to the doctor." James said.

The doctor quickly diagnosed Erica with early onset Dementia. Erica was heartbroken. Two years went by and the disease advanced quicker than doctors expected. Erica kept running off and disappearing, going places, she thought she needed to be at. James tried and sacrificed so much to keep Erica living at home, but after she disappeared for an entire day and the police had to help find her – he just couldn't. A social worker helped find a good care facility that was displayed on a pamphlet in James's hands, close by to their home where he could visit often.

*'The choice is yours to make'* flashed across the darkness

behind my eyes. A scream welled within me and released; hoarse, raspy within my inner soul. It split the silence of the early morning air. I was in a sweat just as Miss Annalee had been, and I quickly threw the covers off and smelled the air around me; I didn't smell smoke. I rushed out of my bedroom and searched the whole house for signs of fire; there weren't any.

I sat down at the kitchen table and began processing what I had just dreamt. It was clear as day in my mind. I quickly grabbed a notebook from the end table by the couch in the living room and a pen. I wrote down all the details from the dream. This must be my next assignment.

*Did I really have to choose between these two women?*

The phone rang and I shot up in the air; startled. I quickly answered it as to not allow it to wake Eli.
"Hello?" I said quietly.
The deep, smooth, calm voice came across the phone line, "Yes that is your answer," Azariah said.
"Well, that was quick."
"We like to be efficient here," he said with a little chortle in his tone.
"Clearly." I stated a touch sarcastically, but in a joking manner.
"You must choose between Miss Annalee and Erica. Both women can't be saved."
"Is this a test?"
"No, merely a choice due to their circumstances currently. They are both in similar situations, and they both have little time. Unfortunately, both arose on our radar at the same time. There will not be enough time to help both."
"Wait... it didn't show me anything of Miss Annalee's current condition, just Erica...."
Azariah cut me off, "and this is where you must do your research, but quickly, before time runs out."

The line went static and then dial tone. I held the phone away from my ear and placed it back on the wall mount.

"Well then... where do I start." I said aloud. I got out my laptop and began researching. I figured I had better start with Miss Annalee as I knew pretty much everything about Erica, but I didn't know where Annalee had ended up. I typed in Annalee Montgomery and Belleville, Illinois. 'White Pages' was the first link, but underneath it was a link to a location in St. Louis, MO. It was a memory care facility in Missouri.

*Did Miss Annalee also have dementia?*

I quickly looked up the murders near St. Louis back in 1974. There were almost thirty connected cases around the St. Louis area between 1974 and 1976. They had never found any of them and never knew who committed the murders.

*Did Miss Annalee never give that letter to the authorities?*
*Did she still have it?*
*Could that be the key to solving all these murders?*

How was I supposed to decide between two sweet ladies? Ladies that had impacted others' lives. Erica gave back to so many people, children, her community. Would she continue to do that for the next twenty to thirty years if I saved her? Miss Annalee might have the key to solving a thirty-year-old serial murder, but what if she didn't? What if I saved her and she didn't have that key piece of evidence any longer? Would her word of mouth alone be able to solve those crimes? Would she even want to speak to authorities? If she did have the evidence, would she want to turn it over to the police?

May 19, 2004. It was a four-hour drive from Eddyville, IA where we lived to St. Louis, MO. My parents lived an hour away from us a little out of the way I was heading, but not too far. I had packed a bag for Eli and me, called my parents and asked them to leave him there for a couple of days, and then headed that way.

I dropped Eli off and continued the three hours to St. Louis. I arrived at the care facility where Miss Annalee was at around ten in the morning. I quickly entered the facility and asked to see her. The nurse said, "well you're in luck, it seems she is having a good day today. She seems her normal self today, not such in a fog."

They led me into a living room area where she was sitting near a window in a light blue high back upholstered chair. She looked stoic; almost regal sitting there with the sunlight shining in on her face. Her dark skin gleamed and was beautifully lit up. As I got closer, she looked lost in thought, her light brown eyes looked dull though... almost in a haze.

"Miss Annalee," the nurse put her hand on her shoulder, "you have a visitor."

Miss Annalee seemed to come back to life a little, her eyes twinkled as she looked up towards me.

"Hello Miss Annalee, my name is Dalene Byrnes, and I was led to come and visit you today."

"Oh my," her thick southern accent was gentle and sweet, "well Miss Dalene it is so nice to meet you."

"Ma'am I have a question for you. I'm not sure if you remember or if you can help me, but I heard that your husband disappeared many years ago, and that he was never found."

"Oh yes ma'am... still one of the worst moments in my life. Many more African American men went missing in the next couple of years too."

"Yes ma'am, I read about it before I came to see you."

"Awful times... just awful." Miss Annalee looked away defeated.

"I can't even imagine what you have been through... the fire that your family went through... and..." I paused, hesitant to continue, "the note."

Miss Annalee looked at me, eyes wide, her delicate gentle features began to tighten, and her brow furrowed. "How ... How do you know about that?" She stammered.

"I was led to you... I know everything ma'am. I'm here to help you to get closure, but I need your help. Do you still have the letter?"

Suddenly Miss Annalee turned her head back to the window, her eyes glazed over once more. I paused and watched her momentarily thinking that maybe she just didn't want to speak to me anymore. After a few moments I placed my hand on her shoulder, "Miss Annalee?"
"Yes dear? Is it time for lunch already?"

She had forgotten everything that we had discussed. I never got an answer, but I knew I didn't have a choice at this point. I had to save her to get the answer, get her out of here and do my best to solve a thirty-year-old crime.
"Miss Annalee, do you mind if I just put my hand on your shoulder a minute. I know that may sound strange, but you are just such a wonderful soul, and I'd love to help you."
"Oh, my dear... well of course you can. I don't think you can help this old mind o' mine, but I miss having others to connect with."

I placed my hand on her shoulder, her hand raised up and she placed it on mine. I prayed with all my heart to help her broken mind, to help restore her memories and to help her find closure, and for many others to find closure as well. My whole body once again felt like it had pins and needles racing throughout my entire body. The burning sensation at the lower part of my back from the mark erasing. This time my whole head felt as though it would pop off my neck, the pressure was horrific, but I held on. As quickly as the rush of pressure and tingling began it ended. I fell to my knees next to her chair and rested my arm on the arm rest. Miss Annalee blinked several times. She lifted her glasses and rubbed her light brown eyes.
"What ... what just happened?" She clamored.
I sat there catching my breath for a minute. "I'm hoping that your memory is fully restored, ma'am."
"I remember everything... everything as clear as day. There's no more fog, no more lost memories, or thoughts. I... I don't understand."
"Call it a miracle from heaven; a second chance at life, but you

53

mustn't tell anyone it was me or that I helped you."

She stared at me for some time in disbelief and then grasped my hands in hers and quietly said, "I won't Miss Dalene, I swear it."

"Miss Annalee, we don't have much time, but I really would like to help you with your husband's case. I know that there are so many, just like you, who would love to have some closure in their lives. I'd love to help you solve his disappearance if you let me. Do you still have that letter?"

"Oh Miss Dalene, I'm not sure if I'm willing to do that. I've been scared all my life that man would come and find me. That he'd kill me."

"I know ma'am, but I will be right by your side... we need to finish this. We need to find the man responsible for making all those men disappear and for burning your home down."

She hesitated for quite some time. Then she stood up, grabbed my arm, and walked me down the hall to her room. "I've kept it with me all this time, even when my memory was failing me. I tried not to touch it much after I slipped it into my robe pocket. I placed it in a bread bag and only transferred it one more time to a Ziploc bag later – to hopefully keep it better protected." She handed the note to me. "I thought it would be my dying confession, to hand it to the authorities with a letter of my own, but my memory began going quicker than I thought and I lost what I wanted to say. I want to see that killer in prison before I die, you're right, I want closure for me, my family and all the other families. Even if it is the last thing I do."

"I know they won't release you yet; without a doctor's approval or something, so would it be alright if I called the authorities to come here?"

"Yes, Miss Dalene I think that'd be a wonderful idea."

I told Miss Annalee to sit tightly while I went to the front nurse's station and explained that Miss Annalee had some important information about an old crime that she'd like to discuss with the authorities. I told them to let the police come to her room when they arrived. I also informed them to make a doctor's appointment for Miss Annalee to be re-evaluated for her dementia as I believed it wasn't as severe as they had previously thought.

The nurse looked at me with confusion but reluctantly agreed to my terms. I dialed the local police department from the nurse's station and informed them that Miss Annalee had information pertaining to the Arch Killer, as the locals called him. Named after the St. Louis Arch. The police officer paused and then said, "I believe that case was passed on to the FBI ma'am. Let me double check in our records quick."
"Thank you."
"Yes, ma'am. That case was one of the most notorious in St. Louis, but they found that the killer crossed state lines and so it became an FBI case. I have the lead detective for the case here on file and his contact number though. I'm not sure if it is still valid, but they're pretty good about updating their records. Let me know when you're ready to copy this down."

I quickly reached across the desk for a sticky note and pen, going so quickly that I clumsily knocked over the pen cup and they sprawled out everywhere. I looked up at the disapproving nurse and whispered, "sorry, I'll pick those up."
She nodded in dissatisfaction but continued with her routine.
"Yes sir, I'm ready." I said louder than I anticipated.
"Alright his name is Detective Luis Fitzgerald." He then rattled off his telephone number, and I quickly jotted it down.
"Thank you so much for your time officer."
"No problem, ma'am... I really hope they can close that case."
"Me too. Thank you." The line disconnected and I quickly dialed Detective Fitzgerald's number. The phone rang and rang until I got a voicemail with a deep resound voice stating that it was indeed Detective Fitzgerald's number and that he was away from his phone. I didn't care and I didn't have time to wait. I hung up and dialed it again. This time on the third ring he answered, "Detective Fitzgerald." His voice sounded even bigger and deeper than his voicemail portrayed.
"Hello sir, the St. Louis PD directed me your way. I am sitting here with Miss Annalee Montgomery who has information on the

Arch Killer case."
Silence followed me and then, "are you sure?" He sounded astonished, "I thought that case would never be closed or have any new information... ever."
"Well sir, I have some for you, and I hope it will eventually solve the case."
"Where are you located right now?" He said sharply.

I told him the location we were at, and he said he could be there in a half hour. We waited in Miss Annalee's room, and she ate her lunch at a side table in her room. A large man engulfed the doorway, and he rapped on the door, "Miss Annalee ma'am?"
"Ah you must be Detective Fitzgerald." She said with her sweet southern drawl.
"Yes, ma'am that's me." He had a large stature. Gray hair swooped over his head, he had tiny eyes for his face, and they were dark in color, a larger sized nose, and tight lips. He wore jeans, black work boots and a navy-blue shirt that read 'FBI' that was tucked into his waist band. A belt held his pants up and on it was a cell phone carrier, gun, handcuffs, and other utility tools.

I quickly introduced myself, pulled up a chair for him and then sat back down. Miss Annalee handed the man the Ziploc bag. She explained about the night of the fire, this letter, and why she had never turned it over to the authorities. She said the last part almost embarrassed, but I placed my hand on her arm reassuringly.
"Ma'am, this is … amazing. You are so incredibly brave, and we appreciate you coming forward with this evidence. If you ever feel scared or receive any threats, please call me immediately."

He handed her his business card, and his cell number were jotted down on the back. "We will be happy to post a police officer outside of your residence immediately for protection. I plan to take it to the lab immediately for fingerprint analysis as a high priority. My hope is we could have results back by end of week so we can catch this son of a ..." he paused a moment catching himself, "well you know what I mean."

Miss Annalee blushed a little with pride for being able to have the courage to move this investigation forward. Detective Fitzgerald stood up, his large frame towering over us. He extended his hand to both of us and then said he would be in contact with any new information.

I spent the next several hours with Miss Annalee getting to know her, understanding her. She was an incredible woman and had lived through so many events in her lifetime. I wished nothing but the best for this woman.

Towards the end of our conversation the nurse came in and said that she had got an appointment for Miss Annalee in a couple of days. Miss Annalee and the nurse had a full conversation and the nurse looked on in awe, "Miss Annalee, I've never seen you so alert and focused."
"Well Ma'am I feel like a brand-new woman and I'm ready to move on with my life and live it to the fullest."
"I hope we can get you out of here, not that we all won't miss you, but I hope exactly that for you," she said before departing the room.

A few minutes later a beautiful young woman entered the room in a hurry. "Mama, are you alright?" She had an eloquent southern accent, flawless brown skin, black spiral curls that went to her shoulders and bounced as she moved, light brown eyes, and a very athletic build.
"Tallulah dear, I wasn't expecting you until later this week!" Miss Annalee looked surprised to see her daughter. "The nurse called me Mama and said you needed to see a doctor this week. Is everything okay?" Tallulah looked at her mother with concern.
"No dear, it is to hopefully get me out of this facility."
"... but Mama your mind is troubled." She said with great hesitation, "...but you do seem different."
"This wonderful woman saved me, but we mustn't tell anyone about what she has done."
"Saved you? Mama, you don't make any sense."

I interjected, "ma'am if I may, what your mother means to say is that the Lord blessed her with a second chance, but I was never here... I didn't do anything."
She looked at me with confusion, but that seemed to suffice. "I'll let you two catch up. I must be on my way home; it is much later than I expected." The darkness began to swallow the lowering sun outside and I still had to go check into my hotel for the evening.

Miss Annalee stood up to give me a hug goodbye. I told her I'd be checking the papers for updates on everything. I shook Tallulah's hand as I left.

I filled up my tank for the next morning to make the trek home, then found my hotel and got checked in, got to my room, dropped my bags, and flopped onto the bed. I was so exhausted after such an intense day. It was a wonderful day full of stories, love, and inspiration; but exhausting.

I woke up in the middle of the night and looked over at the red numbers on the hotel's alarm clock. It was two in the morning. My legs were numb from hanging off the bed for the last several hours. I slowly let them wake up and then proceeded to the bathroom to get ready for bed. I returned to my bed to sleep again, but before doing so my head felt that enormous pressure again.

☼☼☼☼☼

I woke up in a panic, cold sweat. I quickly looked around and soon realized that I was not in my hotel room anymore. I was on the side of the road somewhere, hazards flashing. Dark, ominous trees and massive boulders surrounded the edging of the road as nightfall surrounded them. I tried starting my car up and then saw the neon flash of the gas light on my dashboard. I stepped out of my car hoping to see something, anything that might give me an idea of where I was. Nothing. I pulled the keys from the ignition, locked the doors, and began walking back the way I came. According to my watch it was two thirty in the morning. How could it be two thirty in the morning when I just went back to bed, and I had just filled my car up... it wouldn't be out of gas now. I was completely baffled and disoriented. It felt like I was in an episode of Twilight Zone. Up ahead I could see what looked like a sign, but it was difficult to discern in the darkness. I ran towards it hopeful that if it was a sign, it would give me some answers. It was a sign! As I approached it and began to read, my jaw dropped:

| | |
|---|---|
| *Junction City* | *20* |
| *Fort Riley* | *15* |

"No, no, no... how is this possible?" I wasn't expecting that to emit from my mouth. That drive isn't a short distance. *Did I lose an entire day?* I don't remember anything from the last twenty-four hours. I was in Kansas... how did I get to Kansas? After standing there staring at the sign in shock for several minutes I decided to go back to my car until sunrise. I didn't want to walk in an unfamiliar place in the dark. After returning to my car my head started throbbing again – the pressure rising at the base of my skull and flowing up and over the top of my head. It then dawned on me that this must have been the repercussion of Miss Annalee's dementia. It just happened sooner than Ray's had, but I guess I'd rather it happen now than when I was with Eli. I guess I wait until someone either finds me and can lend a hand, or until daylight breaks and can walk to a gas station.

Daylight broke and no one had passed by. I decided it was time to start the journey to find a gas station. I got out, slung my purse over my shoulder and locked the car. I walked several miles, sweat began trickling down my back even though it was not an overly warm day. A car finally passed by me, slowed down and pulled over. A woman probably in her forties stepped out and asked if that was my car back a way.

"Yes, I ran out of gas."

"Well honey the next gas station isn't for another ten miles. Why don't you hop in, and I'll give you a ride there and back to your car."

"Are you sure? I don't want to be a burden."

"Honey you aren't a burden; it happens to all of us."

I graciously climbed in her passenger seat, and we drove off down the road.

"My name is Emelia, but everyone calls me Emmy," she said.

"It is very nice to meet you, Emmy. My name is Dalene."

"Where are you from honey?"

"I live in Iowa but was doing some work in St. Louis. To be honest I'm not one hundred percent sure how I ended up here."

"You are quite a distance from home. I live on Fort Riley with my husband. We just got transferred here not too long ago. I'm a photographer so I like to come out at dawn and take some landscape photos around the area."

"That is neat and I'm sure glad you were out and about today. Thank you again for helping me."

"No problem honey."

We arrived at the gas station, and I quickly ran in and purchased a gas can. I went out to the pump and filled it and then loaded it in her trunk before departing back to my car. We talked the whole way back about her travels and photography. When we arrived back at my car I got out and filled my gas tank, started up the engine and went back to thank her again for her kindness. We departed with a handshake. I then drove back to the gas station to fill my tank all the way up. I went back inside to ask for directions to the interstate and headed in that direction.

I made it back to my parents' home in Iowa in the afternoon and picked up Eli. We headed home and were home in time for me to quickly throw some grilled cheese and tomato soup together for dinner. It had been a long few days, but I was hopeful that the dementia spell was over with. It was time for some snuggles and a movie with my favorite boy before a good night's sleep.

*Soul 2: May 19, 2004, Miss Annalee, Dementia, Memory Found, Case Solved, Saved.*

June arrived and I felt compelled to search for Miss Annalee's case online. I quickly found an article pertaining to the case that had just been posted the day prior.

*An arrest has been made in a thirty-year-old cold case. Mr. Waylon Thorson of St. Louis Missouri age 63 was arrested June 3, 2004, on multiple murder counts. He was found guilty of forty-one murders all of whom were African American males. A question that was asked of Mr. Thorson during trial was 'why', 'why African American males'. Mr. Thorson responded, "they don't deserve to be in this country unless they're slaves, and I was tired of them being promoted over me, taking jobs that white men should have had." Mr. Thorson was also charged with twenty-four counts of arson. He would leave notes for his victims in case they happened to make it out of their homes alive. They always began with "Congratulations" and ended with a threat to stop hunting for their loved ones. He was also charged with seventeen counts of murder due to the arson charges. Mr. Thorson showed no remorse for the situation. Mr. Thorson's fingerprint was found on a letter that was hidden away by one of his victims. The letter stated to place it in the fire and let it burn with their belongings. This brave woman brought his reign of terror to an end, by risking her life to save the letter. Mr. Thorson readily admitted to his crimes and almost seemed proud of himself. He admitted to stalking each victim as they were leaving their office, hitting them over the head with a tire iron and then loading them into his trunk for transport. He then drove them to a location that he will not provide at this time to kill them by 'spilling their guts as they so deserved' quoted Mr. Thorson. He then buried them, would clean up and then go home to his family. Mr. Thorson was informed that the death penalty would occur unless he gives up the location of all his victims resting places. "The families would like to put their loved ones to rest Mr. Thorson, I think that is the least you can give to them after all these years of torture." Mr. Thorson is in deliberations with his lawyer and the prosecutor of the case.*

*Updated: June 6th, 2004 – Mr. Thorson has given up the location of his forty-one victims. Crime Scene Investigators have been working quickly to uncover all the victims in Forest Park. Mr. Thorson would go at night and bury his victims in the woods. There was no deal made before Mr. Thorson gave up the location of his victims thus leaving the death penalty on the table. Leaving the world to believe that maybe that is what he ultimately wants. Families are coming forward to claim the remains of their loved ones, but the State Crime Lab will still need to examine each body before returning them to loved ones. If you are a family of one of these many victims, please contact the State Crime Lab and leave your information. They will contact you as soon as the victim is properly identified, and all examinations have been thoroughly completed. They ask for your patience during this time as this is an extensive undertaking, and they want to make sure that everyone is reconnected with their family.*

I couldn't believe it. All those victims, those poor families. I just prayed now that they could be buried in peace and that the families could find some closure. I did one more search before closing my laptop: *Miss Annalee – St. Louis, MO.* The first thing that popped up was big bold letters stating, "HE (GOD) HAS FAVORED ME." The origin, and meaning, of Annalee.

Soul two had been saved.

# 6.

October 5th, 2004. Days were going by, and I was embracing the moments spent with Eli. My thoughts often went to the next time I'd be saving a life, but I knew if my thoughts were constantly filled with that of saving, I'd forget to live. My priorities were torn between ensuring I helped others and giving my son a beautiful childhood filled with love and joy. Even though my thoughts flickered back to potentially missing someone to save I had to have my faith within Azariah and God. I knew they would make sure I didn't let a person fall through the cracks.

All day I couldn't shake this feeling and these thoughts that I needed to save someone. No matter how hard I tried… tried to focus on my home life I just couldn't. Something was pulling me; a black hole sucking me into its vortex. I was distracted. I tried to regain focus and began preparing lunch for Eli. I was chopping up an apple and cut my hand between my thumb and pointer finger. I cried out in shock. I couldn't believe I had been so careless. I ran my hand under the faucet to wash off the blood trickling down my arm. At first, I didn't think it was too bad, but after I washed it out, I realized it was deeper than I thought. I wrapped it in a bandage from our first aid kit as a temporary solution. I loved living in a small town until moments like this occurred. Our local doctor's office was comprised of one doctor and his hours were limited. Unless you could wait a couple of days to go in the next closest option was the hospital twenty minutes outside of town. There wasn't a walk-in clinic closer. I packed up Eli's lunch and some snacks. We hopped in the car and drove twenty minutes outside of town to the emergency room.

Eli had finished the majority of his lunch on the drive to the emergency room, but the rest ended up next to him in his car seat or on the floor. I picked out the food from around him and tossed it out of the car along with the big chunks from the floor. I wiped his hands and face with a wipe before removing him from his car seat. We walked through the automatic doors to the emergency room and thankfully there were only a couple of people in the waiting room ahead of us. I got checked in and we found a seat in one of the waiting room's pods.

After about fifteen minutes my name was called to go to a triage room. They checked all my vitals and asked me the basic check-in questions: Allergies, mental health, and then of course how I managed to cut my hand. They ushered me out of the triage room and down the hall to an actual room. My hand was beginning to bleed through my temporary bandage at this point. The nurse came into the room. She looked exhausted, her face worn down, and eyes lacked shine. She had blonde hair styled in a pixie cut, her face was thin, and she looked frail. Regardless of her demeanor she was a very pleasant woman. She stretched a smile across her face and greeted me with kindness in her words. "Hello honey, my name is LeAnn, sounds like that knife and you didn't get along much, huh?" She joked.
I laughed in return. It was nice to feel some of my nervousness leave.
"Oh, my goodness, and who is this cutie pie?" She gestured towards Eli who was quietly playing with a couple of toys I brought on the bed next to me.
"This is Eli. Can you say 'hi' buddy?"
Eli looked up and waved and said 'hi'.

"Such a sweetie. I've got three boys at home, but they're a bit older now." She looked a little sad, but I think it was more so from not having a toddler any more than anything.

"How old are they?" I asked as she began unraveling the bandage on my hand.

"Let's see here, Brady is twelve now, Charles is ten, and Henry is 8." She started cleaning my hand out with water. Her gestures were slow, and her hands tremored as she cleaned. I could tell there was more she wasn't saying, but I didn't know if I should press it. That same urge I felt this morning overtook me and before I could think more my mouth was opening.

"I'm sorry about your husband." I spoke the words, but I don't know where they came from, and I don't know how I knew.

She looked at me with surprise on her face. "Thank you, dear. He passed away about a year ago in a work accident. He was a construction worker and was working on the side of a building. His harness failed and he fell."

"I'm so sorry to hear that. That must have been horrific for all of you. My husband passed away a few years back in a car accident."

She looked at me with sadness in her eyes and then gave me a big hug. She pulled away but held onto my shoulders a moment longer. "I'm sorry that you have to know that pain."

I placed my hand on her hand for a moment. She was such a kind soul.

"Well,' she said, 'I best get this cleaned out so the doc can come in and fix you up."


After she was done cleaning up my hand and the items, she used she turned to leave, but as she did so she stumbled.

"Are you okay?" I asked.

She took a moment to steady herself and regain balance. "Oh yes dear, I've just been having moments where I lose my balance lately. I'm not sure why."

"I think you need to see a doctor."

"Yes, I probably do, but I don't have a lot of time for that. Not with three boys at home and working full time."

"I understand that, but I think it is important. What if this is serious? If you don't get ahead of it, you could be down even longer and away from your boys." She nodded and then left the room.

The doctor came in and looked at my hand. "Oh yes, you are going to need stitches. I'll be right back in to numb this. We will give it a few minutes to work and then I will get this all fixed up for ya."
I nodded and said thank you as he turned to leave. A few moments later he came back in and injected my hand to numb it. "Okay, we will give this about ten minutes to work properly. I'll be back." He left again. Eli and I played for a little bit on the bed with his toys while we waited.

About fifteen minutes later the doctor and LeAnn came back in. He thoroughly washed his hands and then placed gloves on. She un-tied a medical kit that had tools and supplies in it and then set up a screen that my hand could go through. This was to not allow the patient, and in this case Eli, to observe the stitching process. LeAnn was slow in setting things up, her hands tremored again, and she almost dropped the supplies as she untied them. The doctor looked over at her with the noise the supply kit made as she fumbled it. She carried on as if nothing had happened. She began handing tools to the doctor as he began working on my hand. After about ten minutes the job was done, and he informed me of the after-care instructions.
"LeAnn will get you a copy of these instructions to take home with you as well, along with your discharge instructions." He gestured towards her. She nodded.
As he left, she turned back towards me and said, "I'll be right back hun. Just gonna go draw up that paperwork quick."

Upon her return she went back over the paperwork with me to show me where to find all the instructions. At the end I placed my hand on hers and said, "LeAnn, I think it would be wise of you to be checked out by a doctor. I really do. I know we don't know each other beyond this hospital room, but I just feel like I needed to say something." She placed her hand back on mine, smiled slightly, and then turned to walk out. I gathered up Eli and our things and we turned to leave.

A few days later that persistent jabbing at my brain began again. Something insisting that I needed to do something, that perpetual insistent prod. *Really, I thought? So early in the morning… I haven't even had coffee yet.* However, this time I felt as if I knew what I needed to do. I was going to go and check on LeAnn. Something told me our journey together wasn't finished. I slowly got up and gathered myself. It seemed like every year that I moved beyond the age of thirty my body protested more and more at the thought of getting up. I continued with my morning routine until I heard Eli babbling in his room and eventually calling "mama". I went to go get him so we could both get ready for our day ahead.

After we both had our breakfast and got ready, we packed up the diaper bag and headed out the door. We drove twenty minutes to the hospital. We walked into the main part of the hospital; there was a half-circle desk at the center and a beautiful water feature behind it. The sound of the water trickling down was soothing. There were plants surrounding the base of the water feature and around the two sides of the desk. You could look straight up and balconies for the different floors surrounded either side of the water feature. Above the main entrance was straight panels of glass – all windows that spilled in the natural light and highlighted all the features of the water glimmering down the wall.

At the information desk there sat a woman in probably her mid-fifties. A little heavy set with scrubs on and a black jacket over the top. She had brown hair that was gathered in a clip at the back, grey swirls throughout. She wore half-moon glasses that reminded me of something a librarian would wear and she was reading a book. We walked up to her and asked her if LeAnn from the emergency department was working today. She looked up with a smile and slid a bookmark into her page before setting her book down on the desk. She then typed something into her computer, looked perplexed, and then typed something else.

"Well dear, it looks like she is actually a patient here right now instead."

"Oh. We just saw her the other day. We wanted to come by and see how she was doing."

"It looks like her doctors have said it is okay for visitors. You could swing by her room if you like."

"Yes, please, that would be great."

"Room 506 dear. You take this elevator up to the fifth floor. Make a right, go down the hallway and you'll see a nurse's station. You can either ask them to point you to her room from there, or there should be signs on the wall directing you to where the rooms are at."

"Thank you. I appreciate it."

Eli and I made the trek to the fifth floor and down the hallway. There were no nurses at the station, so we looked at the wall and determined where her room was. The hallway toward her door smelled of antiseptic and a slight hint of something lemon. Probably the cleaner that was used. Everything was white and sterile. The fluorescents overhead didn't help with the sterile features of the hallway and instead accentuated it.

When we got to her door it was plastered with a variety of different drawings and pictures. It looked like they were all from her boys. The room was dark, other than the natural light shining through the window. I gently tapped on the door, and a sweet low voice told us to 'come on in'. As we entered LeAnn looked towards us. Her eyes grew wide with surprise and then turned into tears.

"I never expected to see you both again." She cried.

"Well, I had to see if you figured out what was going on, although I expected a quick visit down in the emergency room, not here."

"I fell at work a few hours after you left. Hit my head on the nurse's station. The doctor admitted me for some tests." She paused and looked towards the window. She wiped away her tears and then continued. "You were right… something is wrong."

I didn't say anything, just waited for her to go on. I placed my hand on hers to encourage her.

"I have Fulminate Multiple Sclerosis."

I squeezed her hand gently and paused for a moment to gather my thoughts. "I… I know what Multiple Sclerosis is. It's a disease where your immune system attacks the nerves, but what is the 'Fulminate' part?"

"Multiple Sclerosis also shuts down communication between the brain and body due to the nerves being so deteriorated. The fulminate part means it is one of the most severe cases of MS that reoccurs often. I guess my body is attacking so hard that when I fell it was due to a minor seizure."

"What does this mean?"

"It means I won't be able to work anymore. The doctors think even with steroids or other treatments I could potentially endanger lives. They think to the degree the disease has progressed the treatment may not work or take months to get under control, and then with it being so severe it could relapse every few years. The degeneration is so advanced they are worried about my fine motor skills, which unfortunately you need as a nurse. Long story short, I don't know how I am going to provide for my family anymore. We are barely making it as it is. My husband's social security paychecks aren't a lot, and we have already moved to a smaller place. What do I do? How do I provide for my kids?"

At that moment I felt like someone was watching me. I looked over my shoulder, but all that was there was the sterile hallway staring back at me, the curtain divider hanging slightly closed. Then I felt a pressure on my shoulder. It felt like a hand, but still no one was there. Then it squeezed my shoulder, and as quickly as it came it then disappeared.

*Azariah.*

I knew then what I needed to do – God chose this woman for a reason. I don't think it was due to her unfortunate circumstances financially. I believed it was something to do with her future as a nurse.

"I need you to trust me a minute."

She looked at me a little perplexed but then nodded. I kept my hand on hers and I prayed for her soul to feel no more pain, to have no more seizures, for her body to be restored, and for her to save many more lives as a nurse. That familiar sensation of pins and needles erupting through my body arrived, and the burning sensation to my lower back where the mark was erasing. My whole body felt electrified with pain, as if my nervous system was going to explode. Eli was on my lap, so I tried hard not to cringe or writhe in pain. When the pain finally dissipated my hand slid off hers, I began breathing shallowly but tried to regain control with deeper breaths.

"Are you okay, hun?" She looked at me with concern in her eyes. Then her eyes widened. She started patting herself all over as if she were expecting to trigger the pain to come back to her, as if she were hallucinating. "Wait… what did you do?" she stammered. "I…I don't feel tired anymore. I don't feel pain anymore. My hands are steady again…." She held her hands out as if to double-check that what her mouth was saying was accurate.

"Call it a miracle." I said with a slight smile. This time it really hit me hard for some reason. I was still feeling woozy from the sudden rush that had crept up my body.

"I don't understand," she clamored.

"All I can tell you is that you have been given a second chance at life, but you mustn't take it for granted, and you can't tell anyone that I was the one who helped you."

She looked at me in disbelief. Then nodded.

"I should be going. I need to get little mister home for lunch and a nap."

She reached out and grabbed my hand before I could leave.

70

"Thank you. Whatever this is, whatever you did. Thank you." A tear came to her eye and slowly cascaded down her face. I squeezed her hand gently and then turned to walk away. As I was leaving her doorway I turned and saw her sobbing in her hands.

✦✦✦✦✦✦

Two days went by, and I had started symptoms that LeAnn had exhibited. It began slowly with my joints aching throughout my body. I was able to get Eli down to bed that evening, before the extreme side effects kicked in. I felt it would be safer if I stayed in my bed and tucked in for the long evening that I anticipated ahead of me. I got myself ready for bed as quickly as I could, but it became increasingly difficult as my hands began to tremor, and I started to feel unstable. I stumbled from the bathroom around the corner to my room. My body began to seize as I faltered towards my bed. Convulsions rose throughout my body, and I collapsed onto the bed just as my body went into a paralysis state. I couldn't move, but my body was having a full seizure. I tried to roll onto my side. The seizure continued for several minutes. When it finally stopped, I felt exhausted. My hands still tremored and the pain seared in all my joints. It felt like each individual joint was being ripped apart at the seams. I continued to lie there feeling helpless for hours on end, the pain and tremors never subsiding. . .

The next morning the tremors were still there but not as drastic, and the pain finally had dwindled to a manageable amount. The next week Eli and I would stay indoors and color, watch movies, and play with his toys as I recovered.

*Soul 3: October 5, 2004, LeAnn, Multiple Sclerosis, Kindness pursues – nursing others to health. Saved.*

# 7.

May 2nd, 2005. Spring was finally upon us and with the warmer weather Eli and I were getting out more to play outside. Enjoying the warmth of the sun, the trees, and flowers in bloom. On this particular day we decided to go to the park in town near our church. It was a small community park that the majority of the town went to. It had beautiful mature oak trees encasing either side. A small wooden open-air shelter set off to the side of the playground. A merry-go-round, set of swings, small play structure with two slides, a little bridge connecting the two sides of the structure, and different steps and ladders to access it. Woodchips flooded underneath the equipment and were surrounded by wood beams to contain them.

Eli dashed away to climb up the stairs and go down the spiral slide. He loved slides and swings. There were several children at the park today, but Eli was more concerned about going down the slides. I sat on a bench off to the side and watched as he played. After about one hundred times of Eli going down the slide, he ran back over to me and asked if I'd take him on the swings. I picked him up and put him in the toddler swing and began pushing him, his laughter illuminating the warm spring day. His dirty blonde hair fluttering amongst the breeze as he swung up and back.

A short while later a dad and, what I assumed was his son, approached the swing set. The boy was thin, frail looking, his eyes looked hollow and sunken. It looked as though he was being swallowed into his T-shirt and shorts. The thing that stood out the most was that his head was bald. I felt empathetic towards him, it was clear that he had some sort of illness. Then he got on the swings, and his dad slowly pushed him. The joy rushed over his face and his smile lit up the entire playground. It was intoxicating and I couldn't help but stare. I saw that dad looking at me.
"I'm sorry for staring. His smile is just… it's so wonderful."
The dad smiled and looked back towards his son, "he is amazing."
"May I ask how old he is?" I asked hesitantly. Sometimes parents don't want to engage in communication at parks. They are just there to be with their kid and don't want outside engagement.
"He's six…" he was going to go on but was interrupted by the little boy's sweet frail voice.
"…and a half!" The little boy stated matter-of-factually.
"That's right son." The dad, now officially confirmed that it indeed was his dad, smiled.
I responded, "Well, that is wonderful!" I was thinking how the boy didn't look six and a half. He looked like he was more like four or five due to his condition. He was small for his age.
After a little time, the dad asked, "How old is your boy?"
"Oh, um, Eli is three now, he will be four in the fall."
"My name is Arthur, but everyone calls me Art." The little boy chimed in as he continued to swing next to us.
"I love that name, Art, how cool. It is so unique." I gave him a big smile.
"Ya, my dad says it is unique like me."
"I can tell you are probably one of the coolest kids around."
"It's true." He stated, but not in an arrogant way. He was so sure of himself, so confident.
"I'm sure you get asked this a lot Art, but do you like "art"?

73

Coloring, drawing, painting…" I trailed off to let him answer.
"I love to draw… and color. My dad's helping me set up a
charity,' he stumbled over the word charity, but it was so cute,
'event where I sell my colorings to get money for Children's
Cancer. We gonna give the money to find a… what is the word
dad?"
"A cure, buddy." His dad filled in the blank.
"Ya, that is it. Cure."
"What a wonderful idea. Did you come up with that?"
"Well… I want to do something before I have to go be in the
sky… dad says that I won't have to go be in the sky, but I heard
the doctors talkin'. I want to help other kids while I can."

I just stared at that frail little boy with the biggest heart I
had ever come across. He was simply awe-inspiring. I looked at
his dad who had tears coming into his eyes and looked a little
embarrassed that his son had revealed so much to a stranger.
"Well Art, I would love to buy one of your colorings."
"Really?" he almost shouted with excitement.
"Of course! Do you know where the event will be at?"
"Ya, it will be here in the park at the shelter this Saturday. We
came to make sure we could set all my colorings out."
His dad chimed in, "it starts at 9:00am."
"Well, Eli and I will definitely be there, Art."
He looked up at me and smiled. Eli wanted to get down to go play
on the slides some more before we headed home. We waved
goodbye.

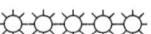

May 7, 2005. Eli and I arrived back at the park around
9:30am that beautiful Saturday morning. Clouds were slowly
passing by creating shadows all around. The sun peeking through
was starting to warm up the air, but not quite ready for no jackets
yet. As we arrived outside of the park there was a big colorful
banner that read 'Art in the Park' and underneath read 'Charity
Event for Children's Cancer'. There was another large yard sign
in the shape of a yellow ribbon. Within the shelter there were

easels set up with several framed colorings, and several more on the picnic tables and set up all around. They were really good for a six-and-a-half-year-old. I was really impressed by the color and depth that each presented. Each drawing had a story with it that explained why Art had drawn it. The one that caught my eye was an abstract coloring with a beautiful golden arch that swooped like an upside down 'J'. It looked like half of a yellow ribbon. Around it was blues, reds, oranges, and a brilliant white surrounding the actual golden swoosh. The name at the top of the story was *My Future.* The story read:

*I am not an illness or disease. I am me. I am an advocate for Children's Cancer. I know that one day I will approach the golden gates of heaven due to my illness. Surrounded in a bright white light. The sun will set around me. I will be sad to leave my family, my home, but I know that I helped while I was on this Earth. I made this painting to show my future and the sadness surrounding me leaving.*

You could tell an adult had written it in more expanded words than a six-year-old would have written, but you could also tell that Art was behind those words too. I searched around for Art and his dad, but I only saw his dad. I walked up to him, he looked worn down, ragged. His brown eyes were surrounded by red, and bags accompanied the redness. His black hair was a bit disheveled and his golden shirt that read 'Art has my Heart' was untucked from his blue jeans.

"Hi, I don't know if you remember us, but we met here this week." I began.
"Oh, yes, I do."
"Where is Art...?" I asked but trailed off because I thought maybe it was too intrusive. I almost winced, expecting a poor reaction. Instead, a tear rolled down from his eye.
"Art isn't doing well. This week he had a big episode with his Leukemia. They are trying an experimental treatment, because really that is all we have left. It didn't go well. He reacted poorly and his body is too weak to do anything now, so they kept him in

the hospital." He then smirked a little and went on, "However, he will be here for a few minutes soon. He begged and begged the doctors and nurses to let him come, and really the only reason I continued on with this event is because he instructed me to do so. I couldn't tell him no, even though I really didn't want to. The doctors were planning on moving him to …" he hesitated and then began to cry. I placed my hand on his arm. He cleared his throat and went on, "the doctors are moving him to hospice today. They instructed the ambulance drivers to "get lost" on the way and bring him here for a few minutes before taking him to the hospice facility. I will join him as soon as the event is done. They are only giving him a couple of days to live." He sobbed into his hands at the words.

"I'm so sorry." I went in for a hug even though I wasn't sure if he actually wanted one. He hugged me back. After a few moments we released.

"Well, I'd like to help." I pointed out the painting from before and told him I wanted to purchase it. He told me the price was twenty dollars, but I didn't think that was enough. I pulled out a one-hundred-dollar bill and passed it to him. He thanked me profusely. I took the painting back to my car and then let Eli go run and play at the park again for a little while. I wanted to see Art before we left. I sat on the bench again and watched Eli play on the slides. The breeze spun around me and within the wind I heard a small voice speak in my ear.

*You will help this boy.*

I spoke softly under my breath. "I was already planning on it, Azariah." The wind picked my hair up and the hood of my jacket and tossed it up over my head as if playing a game. I knew it was Azariah messing with me for 'sassing' back. I laughed a little and the wind stopped as quickly as it came.

An hour passed by and out of the corner of my eye I noticed the ambulance coming down the lane. It pulled up next to the park. The back doors opened and inside was a hospital gurney with a small boy on it. The medic helped unbuckle him and the driver had now come around and grabbed out a wheelchair. The medic inside of the ambulance helped lower the boy down into the other medic's arms.

*Art.*

He looked so much worse. I didn't think it was possible, but his smile was only half what it was. His skin looked almost grey now. The medic placed him in the wheelchair and covered him in a blanket. He wore sweatpants and a sweatshirt that seemed to swallow him even more than his T-shirt and shorts from the other day. The medic carefully rolled him up the sidewalk to the shelter and the other medic closed up the ambulance and followed behind them. Art's dad came to greet him. Several townsfolk were there perusing his colorings. It had been a steady flow since we arrived. I gave Art a minute to be with his dad and the others that were at his event. He looked as happy as he could be to see everyone.

Art wasn't able to stay long before they had to take him to the hospice house. As they turned to walk him down the sidewalk, I grabbed Eli and we approached him towards the end of it. Eli was not pleased that I had drug him away so quickly from the slides, but I told him we could go back for a couple more turns after I talked to Art. That seemed to suffice.

"Hi Art, do you remember Eli and I from the other day?" The medics had stopped rolling him.
"Ya, I do." He weakly looked up at me.
I asked the medics to please give us a minute. They looked at each other and then returned to the ambulance to open it up and prep it.
I knelt next to him. "I really wanted to see you again. I bought one of your paintings. It was called 'My Future'. It was beautiful."
"That is one of my favorites." He coughed into his arm. He looked so sickly. "Sorry, I'm really tired."

"I understand, Art. One more thing before you go, please." I placed my hand on his hand. He grabbed my hand and held it. He squeezed gently. I closed my eyes. I prayed for this sweet boy's soul. I prayed that he would feel no more pain, no more despair, no more pokes, prods, worry. I prayed that he would continue to be an advocate for Children's Cancer. I prayed for him never to have to deal with cancer in his body again, for him to live a normal happy childhood away from hospitals and doctors. My thoughts and prayer trailed off as I felt the mark on my back being erased.

I prepped myself for what was next. The pins and needles followed by the eruption of pain that spread from my toes through my hair follicles on my head. Every pore in my body felt the pain. My head jutted back as the pain almost exploded from my mouth and eyes. It slowly dissipated and I let my hand slide to my knee. I took some big breaths, regained control, my eyes watering from the pain illuminating out of me. I looked up at Art. He looked at me and then pushed the wheelchair back and stood up next to me. His skin looked a beautiful shade of pink again, his eyes looked full, no longer sunken in. His body looked all around healthier. He pulled down his shirt and the spot where his Hickman Line had been removed yesterday was gone. No open wound, no scar. He looked back at me and basically fell on top of me in a huge embrace. I wrapped my arm around him and whispered in his ear. "You have been saved. You can't tell anyone. It is a secret. Keep being an advocate." He shook his head up and down into my shoulder. He let go and ran as fast as his legs would take him over to his dad. I got up quickly and walked Eli back to the park for another turn on the slide before we left the park. I looked over my shoulder at the medics who had come back around the ambulance and were scratching their heads dumbfounded. Then when they realized where Art was, they ran over to him. His dad was on his knees bawling into his son's sweatshirt.

With the advanced stage of Art's Leukemia, I knew that it

would be a long few days ahead. I called in reinforcements, my parents. Alma and Dale showed up in a blaze of glory the next morning. They waltzed right in through the front door as I came around the corner with my coffee. I hadn't felt the effects fully yet, but I had signs that it was quickly approaching. I had hoped it would hold off long enough for me to be able to do a run down with my folks prior to going into hiding for the next couple of days.

My mother immediately ran up to me and threw her wrist against my forehead and down my cheek again. I swear that is a natural instinct when your child tells you they don't feel well. Even if it is a skinned knee. It was engrained the second you gave birth.

I grabbed my mom's arm softly and held it against my face. "I'm okay mom. Just don't want to get Eli sick if I'm coming down with something."

I ran down what was in the fridge for them and Eli to eat and everything else that was typically discussed when you were 'changing over the guard' so to speak. I gave both of my parents a hug and gave my mom the baby monitor to await Eli waking up. I headed back to the bedroom to await my fate; and although I knew deep down that these next few days would be extremely difficult, I knew that what I was able to do for Art was all worth it. I had hung his coloring in my office next to my bookshelf and put the story that went along with it inside the back of the frame. The tag on the front was written in childlike handwriting: *My Future by Art McGavin.*

*Soul 4: May 7, 2005, Art, Leukemia, Making the world more beautiful one brush stroke at a time. Saved.*

# 8.

September 23rd, 2005. Atti Crannell was a twenty-year-old college student at Central College in Pella, Iowa. She was majoring in Environmental Sustainability. She wanted to be able to help the environment and use her free time to travel around the world to volunteer. Helping countries that need assistance with their surrounding environments and show them how to create a sustainable source of food. She had grown up in Ottumwa, Iowa which was a little less than an hour drive away from her college.

She had long, thick auburn hair that fell to just above her pant line. She had freckles that covered her fair-skinned cheek bones and scattered across her nose. Her green eyes were one of the features she actually liked about herself. They were light green, but they were vivid. She wore a vintage off-the-shoulder long-sleeved Bardot blouse that was a rich dark red color. She had gained some 'college weight' that she was trying to get rid of. For instance, when she was sitting in her car, she had started getting a bit of stomach hanging over her jeans. She sucked in her stomach and pulled up the front of her jeans to cover it. It wasn't like it was bad and when she stood up, she still looked thin, but sitting is what she didn't approve of. She was much more judgmental of herself then others probably saw her.

She was sitting in her 1998 silver Honda Civic in the parking lot of her college. She was about to head home for a long weekend; her Monday classes had been cancelled. It was Friday after classes, and she had gone back to her dorm to grab a duffel bag quickly before heading out. It was about 6:00pm and the sun was beginning to go down. She pulled her hair off to the side and braided it. She turned on the radio and her headlights and began on her way.

She was on Highway 63S looping around the outskirts of Eddyville tapping her hands on her steering wheel to the beat of the song. It was now dusk and the trees that lined the highway made it look even more dark and ominous. Out of the darkness, across the median was a black Dodge Neon that was hurtling in her direction. It had jumped the median and was flying up above the ground a bit from the sheer speed of hitting the slope of the median. The Neon's lights were not on. She tried to swerve, but the car came so quickly she didn't have enough time to react.

She braced for impact and twisted her body to the right as quickly as she could. The Neon made contact; metal grinding against metal; glass shattering and shards splintering into her shoulders, neck, and face. She let out a scream as the Neon's front end smashed her door into her side, forcing her against the steering wheel and over towards the passenger seat. The air bag deployed at that moment and slammed her into the back of the seat knocking the wind from her. Metal continued to contort, and she felt her car sliding down the slope on the opposite side of the highway… into the depth of the woods; swallowing her car whole as her car went end over end.

She felt the top of her car compounding inward as it

rolled over and over again. Shards of glass, metal, and random items in the car were flying in slow motion through the air around her until the passenger side finally collided into a tree and came to rest. The Neon pinned her car against the tree. Atti was going in and out of consciousness. As she came to for a moment she looked down at her legs. They were mangled, broken, bones showing through her ripped jeans. Her heart rate rose more than it already was as she took in the sight; she started breathing heavily and sobbing.

She glanced up as her engine began steaming and looked out what was left of her driver's side window. She saw a man inside the Neon, head tilted back against the seat, blood trickling down from his forehead. *Ryan.* She knew who it was … she knew this man. Suddenly a sharpness overtook her. She grasped her left side with her right hand, and a sticky warmth overcame her fingers.

*Blood.*

She saw Ryan stirring within his car and knew, to protect herself, she needed to go unconscious. She didn't need to fake it… her eyes went hazy… blackness overtook her… her body collapsing against the seatbelt, head flopped forward.

✧✧✧✧✧✧

Ryan was an alumnus of the Central Iowa Juvenile Detention Center. He was really popular with the local police, and not in a 'good citizen' type of way. He had a few petty theft charges, breaking and entering charges, but the one that made him so infamous in the area was for his stalking, aggravated assault, and attempted kidnapping. It began when his family moved from Florida when he was thirteen to Ottumwa. The girl that lived next to them was a year older than him, Atti. She was beautiful, and he was the opposite. He was what everyone considered 'goth'. He wore black all the time, baggy pants with chains, hair pitch black and spiked. His mom was a pastor at the local church, she was constantly making him come with her, making him wear dress pants and button ups and combing his hair to the side. He hated it. Despised it. Being forced to believe in a God that he didn't believe was even real. He did everything in his power to go against his mother's wishes. He told her constantly that he was an atheist, but every time he did, she just made him go to church more. It was a viscous cycle, but when he realized that Atti's family went to the same church – and would occasionally come on Sundays he wouldn't protest as much to going. Unless she ended up not being at church that week, then he would make his mom's life a living hell at church in front of her congregation.

He made a sick obsession with stalking Atti. Followed her around school, lurking around her work at the local diner, but the best part was that his bedroom window was adjacent to hers. He would turn off his bedroom lights and look through his blinds at her in the evenings. She mostly lay on her bed and wrote in a journal or did her homework. Like he said, he was the opposite of Atti, but he loved that about her. He wanted to be near her. He had brushed against her in the hallways of school several times... getting a whiff of her citrus medley perfume, the fresh scent of her shampoo, felt the smoothness of her skin against his. He was intoxicated by her. This obsession went on for almost three years.

When he turned sixteen, he bought a cheap black 2000 Kia Rio. He wanted to impress Atti and drive her to school. She didn't have a car of her own but would borrow her parent's car occasionally. He drove up next to her one morning as she was walking to school and asked to give her a ride. She politely rejected him, and that infuriated him. He sped off. That day at school Atti was flirting with a boy in her grade, Jack Winston, in the hallway. Ryan turned his attention to Jack for the next couple of days.

Four days later after school Ryan was waiting by his car for Jack to emerge from the building. He had skipped school that day to prepare for the events that would unwind that afternoon.

When he saw Jack come out of the school, he followed him towards the tree line that led toward Jack's house. He was with a group of friends, but they quickly dispersed. Jack was walking along the thick trees on the sidewalk heading to his cul-de-sac. Ryan left the side of his car, grabbing the baseball bat that he had propped up against the car next to him... waiting. Ryan snuck up behind Jack as quickly and quietly as he could, and bum rushed him; tackling him into the woods that lined the sidewalk. Even though Ryan was thinner and a touch shorter than Jack, who clearly worked out on a regular basis, he caught him by surprise and was able to get him to the ground.

Ryan scurried up and stood over Jack holding the baseball bat above his head. Jack swept Ryan's feet from underneath him, and he fell backwards onto the leaf laden ground beneath him. Jack and Ryan both got on their feet as quickly as possible and before Jack could rush at him Ryan swung the bat as hard as he could. Clocking Jack's left shoulder swiftly and with intensity. Jack stumbled to the right and went to his knee. Now was Ryan's chance.
"How dare you touch Atti. How dare you talk to her." Ryan muttered under his breath before once more hitting Jack, but this time it would be lights out. This time he hit him on his left temple, taking him to the ground, blood emerging from his scalp.

Ryan dropped the bat next to Jack and ran back to his car. Exhilarated. Winded. Ready for Phase Two of his plan. He sped off in his car down the street until he spotted her. *Atti.* He drove up next to her. Her hair shone brightly in the sunshine. He parked the car and ran over to her. He could smell her perfume in the wind. He grabbed her arm. She spun around alarmed by the sudden contact.

"Atti, come with me." He pleaded. "I have my car packed with clothes, food, and supplies. Run away with me. We can be together… just you and me. Forever."

She was trying to wrench away from Ryan's grip. "No." She yelled.

This enraged him even more. He had done so much for her, and this is how she was going to repay him… by being repulsed. "You leave me no choice." He tried dragging her by the arm towards his car, and she sat down digging her heels into the earth, clawing at the earth with her free hand. She was screaming as loud as she could. He kicked her rib cage to knock the wind out of her. Which worked, but only temporarily. She was definitely a fighter. He wished he had a firearm to help subdue her, or even brought the bat with him, but he never imagined she would tell him no.

*No.*

*How could she?*

He grabbed her by the leg while she was down and winded and continued dragging her to his car. She was now on her stomach and trying to grasp at the grass to gain leverage. Neighbors began to appear at their doorways. As he approached the car door, Ryan stopped to open it. Just then Atti whipped around and kicked him square in the back of the knee bringing him down and, before he could put his hands out, his face made full contact with the metal of the door panel. He released her leg, his face flushing with pain.

He screamed as she dug her feet into the grass below her feet and bolted towards the nearest house. Ryan tried to scurry after her, but he heard sirens in the background. He changed his mind and ran back towards his car. Getting in the driver's seat, starting the car, and then stepping on the gas down the road.

Red and blue lights hurdled towards him and just like in the movies, skidded sideways in front of him blocking his outlet. He tried to reverse, but the police officers jumped out of their vehicles and drew their weapons in his direction. One got on the megaphone and instructed him to put his hands out the window. After a few moments of standoff, he decided to comply.

*Someday Atti will be mine.*

☼☼☼☼☼

September 23, 2005. I was heading home on Highway 63S from a day at my parents' house. They were taking Eli for the weekend since it had been some time since we had visited, or they us. It was going to be a weekend full of deep cleaning of the house, old records playing, opening the windows for one of the last few times they'd get to be open prior to winter's arrival.

Don't get me wrong, spending my time with Eli meant the world to me, but I couldn't get the deep clean and organizing done that I really wanted to with him under foot. He would get all the love and attention he could possibly want, and then probably more, and I would get a clean house. As I came around the bend, I thought I saw a car in front of me, but I wasn't sure. It was black and the lights weren't on. I slowed down a little to make sure.

It was a car.

I flashed my lights at them a couple times to let them know they forgot their headlights. As soon as I did the car sped up and then before I could register what was happening, I watched as the car jutted to the left and jumped the median. Airborne, the car hit another silver sedan heading in the opposite direction directly on the driver's side door. *What was happening?*

I found a place to turn around and called the police from my cell phone. I parked along the median and turned on my hazard lights.

"911 what's your emergency." The dispatcher on the other side of the line sounded unamused to be at work. I'm sure she got several calls that were nothing more than false alarms. My call would change her night around.

"Yes, I just witnessed a car accident. A black sedan jumped the median and hit a silver sedan on the driver's side." I explained. "They rolled down the ravine into the woods on Highway 63S just past the bridge that goes over the Mahaska Road."
"Okay I know where you're at." She seemed to perk up a little.
"I'm guessing there will need to be an ambulance. I'm going to go down and check to make sure everyone is okay."
"Please do not go down the ravine and wait for officers to arrive to keep yourself safe."
"I understand." I said but didn't mean.
We hung up after she instructed that officers and paramedics would be on scene soon.

I wasn't about to wait around if there was someone in trouble. I got out of my car and locked my car doors behind me, shoving my keys into my jacket pocket. I looked down into the darkness of the ravine. It wasn't overly deep, but with the dense trees it made it look foreboding. Just as I approached the edge a figure staggered away from the scene. The person was clearly hurt, but my gut was telling me this was not the person I needed to help; to stay away.

I went with my instinct and dropped down the ravine and lay on my stomach. I inched down into the tree line. The person was in all black and threw their hood up. I assumed it was a man by his stature. He hobbled over to my car and tried to get in. Thankfully I had locked it and taken the keys with me. I figured he would try and smash-in the window, but he didn't. He walked towards the bridge, and I watched as he ducked underneath it and out of sight. I couldn't worry about him right now. I slid the rest of the way down towards the wreckage beneath me.

87

I went around the black, what I now knew to be a Dodge Neon, looking inside to ensure no one else was in it. *No one.* I walked over to the silver sedan and saw a slouched body inside. Before I got there something caught my eye. *Blood.* It was written on the front hood and up the windshield in blood. I could just make it out from the moonlight shining through the canopy of branches above.

*You are mine!*

I rushed to the woman inside the car. I shook her shoulder. "Ma'am, are you okay?" I reached in carefully to avoid the glass and metal shards protruding from the damaged side of the vehicle and turned on the interior light above. It was dim, but enough that I could assess more of the situation. Blood soaked her side and what was left of the seat beneath her. Glass shards obtruded from her face, neck, and shoulders, blood trickling down from each spot. Then I saw her legs... they looked to be beyond repair. I felt for a pulse, and found one, but it was weak. If she died, I wouldn't be able to save her.

*Is this someone I am supposed to save?* There was no wind gust, no Azariah whispering in my ear. This was on me.

*I was here, at this exact moment, for a reason. I wouldn't have been here right now if I weren't supposed to.*

I stopped doubting myself and did what my gut was telling me to do. I needed to act quickly before the ambulance and police showed up. I reached in and touched her shoulder. I prayed for her body to be repaired, for her to go on and live a full life away from whatever danger she was in. I prayed for her mind to heal from the trauma of this incident and from whatever ordeal was contributing to this moment in time. I prayed for her soul to be saved.

I felt the burning sensation on my back as the mark erased

for her soul. The tingling sensation appeared and flooded my body instantaneously after knocking me to the ground. The crunch of the fallen leaves beneath my knees as I hit the earth below me. I clutched my chest gasping for air as the pain shuttered through my body. I heard the sirens approaching and could see their flash from above the ravine. I shakily collected myself and got up. I looked down at the woman in the seat as I continued to collect myself. I watched the wound on her side disappear, her legs revert back to normal, and the glass shards dropping from her body, wounds underneath healing instantly.

Blood still stained her shirt, seat, face, and legs, but no longer fresh. Her jeans and shirt were still ripped, but her body was healed. I had only ever done souls that had internal illnesses, nothing external like this. I was in shock of how quickly bones slid back into place, wounds healed… I couldn't believe what was happening before my eyes. The woman began to stir. She put her hand to her head.
"Oh man," she murmured, "what happened?" She blinked a few times and looked around at the scene around her. She became increasingly alarmed. "Oh my gosh, Ryan. Where is he? I have to get out of here."
"It's okay." I put my hand on her shoulder. "He isn't here. He ran off."
She seemed relieved but on edge at the same time.
The police came down the ravine calling out as they came. "Is everyone okay?"
"She's over here." I hollered back. "She's okay."
"Wait…' she hesitated, 'no, my legs… my side… my face…."
She looked and felt everywhere, but could find nothing other than sticky, drying blood. "I don't understand."

The police came up to the cars and searched the other car with their flashlights. Up above the ravine the fire department was setting up spotlights and pointing them down upon the accident. "Are you the witness that called this in, ma'am?" The taller of the two police officers directed his question towards me.
"Yes,' I answered, 'the other man, she said his name is Ryan,

took off under the bridge. He wrote a message on her hood." The officer pointed his flashlight in the direction of the hood and then spoke onto his radio instructing more officers to set up a perimeter around the area. He then directed his attention to the woman in the car.

"What is your name ma'am?"

"Atti. Atti Crannell."

"Where were you heading, Atti?"

She explained that she was coming from college and going home for the weekend. Then she went on to explain how she knew the man from the other car. She told the police officer his whole name, and that his mother still was her parents neighbor, but she hadn't seen Ryan for years. She knew that he was put in Juvenile Detention for the events that had occurred. She was terrified that he would come back to find her.

"I understand Atti but first let's get you out of this car." The police officer took a tool off his key chain and sliced her seatbelt. The fire department had descended the hill and were next to us. They were trying to figure out the safest way of getting her out of the car without harming her. A paramedic was there next to the car too. She came over and began talking to Atti. The police officer and I moved off to the side to let them work.

I gave the police officer my name and phone number in case they had further questions for me. It took about an hour to get her out of the car, because she was pinned in, and the tree was so severely damaged they were concerned about it falling over on the car. The police officers, paramedics, and fire department were all astounded that she hadn't sustained any injuries. I left the scene before I could be confronted more. Local news was arriving on scene as I left. This story will be all over the local papers and news by tonight. Heck it could even become national news with the back story.

Police officers were going to have her go to the hospital overnight to ensure she didn't have any internal bleeding. They notified her parents for her, and they were going to meet her at the hospital. Cops were going to post outside of her room until they could find Ryan.

When I got home, I quickly went and switched on my computer and looked up the previous story on Ryan Franklin – I had learned from the scene – and Atti Crannell. Once I entered in their names and "Ottumwa, Iowa" an article immediately popped up, and it read:

*Ryan Jameson Franklin, 16, was arrested for aggravated assault and attempted kidnapping. After taking a baseball bat to a fellow student, Jack Winston, and knocking him unconscious. He then proceeded to stalk and attempted to kidnap a 17-year-old named Atti Crannell. Mr. Franklin later admitted to stalking Ms. Crannell for almost three years. Jack Winston is currently in the hospital with three fractured ribs, a skull fracture, and a concussion. He is expected to make a full recovery. Ryan will be processed and held until his court date.*

The mugshot of Ryan was attached to the article. From the black and white photo, he looked super pale but had jet black hair that was spiked into what looked like a mohawk. He had a smirk on his face and wore a black shirt that matched his hair. His eyes looked soulless. Empty. Unforgiving.

I switched over to the TV and turned on the local news. A few minutes into the ten o'clock news flashing lights filled the screen. The news anchor was going on to describe the accident and what they believed to have happened. They showed the wreckage and stated that the party that was hit walked away from the incident unscathed but would spend the night in the hospital for observation. "No one understands how this person walked away unharmed." The anchor looked genuinely surprised. "The perpetrator has not yet been recovered. A search is in progress. Police do not believe locals are in danger at this time, but they are instructing everyone to be in their homes and lock the doors and windows just to be safe."

I had dozed off. I woke up and rubbed my eyes looking back at the TV that was playing some sort of commercial about a cereal. I got up and was about to click off the TV when the screen flashed with a breaking news report. I sat back down and turned up the volume.

*"The perpetrator of the accident earlier reported has been caught. He is now identified as Ryan Franklin. He was released from the Central Iowa Juvenile Detention Center on probation and was awaiting a trial date. Mr. Franklin, at the age of sixteen, was arrested for aggravated assault and attempted kidnapping. The family of the boy that was assaulted is pushing for the aggravated assault to be an attempted murder charge and for Mr. Franklin to be tried as an adult. Mr. Franklin is back in custody tonight after police recovered him a few miles away. His injuries prevented him from going further and he attempted to hide in a drainage ditch. K9 Officers quickly located Mr. Franklin."*

They re-played the previous car accident and then the scene of them arresting Ryan. They also flashed his previous mug shot along the screen that I had seen earlier online. Hopefully justice will be served, and he will be behind bars for many years to come so Atti can finally live in peace.

*Soul 5: September 23, 2005, Atti, Car Accident, Stalker, Free. Saved.*

# 9.

April 15, 2006. I was happy to have a long break after my last soul. Atti's injuries were excruciating. I hadn't saved anyone prior to her that had broken bones and physical injuries. It felt as though my bones were breaking repeatedly. I had continuously checked my face for actual glass shards in my face, and my side was on fire. It was probably the worst I had gone through so far in terms of pain, and although it only lasted a day it was so intense, I didn't know if I could have made it any longer. The aftereffects lasted longer than normal, and I wasn't really back to myself for some time… mentally and emotionally.

During the day of excruciating pain my mind continued to relive her fear and anguish from the initial attack by Ryan, when she was only a teenager. Flashbacks occurred like after I saved Ray. My mind flashed to that moment in time when Ryan was dragging her across the grass. I could smell it, could feel it. The fresh cut grass smell, the dirt in my fingernails. The pressure on my ankle and the air removed from my lungs after the swift kick to my stomach. Then my memory would flash forward to the car accident. Feeling each and every bump, twist, contortion.

93

Smelling the rust stench; blood, pine trees around me, sweat from adrenaline. Going in and out of reality to see the dark figure next to me and the fear and anxiety rising once more within my soul again. Heart pounding in my chest, and then darkness. Even after the day I relived the memory and had the anxiety of someone always watching me. This went on for weeks, before I felt like myself again. I was relieved to feel normality sink back in and was happy spending the holidays with my family.

☼☼☼☼☼

I was taking a nap with Eli today after he got home from three-year-old preschool. Since his birthday is in October, he quickly turned four after preschool started, but he would go to preschool this year and next before beginning kindergarten. I guess I just figured since he was an only child it would be good socialization for him, and to start him on his letters and numbers more so than I could help him at home. He went in the mornings, and I would pick him up around eleven, we would eat lunch and then snuggle.

Today we were both tired and took a nap next to each other. The blackness behind my eyes surrounded me and then with a flash a white light appeared. Through the white light there was a figure. Then in the deep, calm, smooth voice through the blazing white light I heard Azariah speaking to me.
"There is a girl that needs your help. She attends the University of Chicago, majoring in engineering. She was just diagnosed with a serious condition called Scleroderma. It is a very rare disorder. Saving her will change her life, and many others. Her name is Isabella Hernandez."

I felt like he was fading away back into the darkness. I quickly responded, "okay," but by the time the word was out of my mouth he had disappeared into the blackness that surrounded me once more.

After Eli and I woke up from our nap I went to the computer and did some searching about the University of Chicago and what Scleroderma was exactly. I had never heard of it before, but if it was rare like Azariah was saying it makes sense. Scleroderma is an autoimmune disease that causes redness and swelling in skin and body. The disease can cause pulmonary hypertension. I made plans to leave the next morning for Chicago, calling my parents to ask if they'd watch Eli for a few days for me. They, of course, happily obliged.

April 16, 2006. The next day I left early to drop Eli off at my parents' house before making the drive to Chicago. Coffee in hand, the aroma of Kona filling the still air in the car, Eli with his chocolate milk and a granola bar in hand. It was about a six-hour drive, with dropping Eli off, from Eddyville to Chicago. I had looked online and printed off a map prior to leaving of how to get to the Central Administration office from home and another of the campus itself.

I arrived at the Central Administration office, fixed my hair, and made sure I didn't have lunch left on my face. It was about one-thirty in the afternoon. I hopped out of the car and walked up through the double doors. When I entered, I saw someone in her mid-thirties at a desk shuffling through some papers. She had thin eyes and a round face. Her hair was pulled back into a ponytail, which did not suit her facial features. She had makeup caked on her face and what appeared to be a fresh manicure on her pointy fingernails. I asked her if she could help me locate a student on campus. She told me she wasn't allowed to tell me where she was located but could call the number on file and see if she would be willing to meet me here.

She called. No Answer.

"I have one more option. She may be in class. Let me look at her class list and see if I can contact her teacher." She clacked away

95

at her computer, an unamused expression on her face as though I
was burdening her, taking her away from her normal duties. Soon
after she was picking up her phone to call a teacher.
"Yes, Mr. Sheffield could you please put Isabella Hernandez on
the phone."
Some muttering on the other end of the line and then a female
voice came on the line.
"Yes, Ms. Hernandez, you have a guest at the Administration
Office. Would you have time to come meet them?"
Silence. Then I heard Isabella say something, but it was inaudible
to me. The lady behind the desk hung up.
"She will be here in the next half hour. You can have a seat over
there while you wait." She gestured towards a row of chairs
against a wall.
"Thank you for your help." I said and went and sat down, but I
saw her huff as she continued to shuffle through the papers again.

A little less than thirty minutes later a beautiful girl walked
through the double doors. She had straight dark brown hair that
flowed below her shoulder blades, a hazelnut skin tone, and
piercing eyes. She was thin but had the natural Latino curves to
her. I stood up as she entered.
"Isabella?" I asked.
She looked towards me. "Yes?" She looked utterly confused.
"Hi, my name is Dalene. I know you don't know me, but I think I
can help you." I didn't know the best way of doing this.
Especially when I just show up out of nowhere and must
introduce myself.
Silence as she stared at me. Finally, she spoke, "I'm not sure what
you can help me with."
"Could I buy you a cup of coffee and we could discuss it?"
"Um…" she looked at her watch, "I have two hours until my next
class."
"That is plenty of time. Is there a good coffee spot on campus?"
"There is a coffee cart nearby." She said hesitantly, but then
headed for the door, and I followed.

As we walked towards the coffee cart, she started to ask me

some questions, still a little defensive.

"Do you live around here?" She questioned me.

"I'm actually from a small town called Eddyville in Iowa."

"So, you drove all the way to Chicago to... help me?" She now looked at me like I was some sort of criminal.

I nodded. We both fell silent and then I tried to bring up some small talk to fill the gap, before she decided to bolt.

"What are you majoring in?"

"Um... Aerospace Engineering."

Azariah had said engineering, but not what type of engineering.

"Wow, that is very impressive. What would you like to do with that degree?"

"I really want to work at NASA and help create satellites."

"That is an incredible goal. I'm sure you'll achieve it."

"Ya... well I'm not so sure anymore." She said it but then looked as though she regretted saying it.

"Oh... why is that?" I had a feeling I knew where this was going.

We arrived at the coffee cart before she got the chance to answer. We ordered our coffees and sat at a bench nearby. I waited a little bit hoping she would pick up where she left off. When she didn't, I re-started the conversation.

"You were saying that you weren't sure about your goals?" She fiddled with her coffee lid. Hesitating and delaying her response. Her hands were swollen, and her fingers were starting to almost bend like when you have an advanced stage of arthritis.

"Ya... I was diagnosed with a condition, and it will probably prevent me from meeting my goals."

"Oh, I'm really sorry for that."

Looking towards me quizzically she asked, "you said you could help me... how exactly and with what?"

"Well, I have this ...uh..." I still hadn't figured out how to describe this to people, because I wasn't supposed to really tell people anything about my mission. "Let's just call it a gift."

"Okay... and this gift will help me how exactly?"

"You first tell me more about why you don't think you'll be able to become an aerospace engineer and then I'll tell you more."

97

She gave me a side eye and then slowly decided to proceed. "I was diagnosed with a condition called Scleroderma. Basically, an autoimmune disorder that attacks my body and causes this reaction." She held her hand up towards me to let me see the damage it was causing better. "The doctors say that I am at a high risk of having my heart fail with this disease. Regardless, with my hands like this, and only getting worse, it is unlikely that I will be able to work on satellites. So…ya. Not much I can do about it unfortunately." She paused. "Your turn."

"Mine isn't so much telling as showing." I said, "may I?" I gestured towards her hand. Again, she looked at me with skepticism. Maybe it helped because I was a woman, or because she was just so desperate for help. It is interesting what people will do when they are desperate for help and don't have any other choices in their life. Either way she seemed to trust me at that moment.

She gave me her hand. I held it and I prayed. I prayed for her to feel no more pain, for her body to stop attacking itself, for her to have a vast future and to achieve her goals. . . Before I could pray anymore the burning sensation appeared where the mark on my back was erasing. Then the pins and needles arrived and extended throughout my body. My skin felt like it would melt off from the burning sensation that filled within me. I sat frozen on the bench still clutching her hand.

"Are you okay?" She looked at me like I was on my death bed, which at this point it sure felt like.

"Yes… sorry, yes." It came out much more winded than I anticipated.

She must have felt something within her hands because she pulled the one away from me and held them up to examine both. The redness went away; her fingers began to straighten back out to normal. She sat there in shock as she stared. I collected myself and got up to leave hoping not to have a bigger conversation than what needed to be.

"Wha…how…?" She stumbled over her words.

"Don't worry about the how, just know that you were given a second chance. Also, you never met me, and I did nothing for you." I gave her a "mom" look if you will.

She stared up at me from the bench, and finally she smiled and nodded. As I was leaving, I looked over my shoulder and saw her still sitting there staring at her hands. Tears rolling down her beautiful hazelnut cheeks, hair flowing down around her.

I decided to drive back home that afternoon instead of going to my hotel. I would rather go through whatever was about to come at home in my own space then a random hotel. It was about eleven at night when I got home. I dropped my bag at the door, locked up, quickly got ready for bed, and then crashed.

Update: May 3rd, 2006. I received a letter in the mail today from Isabella Hernandez. Letter is paperclipped to the back page.

*Dear Dalene,*

*I remembered you telling me that you lived in Eddyville, IA. I apologize for 'hunting you down' so to speak, but I really wanted to thank you. I haven't taken what you did for me for granted. I wanted to let you know that I changed my degree from Aerospace Engineering to becoming a Chemist. I want to help discover medications and treatments to help those with Scleroderma and other disabling diseases. I think that maybe you helped me so I could help others. I'm not sure why you chose to help me, but regardless I am so appreciative.*

*Thank you,*
*Isabella Hernandez*

*Soul 6: April 16, 2006, Isabella, Scleroderma, Chemist, Going to Change the World one rare disorder at a time. Saved.*

# 10.

November 20, 2006. I was starting to get used to the months in between souls. It was nice to be able to enjoy the time with Eli. He was now five years old, which didn't seem even remotely possible. He was in four-year-old preschool this year since his birthday was just a little over a month after school began. He was the oldest in his class but loved every minute.

Around lunch time my mom called me. She mainly wanted to catch up, but she also told me about her friend's granddaughter who had been diagnosed with cerebral palsy at birth.
"It's just awful." My mom went on. "She is only nine years old, and such a sweetie."
"What is happening that is so awful? I mean I understand that cerebral palsy on its own is incredibly difficult, but is something more happening?"
"She is being bullied something awful. She is so depressed."
"Kids can be so cruel."
"She is the one I was tellin' you about that does the lemonade stands and lemonade gift kits to raise money for kids with cerebral palsy."
"Oh... I remember that."
"She sits out almost every day after school at her lemonade stand,

while it is warm anyway, and was making new kits to put up on her little shop site. Now she is so depressed she doesn't sit outside anymore and doesn't make kits anymore."

"Is the school doing anything about it?"

"Not much they can do I reckon." I loved it when my mom used the verbiage from her generation. She continued, "They can tell the kids not to bully and to leave her alone, reprimand them… but heck sometimes I feel like that just makes it worse."

"That poor kiddo." I rubbed Eli's head and hoped that nothing like that would ever happen to him.

We talked for a few more minutes before we hung up. I went about my day as though that conversation wouldn't rattle my heart and mind, but it did. It rattled my heart with vengeance. I wanted to help that little girl… all she was trying to do was some good for this world… live her life to the fullest and these kids wanted to treat her selfishly and menacingly. I couldn't take it.

After Eli went to bed, I googled the little girl's shop. Her name was Eleanor Flynn. She lived in Gretna, Nebraska which was fairly close to Omaha. Her shop was adorable. It had little lemons and lemonade pitchers filling the background of the screen. The shop name was 'Eleanor's CAUSEation Sensation Lemonade". There was a picture of her sitting in her wheelchair by her lemonade stand. She had beautiful wavy blonde hair that fell to her shoulders, and bright blue eyes. She had a smile that could make the unhappiest person smile.

There was an 'About Me' section that gave her backstory:

*Hi! I'm Eleanor, and I have cerebral palsy. I set up a lemonade stand outside my house and this online shop to raise money in support of other kids with cerebral palsy. I hope to raise money to give them better medical equipment so that they can live their lives to the fullest like I am. I live with my mommy and daddy and baby brother Spencer. Oh, and our dog Franklin. Thank you for visiting my page and supporting me in my adventure.*

There were several more pictures on this page. One of her whole family with Franklin, smiling up at the camera. Her and her brother alone, her and her mom and dad alone. They looked happy. At peace with their circumstances, but pictures can tell a whole different story to reality. Maybe those photos were from happier times, less painful emotionally and mentally. Now her story has altered. Changed.

I went to her "Shop" tab. There were a slew of beautiful gift sets all focused-on lemonade. Little baskets with lemon printed ribbon encircling them. A lemonade pitcher, stir sticks, cups, lemonade mixture in fun mason jars with lemon fabric covering the top and pink or yellow ribbon tying it together based on if it was pink or regular lemonade. She even had a half and half basket for those that enjoyed tea and lemonade together. At the very bottom was an item that said, "Lemonade Stand" and it had an address of where to go for the stand and the hours of operation. My heart sank as I pictured the empty stand outside of her home. Locals driving by hoping to get some lemonade and no one being there. All her hard work, her stand, fading away, deteriorating.

I don't know if this was part of Azariah's plan or not, but at this point it was on me. This was my decision, and I was going to Gretna, Nebraska to help this little girl. It was a three-and-a-half-hour drive from our home to Gretna. It was only Monday, so I had two choices. Either I called my parents to stay with Eli here while I went since he had preschool, or I waited until Friday after preschool to go.

I quickly called my mom, because I couldn't stand the thought of Eleanor having to withstand one more week of torture. I told my mom it would only be two days. I'd leave tomorrow after they arrive and would return by Wednesday evening or Thursday morning at the latest. I would get a hotel and then let the pain ensue there versus coming home to endure it around Eli. I had no clue what cerebral palsy that a little girl has had for nine years might do to me and for how long, but that didn't matter.

My mom and dad of course agreed and would be here first thing in the morning.

✿✿✿✿✿

November 21, 2006. My parents arrived around seven in the morning, and I instructed them on what to do with Eli to prepare him for preschool. They had come a few times with me to pick Eli up from preschool, so they knew where to go and what to do. It was more my mental checklist and for the sake of my sanity, needed to be verbalized. Around seven-thirty I was off and, on the road, making the three-and-a-half-hour trip to save a little girl. Maybe it was the fact that she was in fact a little girl that made my heart want to find her. Save her. How many little girls out there start a business strictly to help other kids? At nine-years old? She has accomplished more than half the population and hasn't even made it to double digits. To have other kids trample that confidence, I couldn't stand it. I needed to find her, to help her. The drive inside me was urging me to save this little girl.

I'm not sure why this particular girl lit such a fire within me. My thoughts were racing as I continued the trek down I-80 towards Nebraska.

*Where would I be if my mom had told me that story back before 2003?*
*Would I have helped her in a different way?*
*What could I do for her? How could I help her?*
*Would I have given up and succumb to the fact that there wasn't anything I could do for her?*

I pulled off around eleven and went into a McDonald's to use their restroom and to grab a quick lunch as I finished up the final few minutes of my drive. Eleanor would be in school and when I had looked at the map last night, I found only one elementary school within Gretna. Not a big surprise considering how small a town it truly was. I drove the last few miles to the school as I finished up my fries and swallowed the last few swigs of my Sprite. I found a parking spot, made sure I didn't have any food on my face, grabbed my things and headed for the door.

They had a basic security system. There was a buzzer on the outside of the door, an intercom of sorts. I assumed it was the secretary that questioned my existence outside of the school. I explained that I wanted to visit Miss Eleanor Flynn. The secretary, clearly hesitating, finally pushed the buzzer and let me enter.

Entering into the school, it immediately smelled of disinfectants that stung your nostrils and made your throat itch. I swallowed hard adjusting to the smell. I walked the couple of steps to the administration office and a slender woman in slacks and a purple button up shirt emerged from the office and headed in my direction. Her jet-black hair was pulled into such a tight bun at the back of her skull I thought her skin would tear across the front of her face. Not a single hair was out of place. She wore thick, square, black glasses and dark maroon lipstick. Her cheekbones were high, and the sides of her mouth were so thin that it accentuated them even more. Heck if she had half-moon shaped glasses with a beaded eyewear retainer, she would look very similar to Professor McGonagall from the Harry Potter series. She was definitely not someone you wanted to get on the bad side of.

"What exactly do you want with Miss Eleanor Flynn?" She questioned me with a piercing stare that I felt within my soul. She removed her glasses from her face and hung them from the pocket of her button-up shirt.
"Um…." I hesitated, clearly nervous about her sheer appearance. "Her family are friends of my family, and my mother informed me that she was going through a difficult time. I was in the area and thought I'd swing by to check in on her."

Some of that may have been an extension of the truth… or a

105

lot.

She gazed at me longer with that piercing stare and then informed me, "I will need to contact her parents prior to you speaking with her."

"I understand."

"What is your name so I can inform the family?"

"Dalene Byrnes. My mother is Alma Smith; they may not know my married name."

"You may wait here." She turned curtly and walked back through the administration door.

After what seemed like hours she returned and informed me that I could speak to Miss Flynn in the Counselor's office. "This way." Again, turning with military precision as if annoyed by my presence. I almost saluted behind her back, but I refrained. She led me down some intertwining halls until we came to a little office. The counselor popped her head out at the secretary's appearance at her door. She gave a little nod as she saw me out of the corner of her eye. The secretary turned and walked away, but not without giving me another quick stare down prior to departing. The guidance counselor then ushered me into the room where that sweet blonde haired little girl sat. Head down, shoulders slumped, the beautiful smile gone. The counselor stated that her parents were okay with me speaking to her, but the counselor would just be down the hall if we needed anything. She gave a concerned look as she walked out the door.

Eleanor didn't lift her head to see the counselor out, didn't even acknowledge my presence. She was sitting in a chair and had her arm braces next to her.

"Hi Eleanor." I said as quietly and calmly as I could. No noticeable change to the little girl's face, and still, she didn't look up at me. "My name is Dalene. My mom knows your family."

Still nothing.

I figured now was the time to get straight to the point.

"I hear you are being bullied here at school."

There was a flinch, almost a slight grimace, and her face turned down and to the right if trying to avoid the conversation even more. A tear came into her eye.

"These kids are really breaking your spirit, aren't they sweetheart?" I sat down in the chair next to her and touched her little arm. It looked so frail underneath my ageing hands. That seemed to spark a bigger reaction. She didn't move away but turned her head straight on again.

Finally, she spoke. "Yes Miss Dalene, they are." As if my heart wasn't already broken enough for her, she had to be the sweetest little thing ever on top of it. Tears started rolling down her cheeks more steadily now. Her voice was shaking, but I don't think all of it was from crying... some from her condition. "Can I ask what they say or do?"

After taking a few minutes, she told me, "Well Miss Dalene, my mama told me not to talk ill of other people, but their words hurt a lot. They make fun of how I walk, how I eat and speak, and how I hold things. It makes me sad because I don't ever make fun of anyone, and I like who I am.' She paused for a little while longer. 'I guess what makes me the saddest is that if you take away what is on our outside then we are all the same on the inside. Like, if you look at an x-ray everyone looks basically the same. We are made of bones... I guess why does it matter how I walk or eat or talk? Why can't it matter what is on my insides? How I treat people, care about others, ya know? Why does everyone have to see only the outside?"

I realized after she was done talking that my mouth was wide open. How can this little girl who has only been on this earth for nine short years already be wiser than most adults. I reached over and gave her a huge hug. I think it startled her for a moment, but then she wrapped her arms up around mine and sank her head into me. We sat there for a moment embracing the fact

107

that we both knew the world would never fully understand her wise words. People went through the motions of their day, caring about themselves and struggling to get through another day. Not paying attention to the bigger picture... holding grievances close and holding kindness away from our chests as though it was the plague.

After a few moments I pulled away from her and moved in front of her, crouching down and holding her little hands.

"Miss Eleanor, if you could have one wish what would it be?" She thought for a long while and then finally spoke, "Well... my mama always taught me to think about others first, so I'd have to say I would really like it if the world would be kind to everyone, be aware that everyone is a person, regardless of how God made us... but deep down, and selfishly, I wish for my cerebral palsy to go away. I guess if that did happen would it be right? If somehow my cerebral palsy would go away would everything I've worked for to bring awareness to my condition, would it be worth nothing... and what would that prove to the kids who are bullying me? They should be the ones to change their insides... I shouldn't have to change my outsides."
"Oh honey, I agree completely." I paused and thought about her words.

*Would it be right if I saved her?*
*Would it prove anything to the kids who bullied her?*
*Would it show them that good people can be healed, or would they still act however they want?*
*Should I take everyone else out of the equation and just think about Eleanor? Look at what she has accomplished with Cerebral Palsy... what else could she show the world? Her disease wasn't the most severe case of Cerebral Palsy... but it wasn't going to get better for her, and with other complications occurring in her body, and the lack of motivation to do her therapies due to depression, she wasn't making any progress. What if she continued to be bullied? Would she eventually resort to suicide?*

I couldn't even stand the thought of that.

"Eleanor, what if you could do both? What if you could be healed, but continue to prove to the world around you that insides matter more than outsides? What if you could still support cerebral palsy and bring awareness to the world, but be healed from it?"

She just looked at me, "well… I guess that would be amazing, but that is only a dream." She slumped her shoulders down again and turned her head away. Tears coming back to her beautiful blue eyes.

In that moment I knew… I knew that this was the right path. Azariah said that God wanted people to be saved that would truly make an impact on the world and spread kindness, faith, and hope. She was simply the definition of all those things, and I had complete faith that she would spread it to every inch of her capabilities. I knew that she needed to be helped; to be saved.

I prayed for her to feel no more pain, for her body to be healed, for her to stop being bullied, and for her to continue to fight for those that needed to be fought for, for her to continue to bring awareness to the world. The burning sensation appeared where the mark on my back was erasing. Then the pins and needles arrived and extended throughout my body. My body seized up as the attack on my body began. The deformation from the cerebral palsy wreaking havoc on my muscles, stiffening my body. I've learned now to breathe through it, because holding my breath only made it worse. I guess those Lamaze classes for Eli really are coming in handy. What a silly thought at a moment like this…

I went from kneeling in front of Eleanor to sitting down as Eleanor's body softened, loosened with the cerebral palsy leaving her body. Her arms and legs didn't look bony and bent. Her face had a new and different glow about it. She looked at me with a little concern as I sat down in front of her, but then a new look crossed her face. One of bewilderment. Like the ones before her –

the same look. The look of impossibility. The look of "I must be dreaming". Finally, after looking at her hands for some time, she stretched her arms out…then she stood up. She took some tentative steps forward holding onto the chair and desk. She stretched her legs out and bent them. Then she spoke…

"I… I can walk without my braces." She gasped and then slapped her hand over her mouth.

"I can talk without my voice sounding different."

She looked down at her body, looking at what she never thought could be possible.

After a few moments of staring at her limbs she began walking around slowly again. Getting her bearings. She looked up at me, "how is this possible?"

I paused for a few moments, still not knowing exactly how to respond to this question.

"All you need to know is that you are healed, and that I hope you take this second chance and continue your mission in this world. Stick up for those that need support and show the world exactly what you want it to be. You just have to do me one favor and not tell anyone that I helped you. Do you understand?"

She looked at me perplexed and then nodded – knowing from my face that I couldn't say more than I did but also knowing that it was enough.

She came over to me, still sitting on the floor against the desk, and gave me a hug, one as tight as her little arms and body could manage. She whispered, "thank you."

"You're welcome sweet girl. Go prove to this world that everyone deserves to be treated fairly."

After we both stood up, I told her I'd go get the counselor and that I'd leave first. She nodded again, tears of joy in her eyes this time.

I walked quickly down the hallways, and the counselor pointed me in the right direction to get back out of the passages of hallways to the front doors. I walked briskly to my car and sat down breathing heavily. Finally, after my heart rate returned to semi-normal, I turned the car on and found my directions to the

hotel a couple of towns back towards home – hoping that my time
at the hotel would be short lived and bearable.

Needless to say, the pain was immense, but a hot bath
seemed to ease some of it. It began smack dab in the middle of
the night, which was typical. It began with my joints feeling
distorted, burning and if physical changes were to occur, I think
you could have heard actual snaps and cracks. I felt like my body
thought I was Gumby and could just do whatever I wanted.

Then the visions happened. The mental strain on that sweet
girl appeared behind my eyelids as I sat in the tub. I tried opening
my eyes to avoid the pain, but my eyes wouldn't open. They were
glued shut and I couldn't peel them open – which I should know
by now, but still I had to try. Kids verbally abused her, breaking
her spirit, telling her she wasn't good enough. Telling her she
should give up on life because she would never amount to
anything. Making fun of her walk instead of encouraging her,
making fun of how she talked instead of being kind and learning
how to adjust their ears. Making fun of how she ate and held her
pencil instead of ignoring it and realizing that it is just who she is,
and it doesn't matter. Kids kicked her braces out from under her
and several times had her fall to the ground because of the
impact. Teachers not doing anything to stop the madness and just
telling her family that kids will be kids, and she has to stick up for
herself too. I started shaking with fury, I was crying, fists
clenched, and my face was flushed with hate and anger.

What has this world come to if we are always judging a
book by its cover and never by the soul housed within an outer
shell. Shells can be different colors, scratched, bruised, cracked,
broken, colored and dyed, disformed, burnt, scarred… but inside
lies a soul, and even if they don't always appear to care that soul
feels. It has emotions. It hurts, cries, feels… if people would
simply look past exteriors and focus more on the interiors
everyone would be a lot better off.

My mama always taught me that chicken eggs are all different. They are brown, blue, speckled, white, blue, and grey on the outside. Some are smaller and some larger. Some have disformed outer shells and others are smooth. At the end of the day when you go to crack an egg the interior is the same. A whitish translucent outer albumen and the yellow yolk. At the end of the day, for a chicken egg, the inside is what matters – not how the outer shell looks. And at the end of the day, our soul is what matters more than our exterior. Now, if only the entire world would see that and jump on the bandwagon.

I spent the remainder of the night in the bathtub, re-filling it three more times to re-heat the water around me. I was still very sore when I finally decided to leave the realms of the porcelain walls that became my oasis overnight. I moved gingerly and felt extremely disoriented with my ability to do basic functions. I decided I wasn't ready to drive home yet, and after struggling to get dressed I decided to lie down for a bit on the horrible floral print comforter on the inelastic mattress. I don't know if that actually helped resolve my issues or not, but at least it was better than fumbling my way through pedals to get home.

Two in the afternoon arrived and I finally felt a little less disoriented and was at least feeling more reassured about making the trek home. It was about three hours to home from the hotel, and when I arrived home my sweet little Eli came running towards me yelling, "mama", and in that moment I realized that saving that little girl was one hundred percent the right choice.

*Soul 7: November 21, 2006, Eleanor, age 9, Cerebral Palsy, Best darn lemonade the world has ever had. Saved.*

# 11.

January 19, 2007. The holiday season had come and gone, and I had enjoyed every minute with my parents, Eli, and Allen's parents. It was a wonderful holiday full of love, memories, laughter, and joy.

Now that everything had wound down it seemed strange not to be going non-stop with cooking, baking, wrapping presents, and going to different holiday events around town. The smells of Christmas were now dissipating, but the snow lingered, and the bitterly cold wind remained. It was nice to relax though and take a break from the chaos. Eli was even back in preschool now and loving it of course. Everything seemed surreal, especially being home alone for the mornings again.

After putting Eli to bed this evening, I sat down to watch the news before bed. I do this occasionally, but sometimes it gets to be too negative. Tonight, something was telling me I needed to watch.

After a few minutes of watching a Breaking News announcement flashed across the screen. The newscaster began to broadcast about another fire in Iowa City. This is just under two

113

hours from where we live. There had been an outbreak of house fires that were taking place in residential areas and taking the lives of families. The latest house fire took the lives of a mother, father, and two children, ages eleven and fifteen. My heart broke for those families. The arsonist was engulfing the entire home, so the families had no way out of their homes and used a lot of gasoline to raise a fire fast and in a hurry. I had a feeling that Azariah would be contacting me soon about this. I just had a feeling… and I was scared.

It took quite a while for me to finally fall asleep, because I was scared to see what was to come. When I finally fell asleep, as I predicted Azariah took over my dreams and began giving me information via pictures. The first picture that blasted behind my eyes was a photo of a two-story white vinyl sided home on a cul-de-sac. It had a dark colored metal roof and a beautiful porch with cedar columns, a Christmas wreath on the door, and garland all around the railings. The house number then flashed across the screen: 5682, and then the street sign with the name: Arnold Drive. A beautiful family photo came across the screen. A mother with blonde hair and blue eyes holding a fuzzy topped toddler that was about two or three. A father with black hair and brown eyes that stood almost a foot over the wife, and he was holding a five-year-old blonde-haired girl. Then there were a set of black-haired twins – one girl and one boy that looked to be about thirteen. Six family members in total. Six lives are about to be lost. A calendar date flashed across my eyes that said January 20th, 2007, and then a black alarm clock with bright red numbers that read eleven seventeen at night. Then a flash of flames and smoke, and the family photo became engulfed in fire. It curled at the edges, and spots faded throughout the photo as the heat took hold of the glossy photo and the families' faces.

I woke up coughing and gasping; my eyes were watering profusely. All I could see was white from the bright flash of fire at the end of the dream, like when you look at fresh snow fallen ground too long. I couldn't even see my hands. I blinked what felt like a million times to try and adjust to my surroundings.

After what seemed like forever my eyes adjusted, my throat stopped burning, and my eyes stopped watering. I quickly grabbed the pen and small notebook off my nightstand to write down the information that I had seen. I started leaving a small notebook and pen next to my nightstand after the first soul was saved in case I needed to write down any details. I quickly jotted down Jan 20, 11:17pm, 5682 Arnold Dr. Iowa City, IA. It was three in the morning, but I knew I wouldn't be able to get back to sleep with this information in my head.

I got up and began packing a small to go bag so that I could leave tomorrow after I dropped Eli at my in-laws. I did have the forethought to google what the best clothes to wear around fire were. It told me that one hundred percent polyester was one of the best that most people had around their house. I did have a pair of Under Armor warm up pants that I thought were polyester. I went and checked and sure enough they were, but they had zippers at the bottoms of the ankles. I thought the metal might be an issue with the fire. I quickly seam-ripped the zippers out of the pants and did a loose stitch up so I could still get the pants off and on without issues. I also had a workout shirt that was polyester, and although it was short sleeved, I figured warmth wouldn't be an issue around fire.

It was a Saturday so there was no preschool or anything else to worry about. I would have to be home by Sunday though so I could take Eli to preschool on Monday, so I'd just have to figure out how to combat my symptoms while taking care of Eli this time around. I grabbed some clean clothes out of the basket in the laundry room for Eli. I stood there holding one of his shirts out in front of me for a moment.

*How had my little boy gotten so big?*

It seemed like yesterday I was holding up onesies. I held it to my chest and let the silence engulf me for a moment; I felt my heart beating in my chest. I thought about my son, my husband, and where my life was going... this is not the life I had hoped for,

115

but it is the one God wanted for me. I was thankful that He had a plan.

I woke Eli up about seven-thirty in the morning. He wasn't a morning person – like I am usually not – so I let him sleep in a bit. I had called my mother-in-law about six-thirty in the morning, because she was a morning person, and she usually got up to walk around six. She gladly agreed to take Eli for the weekend seeing as they hadn't seen him since Christmas. We left around nine in the morning to start driving for an hour to their house.

Once I got Eli settled at my parents' house, I headed towards Iowa City. It was another forty-five minutes or so. I drove directly to the home I would be spending my evening. I wanted to see the area, see the house in person, see what obstacles might be in place – other than the apparent fire hazards and arsonist on the loose that is. When I arrived at the cul-de-sac the first thing I noticed was the house. It blended in with the snow surrounding it, other than the dark metal roof and beautiful cedar columns, but mostly I noticed the garland strung in place. Then I imagined this beautiful home up in flames, the garland singed and engulfed by the flames, the family inside.

I looked around the cul-de-sac for obstacles. There weren't any that were apparent, but I didn't see a fire hydrant in the area. I looked in my rear-view mirrors and spotted one at the very end of the lane heading back out of the cul-de-sac.

*Would that prevent fire fighters from responding quickly?*

I wasn't super savvy on fire techniques. The neighbors two houses down had a giant ladder outside, and I may not be the ideal candidate to put out fires, but I did know how to work a ladder!

*Would that still be out?*

116

*Could I collapse it and drag it down the two houses and get it set up to the second floor?*

Probably not in the time I needed to.

*How in the world was I going to get into this house to help this family?*

I thought about warning them ahead of time, but if I did that would the arsonist find a different family instead? Then I would have saved one family, but another would be lost. I had to follow this plan... Azariah was doing this for a reason.

I knew I needed a fire extinguisher of some sort... would it help a fire of this magnitude? Probably not, but I needed some sort of line of defense. I went out of the cul-de-sac and headed back towards one of the main roads through Iowa City – Hiawatha Pioneer Trail. I kept following that road until I entered the town of Coralville. I found a Lowe's Home Improvement Store and went in to find some tools to help with my upcoming battle.

I found where the fire extinguishers were located and began looking at the tags. I quickly discovered that I would need a Class B fire extinguisher to help me with a gasoline fire. I picked up two of them and put them in my cart. On one of the end caps near the fire extinguishers were fire blankets. I thought that maybe I could wrap myself up in one if necessary or even drag family members out on them. I grabbed two of those. Then I thought I might need something to pry open a door or break a window to get inside. I went to the hand tool aisle and picked out a two-pack of crow bars and a hammer. Lastly, I thought I would need something to help protect my hands, so I went to the work glove area and searched through all the gloves. I finally found two pairs that were rated for heat, but I don't think they were necessarily meant for a gasoline fire type of heat. Regardless, something was better than nothing. I picked one and headed for the checkout.

I left Lowes and realized it was already two in the afternoon. I needed to find a hotel to crash at for the night after the events and find some food. I decided on food first and decided to swing through the drive-thru of Hardee's on the same road that Lowes was on. I asked the person behind the window if they knew a semi-inexpensive hotel to stay at. They recommended two different places, and I ended up choosing the Comfort Suites in Coralville. I grabbed my to-go bag and my food and headed in to get a room.

After eating my late lunch, I decided to get some sleep before this evening. I set an alarm and decided to wake up around eight in the evening to begin preparing the equipment I purchased and head over to the cul-de-sac. I wanted to be outside and waiting when the arsonist arrived. If I could call the fire department the moment the arsonist would set the fire, they could get there in a few moments versus after the home was already in ruins, along with the police and medical teams. Maybe the police could actually catch this guy with early warning.

✦✦✦✦✦

Eight o'clock arrived with a loud beeping tone. I didn't realize how tired I had really been, but the lack of sleep the night before had apparently done me in. I got up and put my hair into a tight bun at the nape of my neck, hoping that the blanket would cover it enough that it wouldn't set on fire.

✦✦✦✦✦

I arrived at the cul-de-sac just after 10:30 p.m. The snow had hardened into a crusty sheen, and the wind bit through my coat like needles. I parked two houses down again, just like earlier, and sat in silence. The house at 5682 Arnold Drive glowed softly—porch light on, garland still strung, wreath still hanging. Inside, I imagined six souls tucked into beds, unaware of what was coming.

I checked my watch.
*10:58 p.m.*

I slipped on the gloves, wrapped the fire blanket around my shoulders, and positioned the extinguishers within reach. My heart thudded against my ribs like a warning drum. I whispered a prayer—not for courage, but for clarity.

*11:10 p.m.*

A car crept into the cul-de-sac. No headlights. Just the crunch of tires on snow. I ducked low, watching. The driver parked directly in front of the house. A figure emerged—hooded, tall, carrying a red gas can. He moved with purpose, like he'd done this before.
I dialed 911.
"5682 Arnold Drive," I whispered. "Arsonist. Gasoline. Please hurry."
I hung up and stepped out of the car, crowbar in hand, extinguisher slung over my shoulder. The figure was already at the side of the house, pouring gasoline along the foundation. I ran.
"Stop!" I shouted, voice cracking through the silence.
He turned, startled—and dropped the match.
The flame caught instantly. A flash of orange raced along the trail of gasoline, igniting the garland, the wreath, the porch steps. The fire roared to life, licking up the cedar columns like they were paper. Smoke billowed upward, thick and fast, curling into the night sky.

I ran toward him, foam spraying from the extinguisher, and swung the crowbar with everything I had.
It connected with his shoulder. He stumbled back, cursing, and tried to flee—but police lights flooded the cul-de-sac. Officers tackled him before he reached his car.
I turned to the house. Smoke was already seeping through the windows. I pounded on the door, coughing as the fumes reached me.

The mother opened it, eyes red and watering, clutching her toddler who was wheezing softly. Behind her, the older children stumbled into view, disoriented, coughing, eyes wide with fear. "You need to get out—now!" I shouted.

She nodded, dazed. The father appeared, scooping up the twins and ushering everyone out. I helped them down the steps, shielding them with the fire blanket. The extinguishers hissed behind me as the fire department arrived, hoses snaking across the snow.

The family collapsed onto the lawn, coughing, gasping for air. The toddler cried weakly. The mother knelt beside her children, her hands trembling. They all had burns, the mother worst of all. All of them had inhaled far too much smoke.

I knelt beside them and placed my hand gently on the mother's shoulder. I prayed for them to feel no more pain, for their lungs to be healed, for the burns to fade, for their minds to be free of fear. I prayed for strength to return to their bodies, and for peace to settle in their hearts.

The burning sensation ignited across my back—six marks glowing, then fading. Pins and needles spread through my limbs. My body seized as the attack began. My chest tightened, my throat burned, my skin prickled as if scorched. I gasped, trying to breathe through it.

I collapsed onto the snow beside them, trembling, tears streaming down my face. The pain was unbearable—but they were alive.

Six souls. Saved.

☼☼☼☼☼☼

January 21, 2007 – 3:12 a.m. *Comfort Suites, Coralville*
I woke up gasping for air, my throat raw, my chest tight. The ceiling fan spun above me, but the room felt thick—like smoke was still lingering in the air. My skin prickled, my lungs burned,

and my muscles ached as if I'd been dragged through fire myself.

I tried to sit up, but my body refused. I rolled onto my side and collapsed onto the floor, trembling. I crawled to the bathroom, gripping the doorframe like a lifeline. I turned on the faucet and let the tub fill, the sound of rushing water grounding me.

I lowered myself into the warmth, wincing as the heat met my scorched-feeling skin. I closed my eyes, just for a moment. That's when I saw them again.

The mother was coughing, clutching her toddler. The twins stumbling through smoke. The father was trying to shield them all. Their faces—red, wet, terrified. The fire licked the porch. The garland igniting. The wreath curled into ash.

I snapped my eyes open, heart pounding.

I knew this would be a long recovery.

Regardless of the recovery time I knew I had to get home. I wanted to take Eli to preschool on Monday. I picked up Eli from my in-laws and held him close, breathing in the scent of his shampoo, the warmth of his little body.

We curled up on the couch and watched *Frosty the Snowman*. He giggled, and I tried my best not to cry in front of him.

*Souls 8–13: The Arnold Drive Family. January 20, 2007. Fire inhalation. Burns. Fear. Saved.*

# 12.

November 14, 2007. Eli turned six last month. October
17th. He's growing so fast it's hard to keep up. He's reading
now—really reading—and asking questions about everything. He
told me he wants to be a firefighter, then a paleontologist, then a
"banana scientist," whatever that is. I laughed so hard I cried.
He's perfect.
He's strong. And I thank God every day for that.

Last night, I had a dream. One of *those* dreams. It began in
a hospital room. Pale green walls. A crib with a mobile spinning
slowly overhead. A toddler lay curled up, her body small and
stiff, muscles trembling. Her name was written on the chart at the
foot of the bed: *Brooklyn St. James*. Diagnosis: *Duchenne
Muscular Dystrophy*. The hospital's name was clear—*University
of Iowa Children's Hospital*.

Then came the flashes. Brooklyn's future. Wheelchairs.
Breathing machines. Surgeries. Her body weakened while her
spirit remained fierce. I saw her mother beside her, holding her
hand, praying silently, her eyes swollen from crying.

I woke up with tears soaking my pillow.

✧✧✧✧✧

November 15, 2007. The next morning after dropping Eli off at school, I drove straight to Iowa City. I didn't know what I was looking for exactly—just that I needed to be there. I parked in the visitor lot and walked into the hospital, my heart pounding, hands shaking, but taking deep breaths to try and control the anxiety washing over me. It never gets easier to figure out how to introduce myself or to interject into someone's life that is emotionally vulnerable – while not giving away what I am currently gifted with.

I wandered the halls for a while, unsure of what to do. I didn't know what room she was in, and I knew that the nurse wouldn't just send me their way.

I stopped at the coffee kiosk. The line was short. A woman stood in front of me, her shoulders hunched, her hands trembling slightly as she reached for her wallet. She looked exhausted, but familiar.
She turned slightly, and I saw her face. The same face from my dream.
"Excuse me," I said gently. "You look absolutely exhausted. This coffee is on me."
She blinked, startled. "Oh, um… thank you."
"My name is Dalene." I handed a few bills over to the barista and the woman took the coffee from her before replying, "my name is Marie."
"It's nice to meet you, Marie. It looks like you've had a tough couple of days."
She chuckled lightly, "more like a tough couple of years."
"I'm so sorry to hear that." I left it at that hoping she would expand, and I was in luck.
"My daughter, Brooklyn, she was diagnosed with Muscular Dystrophy. She's 3 now, but we've been dealing with issues since about the age of 1 and a half. She is so resilient and always smiling, but she is in pain."

123

"Wow… you both sound resilient."
"I guess you must be in these moments." She smiled meekly.
"Well, I best get back to her – she was napping."
She turned to head back towards the elevators.
"Wait." She turned around. "Can I meet her? I mean… I know you don't know me, and I know that is a weird question, but you've just been through so much and I…"
She cut me off with a simple smile and a nod. I followed her to the elevators.

☼☼☼☼☼

Brooklyn was even smaller than I imagined. Her eyes were bright, though, and she smiled when her mother came into the room.
"Hi baby. I brought a friend to meet you."
Brooklyn looked cautiously at me; hesitant.
"Hi Brooklyn." I smiled and waved.
Brooklyn clutched her mother's arm and hid her face. "Its okay baby, I promise she isn't a doctor." She looked towards me, "She is scared of medical staff for obvious reasons, but they are only trying to help."
"I can't imagine how terrified she must be."

I walked across her room to the fish mobile close to her bed – the one from my dream. It was wooden fish strung at different lengths and not connected to a motor. I took one of the fish in my hand, Brooklyn peeking her little eyes around her mother's arm – watching me. I gave it a slow spin around. The whole mobile spun in a rainbow fish circular wave. Brooklyn peered up at the mobile and smiled.

I reached out my hand to Brooklyn – she watched and when I thought for sure she wouldn't reach for my hand – she did. That is when I prayed for her muscles to be loosened, for her body to be strengthened, for her spirit to remain unbroken.

The burning sensation ignited across my back—one mark

124

glowing, then fading. Pins and needles spread through my limbs.

My body seized as the attack began. I tried to keep my composure, but my legs and arms stiffened, my spine arched painfully. I gasped, unable to move.

Marie stared at me. Shocked, scared, and concerned.
"So sorry, I'm alright." Brooklyn's body started changing in front of our eyes. She looked fuller, healthier, stronger.
"Mama, I no hurt." Brooklyn started kicking her legs, clapping her hands, and pulling herself up to stand by one of the crib walls. Marie began weeping, laughing, and smiling. While she was celebrating with her daughter, I slowly left the room.

I hobbled to the nearest bathroom and locked myself in a stall. I curled into myself, tears streaming down my cheeks. My muscles twitched uncontrollably. My breath came in short, shallow bursts. I felt trapped inside my own body.
And then, slowly, it passed.

It was an excruciating night, and I soaked in the tub again for most of it. By morning, I could walk again – stiffly mind you, but it was walking. I made pancakes for Eli and watched him pour syrup like it was liquid gold. He looked up at me and said, "Mama, why are your eyes puffy?"
I smiled. "Just tired, baby."
But inside, I was holding the weight of another child. Another soul. Another miracle.


*Soul 14: Brooklyn St. James. Duchenne Muscular Dystrophy. November 15, 2007. Pain. Weakness. Courage. Saved.*

# 13.

May 9, 2008. Eli tugged at my hand, bouncing with excitement. "Mama, they have the dinosaur book I wanted!" We walked past the rows of shelves, his little feet pattering against the tile. He darted toward the children's section, and I followed, scanning titles as he pulled books off the shelf with the urgency of a treasure hunter.

That's when I saw him.

An older man, maybe late sixties, walking slowly with a cane. He moved carefully, but his right leg dragged slightly behind the other. As he reached for a book on the lower shelf, his balance shifted—and he fell.

I rushed over, kneeling beside him. "Are you okay?"

He winced, trying to sit up. "I'm fine. Just clumsy. Happens more than I'd like to admit."

I helped him to his feet, steadying him as he leaned against the shelf. My hand lingered on his arm—warm, fragile, trembling. "I'm Dalene," I said softly.

"Anthony Lead," he replied, catching his breath. "I had polio back in '55. It left me with a limp and a tendency to trip over air." He chuckled. I smiled gently. "I'm glad you're alright."

He nodded, then looked down at the book he'd dropped—
*Grandparenting with Purpose.* He smiled. "My daughter's
expecting. First grandchild. Due in June."
"That's wonderful," I said, heart warming.
"She says it's a girl. I've been practicing my storytelling voice,"
he added with a grin. "I want her to know her grandpa's not just
the guy who falls down in libraries."

I laughed softly, but something stirred in me. A quiet
knowing. I didn't have a dream. I didn't hear a voice. But I felt it.
Anthony Lead was someone I was supposed to save.

And then—just for a moment—I wasn't in the library
anymore.
*I saw a dirt road split by wind. I saw a playground swallowed by
leaves. Swings flipping and tossing in the wind. A funnel cloud
twisted in the distance, ripping shingles from rooftops and
flinging branches like arrows. A little girl screamed, her voice
swallowed by the roar. Anthony turned toward her, his leg
dragging, his breath ragged. He ran—not fast, not smooth, but
with everything he had. He couldn't reach her...a sharp scream
impaled my ears...*

Then the vision vanished.

I was back in the library, my hand still resting on Anthony's
shoulder. I knew right then while I still had contact with Anthony
I needed to save him. My heart was pounding through my chest
still hearing the echoing scream in my ears.

I closed my eyes, and I prayed for his legs to be
strengthened, for his lungs to be clear, for his body to remember
how to move when it matters most. I prayed for his
granddaughter, who will one day need him to run—with strength
and power. I prayed for time to bend in his favor, for courage to
rise in his bones.

The burning sensation ignited across my back—one mark
glowing, then fading. Pins and needles spread through my limbs.

My breath grew shallow, my legs felt weak and unable to function. I gasped, but kept my hand on his shoulder, grounding myself in the moment.

Anthony looked at me, startled. "Are you alright?"
I nodded, barely. "Yes. Just… noticed my shoe was untied. I don't want to trip in the library too." I laughed breathlessly. He smiled as I crouched down, pretending to tie my shoe, letting the tremors pass. My muscles twitched. My breath came in short, shallow bursts.
And then, slowly, it passed.

Eli came bursting through the aisles with a bag full of books. "Come on Mama, I already checked out."
I turned to Anthony, "it was so nice to meet you. Congratulations on your future promotion to grandpa."

He nodded. He was about to turn away when he looked back at me and said, "you know… I haven't felt this strong in ages."

☼☼☼☼☼☼

Eli and I went home and scoured through the books he had checked out. Many about dinosaurs. We had our dinner on the living room floor surrounded by books. He only had a couple more weeks left of kindergarten, and we took every minute we could get to soak up reading and enjoying the moments we had together. As I was putting him to bed, I began noticing that minimal tasks were taxing. My breathing became labored, and my right foot lagged. I felt weak. . .

☼☼☼☼☼☼

After a couple long days of weakness, exhaustion, a lot of bath tub time, and breathing complications I began to recover. Thankfully Eli and I had plenty of books to keep us entertained. We sat outside and soaked up the sun, watched all the flowers start to bloom, and watched the world come to life again.

I held Eli close that night as we read the same dinosaur book, we had already read twenty times, grateful for every step we both could take.

*Soul 15: Anthony Lead. Polio survivor. May 9, 2008. Strength. Savior. Saved.*

# 14.

July 6, 2010. It's been almost two years since I met Walter Griggs in the library. Two years, five souls, and more pain than I know how to name.

I've stopped trying to explain it to anyone. Even Eli, who's now seven and starting to notice the days I disappear into myself, the nights I sleep on the floor because my body won't bend the right way. I tell him it's just "mama's-tired days." He believes me. For now.

☼☼☼☼☼

September 17, 2008. He was sitting on the edge of a bridge when I found him. I didn't know his name—just that I was supposed to walk that way. Divorce papers in his coat pocket. Pink slip in his glove compartment. A flask in his hand. I sat beside him, placed my hand on his back, and prayed. He sobbed onto my shoulder. I felt the mark burn. I couldn't stop crying for two days.

*Soul 16: James Holloway. Depression. Alcoholism. September 17, 2008. Saved.*

April 2nd, 2009. The florist's shop smelled like blood and lilies. She was curled behind the counter, clutching her stomach, whispering the name of her daughter. I knelt beside her, pressed my hand to her abdomen, and prayed. She went unconscious, but her breathing steadied. The police arrived shortly after I slipped out of the back door. I curled into a ball for a 24-hour period, and after I was able to uncurl, I remained hunched over for an extra couple of days.

*Soul 17: Mel Sweets. Gunshot wound. Robbery. Florist. April 2nd, 2009. Saved.*

December 10th, 2009. He was a lawyer. Sharp, proud, tired. The client he was working with lost his case due to details he didn't inform the lawyer of. The client needed someone to blame and that was of course the lawyer. The attack happened outside the grocery store. I found the lawyer in the alley, unconscious, ribs shattered, bleeding internally. I touched his hand and prayed. He woke up gasping. I collapsed beside him.

*Soul 18: Daniel Cho. December 10, 2009. Law. Assault. December 2009.*

July 6, 2010. Tonight, Eli went to bed early. He'd spent the afternoon building paper airplanes and quizzing me on flight paths, so I wasn't surprised when he crashed hard after dinner. I tucked him in, kissed his forehead, and lingered a moment longer than usual. He's eight now. Still small, still mine—but growing faster than I can hold.

I needed something to quiet my mind.

I went to the living room and scrolled through the movie list. *Skyjacked*, 1972. Charlton Heston. I hadn't seen it in years, but something about the title tugged at me. I pressed play.
Halfway through, the screen flickered.

Suddenly, I wasn't watching a movie. I was *in* one.

I was driving down a long, empty road in Nebraska. The sky was bruised with dusk, the horizon flat and endless. The air felt heavy, like something was about to break. The ground began to tremble beneath my tires. I slowed the car, rolled down the window, and looked up.

A jet screamed overhead—low, too low. Its left engine sputtered, trailing smoke. The plane tilted, dipped, then steadied. I pulled over and stepped out, heart pounding.

*Then I saw it.*

Inside the plane, chaos. A man stood near the cockpit door, waving a pistol. His uniform was rumpled, his face red with rage. He was shouting demands—money, justice, revenge. A disgruntled employee of the airline, betrayed by the company he'd served for years. He'd boarded the plane with a plan: hijack it, force the airline to meet his terms, and make them pay.

The captain tried to reason with him. Calm voice. Hands raised. But the hijacker was unraveling. When the captain reached for the radio, the man fired.

The bullet struck the captain in the chest. He collapsed against the controls, blood blooming across his shirt.

Screams erupted. Passengers ducked, cried, clutched each other. A stewardess—young, fierce, trembling—lunged at the hijacker. She slammed a metal tray against his head. He staggered, dropped the gun, and fell unconscious.

132

But the damage was done.

The plane began to descend—too fast, too steep. The stewardess scrambled into the cockpit, trying to stabilize the controls. No copilot. No backup. Just blinking lights and a dying engine.

The plane clipped a power line, spun sideways, and crashed into an open field.

Metal shrieked. Fire bloomed. The ground shook. . . my couch shook. I was back. Back on my couch. Back in my living room. Skyjacked playing on the TV.

I called my mom immediately and asked if Eli could come stay with them for the next week. Thankfully, my mother doesn't ask a lot of questions and is always grateful to spend time with Eli.

Eli was only a little upset in the morning when I told him the change of plans, but he quickly got over it when he realized he would be spoiled rotten for the next week. I packed his things, and we headed to their house, and then I began my journey to a location I didn't know. I was just trusting my intuition. Trusting my gut. Trusting God.

Daylight turned into dusk. I felt tired from driving all day, but alert at the same time. Exhilarated by anxiety, on edge with nerves. Then it happened. The jet was overhead. The road rumbling, shaking, and smoke filling the sky. I knew what was next. I knew what was coming,

I parked and I ran toward the wreckage, heart hammering. The field was littered with debris—suitcases, seat cushions, twisted metal. Smoke curled into the sky. The air reeked of fuel and scorched plastic.

Bodies lay scattered. Some moved. Some didn't. I didn't know who to save – who had life altering damage – who didn't. I didn't know what to do. The anxiety was overwhelming… so I did the only thing I knew what to do at that time. I helped whoever needed it. Why else would God point me in this direction…

I dropped to my knees beside a woman with a broken leg, her face streaked with blood. She was whispering the name "Jesse." I touched her arm and prayed.

The mark ignited across my back.

I crawled to a man pinned beneath a seat, his ribs crushed. I tried to lift the seat, but it was pinned tight. I laid on my back and kicked the seat upward. It finally moved off the man. I touched his shoulder and prayed.

Another mark burned.

I moved from soul to soul—twenty in total. Some conscious, some fading. I whispered prayers through tears, through smoke, through the ache in my limbs. My body trembled. My breath grew shallow. My muscles locked.

I collapsed beside the final soul – a teenage boy with a gash across his forehead and bruises all over his stomach, exposed from his ripped shirt. His eyes wide with fear. I touched his hand and prayed.

The pain surged through me like fire. I felt my whole body ignite. I couldn't move, but I had to. I had to get back to my car. I crawled, stumbled, and pulled at the earth below me. Hands bloody, dirty, sweat trickled down my face. Smoke burned my eyes. Muscles igniting with every movement. Grasping at anything I could to get me closer to my car… I dragged myself up and into the driver's seat. I drove as best I could to the nearest town. The nearest hotel. I had baby wipes in the car, and I cleaned up as best I could so that the hotel clerk didn't question me. I got a room. Fell on to the bed. Blackness surrounded me.

✹✹✹✹✹

I awoke bleary eyed. As I tried to sit up my muscles gave way, and I fell back onto the bed. My lungs ached from smoke inhalation, and I couldn't get my eyes to focus. It was dark in the room, but I could see a little light peeking under the curtains. I'm not sure if that is from a streetlamp or the sun. I tilted my head slowly to try and see the red numbers illuminating on the nightstand, but it was a blurred mess. I think it said 3:05. Now if that is PM or AM, I'm not sure. What day I'm not sure, and if that is even the time is a clear guess. I lay there, eyes staring up at the ceiling. Vivid images raced before my eyes. Closing my eyes was worse. I tried to get up again. This time with more success. I was able to prop up onto my elbows, but it made my head pound. I wasn't going to give up though. I needed to know what day it was at least.

I could see my purse lying on the floor where I must have dropped it on the way in. I got up onto my hands slowly to not raise the ache in my head. I sat there for another few minutes. This process continued until I was able to gain enough momentum to stand and prop myself up against a wall. I was able to walk forward enough to grab the handle of my purse with my foot and drag it over to the bed. I sat back down and grabbed it. My phone said 3:12AM on July 9th, 2025. I've been asleep for two and a half days. I felt nauseous. I had 17 missed calls from my mom. It was too early to call her back, but if I don't call back first thing at 6:00AM she will for sure have the calvary out for me if she hasn't already… and poor Eli. He must be so worried.

I was able to get up again slowly and head to the bathroom where thank goodness they had a bathtub. I soaked for the next two hours before getting out and calling my mom and Eli.

I spent the next three days in the hotel – recovering, regaining, taking baths. That last day I was still very weak, very sore and still

135

had a raspy voice due to the smoke. My lungs still ached. I went to go pick up Eli and we spent the evening talking about all the fun he had. How spoiled he had been and all about the paper airplanes that he made with Grandpa. He flew them around the house, laughing, playing, and me soaking up every minute.

After Eli went to bed, I looked online to see the news articles about the plane crash. The headline read: *Nebraska Plane Crash Leaves Six Dead, Twenty Survivors.*

**LINCOLN, NE** — *Federal investigators are continuing to examine the wreckage of a small commercial aircraft that crash-landed in a rural field outside Lincoln late Saturday evening, following a mid-flight hijacking attempt by a disgruntled airline employee.*

*The plane, operated by Regional Air, was enroute from Denver to Des Moines when the incident occurred. According to preliminary reports, the hijacker—identified as a male flight steward, his name will not be disclosed until the investigation is completed, employed by the airline—brandished a firearm and demanded the flight be diverted to New York, citing grievances against the company. When the captain attempted to override the hijacker's demands and reach air traffic control, he was shot in the chest.*

*A second crew member, a female stewardess, managed to subdue the hijacker with a blunt object, rendering him unconscious. However, the aircraft had already begun a rapid descent. With the captain incapacitated and no copilot aboard, the plane ultimately crash-landed in an open field near Highway 77.*

*Of the 26 individuals on board, including the captain, two crew members, and 23 passengers - 20 survived, including the captain and stewardess. Six fatalities were confirmed; among them the hijacker and five passengers seated near the front of the aircraft.*

*Emergency responders arrived within 30 minutes. The signal had been corrupted by the disgruntled employee – rendering it difficult for the airline to figure out where the plane had gone. Residents nearby saw smoke and called it in. Survivors were only treated for minor cuts and scrapes, according to hospital officials. FBI agents and hospital officials can't explain how so many passengers walked away with so few injuries. "An act of God..." Fire Chief Meyers stated.*

*The FAA and NTSB are conducting a joint investigation into the incident. Officials have praised the stewardess's quick thinking, which likely prevented further loss of life.*
*"This could have been far worse," said Fire Chief Meyers. "The fact that twenty people made it out alive is nothing short of remarkable."*

*Regional Air has issued a statement expressing condolences to the families of the deceased and gratitude to first responders. The airline has suspended all flights pending further review.*

Twenty souls. Twenty prayers. Twenty marks.

*Souls 19–38: Plane crash victims. Nebraska. July 6th, 2010. Hijacking. Fire. Survival.*

# 15.

January 7, 2011. Eli turned nine last October. He's taller now, sharper, asking questions I'm not always ready to answer. He watches me more closely, especially on the days when I wince climbing stairs or pausing mid-sentence to catch my breath.

It's been almost six months since the plane crash. I'm still recovering. The stiffness comes and goes. My lungs tighten when I push too hard. My legs cramp at night. But I'm getting better. Slowly.

I was sipping coffee at the kitchen table when the headline caught my eye: "Four Years Later, Family Still Holds Vigil for Comatose Firefighter".

I unfolded the paper and began reading.

*Kevin VanderLeest, 39, has remained in a coma since*

*January 2007, when an explosion at a warehouse fire left him with severe head trauma and internal injuries. His wife and two children continue to visit him weekly at Mercy Hospital in Rogers, Arkansas, praying for a miracle.*

    I stared at the photo. His face was thinner now, but I recognized the eyes. I didn't know how—I just did.

Then the flash came.

    *I saw the warehouse—flames licking the rafters, smoke curling into the sky. Kevin was inside, shouting for backup, dragging a hose toward a trapped worker. The explosion hit like thunder. He was thrown backward, pinned beneath debris. Fellow firefighters pulled him out, shouting his name. Sirens. Stretchers.*

*Mercy Hospital.*

I gasped, clutching the table.

Kevin VanderLeest was one of mine.

    On Tuesday I dropped Eli off at school and then I came home and packed a bag. My parents were coming to stay with Eli so he wouldn't miss school while I was away. The best part about my parents is that I never really need an explanation. They are just more than happy to be with Eli and spend time with him.

    The drive to Rogers, Arkansas took seven hours. I didn't stop except for gas. The sky was gray, heavy. They looked like they were ready to unleash snow or sleet at any moment, but the roads were quiet. I arrived around eight at night, grabbed some food and checked into a motel. I ate dinner and then tried to get some sleep, but the vision from earlier just kept replaying in my head.

I finally gave up around five in the morning and started getting ready. I entered Mercy Hospital and asked the information desk what room Kevin VanderLeest was in. Thankfully they allowed visitors to his room instead of just family. Probably due to the numerous firefighters and their families that would want to visit.

Room 256.

Kevin lay motionless, machines humming beside him. He looked gaunt from his original picture in the paper, and his skin was pallid. I stepped closer, I took a deep breath, and I placed my hand on his shoulder. I prayed for his brain to awaken, for his lungs to strengthen, for his body to remember how to live. I prayed for his wife, who never stopped believing. For his children, who still talk to him like he hears. I prayed for him to wake up and live his life wholly.

The mark ignited across my back. My legs buckled. My breath vanished. I collapsed into the chair beside him, trembling. It took me several minutes to regain my composure. Enough to leave the hospital without a nurse trying to admit me.

I drove back to the motel and collapsed – I feel like this is becoming a new pattern for me – I then slept for four days. I didn't dream. I didn't wake up. I just let my body rest. It was like I was in a coma myself. A day for each year Kevin was in a coma.

✺✺✺✺✺

When I finally opened my eyes, the sun was rising. I turned on the TV, flipped through the channels until I reached a news station, and I waited. Finally, a local news anchor was smiling, holding a photo of Kevin VanderLeest.

*"After four years in a coma, firefighter Kevin VanderLeest*

*opened his eyes Wednesday morning at Mercy Hospital in Rogers. Doctors are calling it a miracle."*

They showed him sitting up in bed with his family surrounding him. Hugging and kissing him. He looked so healthy. His skin had color in it and he looked filled out.

*"They are saying he could be released as soon as tomorrow. He is up and walking, passing all his physical fitness tests, and he says he is so ready to go home and make up for lost time. It truly is a miracle."*

I left that afternoon to make the drive home. I couldn't wait to hold my sweet boy and embrace the moments we have together. Never take time for granted. It can come and go so quickly.

*Soul 39: Kevin VanderLeest. Explosion. Coma. January 9th, 2011.*

# 16.

May 31, 2011. The house was too quiet. Eli had left the day before for two weeks at Phyllis and Larry Byrnes' house. He'd been buzzing with excitement about fishing with Grandpa Larry and making cinnamon rolls with Grandma Phyllis. I'd smiled and waved as they drove away, but the silence that followed felt heavy.

I got caught up on laundry. Ate dinner alone. I stared into Eli's room for quite awhile and then decided to turn in early. I tossed and turned for what seemed like hours before finally falling asleep, but when I did a bright light blazed the back of my eyes.
It wasn't gradual. It was *there*.

Azariah's presence pressed into my mind, and then the dream came—sharp, fast, and unrelenting. *Two girls, maybe ten or eleven, running through dense woods. Laughing, running, carefree. Then a crack – ear shattering in my head – thunder. Rain poured down, turning the forest floor into a slick mess of mud and leaves. Their hair plastered to their faces with rain. The girls ducked under a rocky overhang, huddling together as the storm raged.*

*When the rain stopped, they tried to find their way home. But the trees all looked the same. The paths twisted. The light faded. They were soaked, shivering, calling out for each other's mothers. Night fell. They curled up together near the rocks, knees to their chests, whispering to keep the dark away.*

Then the dream shifted.

*A map bloomed in my mind—Shawnee National Forest, Illinois. A pinpoint deep in the green. Police lights flashing outside two homes in Makanda. Parents crying on front porches. Neighbors gathering. A search party forming.* Then the bright light again burned behind my eyes.

I gasped and sat up.

Azariah didn't speak, but the message was clear.

It was almost a six-hour drive. I didn't pack much - just water, snacks, a flashlight, my hygiene bag, and a couple pairs of clothes. When I woke up from the dream, I drew the map that had been given to me. It had entrance markers to the forest and where to go to get in.

I thought about calling the police in Illinois and telling them where the girls were at... but how would that sound? Like I was some sort of psychic, like I had kidnapped them? I didn't need interrogated, and if Azariah sent me this specifically – then there was a reason behind it.

The miles blurred. Cornfields gave way to rolling hills, then to the dense, endless green of the forest. The sky still looked as if it could unleash at any moment. Dark clouds masked daylight. I parked near the Bald Knob Cross and followed the map I was given to the point where my mind knew I was supposed to go into the trees. It wasn't a marked trail – just a separation in the trees.

143

The air was damp, heavy with the smell of wet earth. My shoes sank into mud. Branches clawed at my arms. Somewhere in the distance, a dog barked—part of the search party, maybe—but I kept moving in the opposite direction.

I stumbled over roots, rocks hidden by fallen leaves, sweat trickled down my back from the increasing humidity. I walked for over an hour before I began recognizing some of the areas that were in my dream, and then I saw it. The rock formation was to my right – the rock formation that should house the girls. I went around the edge, and there snuggled up together – were the girls. Their breathing was shallow. Their lips were turning blue, and their skin had a sallow coloring.

I bent down to rouse them, but only one girl's eyes fluttered. I quickly placed my hands on the girls, and I prayed for warmth to return to their bodies and for fear to leave their hearts. I prayed for their parents' arms to close around them tonight. For the trauma of this event to not terrorize their dreams. I prayed for the memory of this night to fade into something they could survive.

The two marks burned across my back. I felt an icy chill rise from my toes to my head, creating goosebumps along my skin. My body trembled and seized. I kept my hands on them until the pain peaked, until I knew it was done.

Somewhere behind me, voices called their names. Flashlights cut through the trees. The girls stirred, blinking at the light. I stepped back into the shadows, and I waited. I waited until the girls woke up completely and their little shouts cut through the woods, through the dark. Lights surrounded them, people rushed forward and encircled them in blankets. They were safe. I retreated through the forest, back the way I had come.

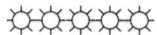

By the time I reached my car, my body was shaking. I drove to a small motel in Makanda. I turned on the bath, and I got out of my muddy clothes and undid my bun. Twigs, leaves, and dried mud fell off me. I dropped myself into the steaming water and soaked for a few hours. I had chills I couldn't get rid of, and I had to keep re-warming the bathtub.

When I finally emerged from the tub, I put both pairs of my spare clothes on to help warm up. I grabbed the extra blankets the hotel provided in the closet and piled them on top of me.

I turned on the news to see if they were airing anything about the girls yet, and sure enough the third news story in was about the girls.

*"Two young girls were found safe last night in Shawnee National Forest after being missing for nearly twenty-four hours. Authorities credit the quick response of search teams and the girls' ability to stay together and find shelter during the storm. They are being treated at a nearby facility for minor scrapes and will stay overnight for observation. They are expected to be home by the morning."*

They displayed the moment the girls were reunited with their parents. Tears, wails, and hugs. I smiled faintly, before turning the TV off and closing my eyes.

*Souls 40 & 41: Shawnee National Forest. June 1, 2011. Lost. Found. Saved.*

# 17.

November 3, 2011. Eli is ten now, in fourth grade. He's growing fast—more questions, more independence, more moments where I catch glimpses of the man he'll become. He left for school this morning with a backpack full of spelling words and a lunchbox packed with apple slices and peanut butter crackers. Today on our way to drop-off we picked up Eli's friends, Charles and Bennett, the twin neighbor boys. On the days their mom has an early shift at work I pick the boys up.

I went grocery shopping after dropping off the boys. The store was quiet. I was reaching for a can of soup when I overheard two women near the cereal aisle.
"...Josie Ferguson. She's only twenty weeks, but the preeclampsia is severe already. They don't think the baby will make it, or they might even have to terminate."

I froze and strained my ears to try and hear more.

"They are devastated. They've been trying for years. This was their rainbow baby."
"Oh, I can imagine. They have tried so many different things, this baby was with IVF treatments."

"The doctor's told Josie she can't do another pregnancy after this. Her body isn't taking it all well, and they are concerned that she might not even live through this pregnancy."

Rainbow baby. A child born after loss. A promise after grief.
I didn't know Josie or Matt. But I knew the ache in those words. And I knew what I had to do. I left my cart abandoned in the aisle, grabbed a container of soup from the deli area and headed out.

Back home, I pulled out the phone book. Their address was listed on Maple Street, just a few blocks away from the grocery store. I didn't call. I didn't plan. I just went.

The house was modest, white siding, a porch swing swaying in the November wind. I was nervous, but I didn't let myself hesitate or I'd probably chicken out. I walked up to the door, and I knocked softly.

Matt answered. His eyes were tired, his face drawn. I smiled at him and held out the container of soup I'd picked up at the store.

"Hi. I live near you guys and heard about what was going on. I thought you might need this," I said simply.
He hesitated, then nodded. "Thanks."
He stepped aside, and I entered.

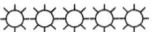

Josie lay on the couch, propped up with pillows, her skin pale and her breath shallow. She looked at me with wary eyes but didn't speak.
I sat beside her, placed the soup on the table, and gently reached for her hand.

147

"How are you doing?" I asked… seems like a ridiculous question, but I wasn't sure what else to say.

Josie looked at me with a tear rolling down her cheek, "I can't believe we are going to lose the baby."

Matt interjected, "We are supposed to go to the hospital this afternoon to monitor her and the baby and make the decision to… to terminate or to try and continue." He closed his eyes and turned away.

This family needed hope… which is why Azariah had me help with this mission anyway. To provide hope to God's followers and remind them that He is there. To bring faith and love back to this world… even if it is so small, because a drop in a pond can create the biggest ripple of all.

I squeezed her hand. I closed my eyes and prayed. I prayed for her blood pressure to be steady, for her body to hold strong, for the child within her to be shielded. I prayed for the promise of life to outweigh the shadow of loss. I prayed for Matt's arms to hold his child, for Josie's tears to be tears of joy, not grief.

The mark ignited across my back. My chest tightened. My muscles seized. I gasped, but kept my hand on hers, grounding myself in the moment. I rose slowly trying to regain my composure.

"I'm so sorry this is all happening to you. I wish there was something I could do." I headed towards the door.

As I was walking through the door. Josie startled and sat up straighter. I knew what was happening and I quickly rushed out the door while Matt ran over to her side.

"She's moving," she almost yelled. "She hasn't moved like this in days."

My last glimpse as I looked back over my shoulder was through their window. Matt was smiling ear to ear and pressing his hand to her stomach… feeling those tiny kicks.

☼☼☼☼☼

I drove the few blocks home, and I collapsed onto the couch and slept until Eli came home. I take Eli to school, but he likes to ride the bus home to be with friends. He sat on the couch with me and told me all about his day. I loved hearing all his stories.

The rest of the week I felt like my blood pressure was way too high, and had a constant migraine, shortness of breath, and I didn't feel much like eating, but to me it was worth it in the sense that this family could now be just that… a family.

*"Josie and Matt Ferguson welcomed their daughter, Amari Hope, on March 14, 2012. Both mother and child are healthy. The Fergusons call her their miracle. The name Amari means 'Gift from God.'"*

*Soul 42: Amari Hope Ferguson. Rainbow baby. November 2011. Family. Saved.*

# 18.

April 12, 2012. I woke up before dawn with a weight in my chest. Not pain—just pressure. I felt this incredible sudden urge that I needed to be in Kansas City, Kansas. I didn't know why. I just knew I had to go. I quickly got up and began my day... not a question in my mind – just I needed to go.

I got Eli off to school like any other Thursday. A whole new level of independence happened sometime during this fourth-grade year where he suddenly wanted to pack his own lunch—PB&J, apple slices, and some carrot sticks. I still slipped in a note and sometimes a rice Krispie treat or small, sweet treat when he wasn't looking.

After I dropped him off at school, I called my parents. I already had a bag packed and in the trunk of the car – before Eli even woke up.
"Can you come stay with Eli for a couple of days?" I asked.
My mother didn't question it. "We'll be there by noon."

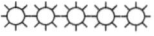

The drive was long—three and a half hours of farmland, highway, and silence. I didn't listen to music. I didn't pray. I just drove, the pull growing stronger with every mile.

Twenty minutes outside Kansas City, I turned on the radio to see if I could find any news about why I might have been called this way. After a few pushes of the "seek" button I came across a news report midway through.
"...again, reports of an active shooter at Wyandotte High School in Kansas City, Kansas. Police are on scene. Parents are being asked to stay clear..."

I gripped the steering wheel, heart pounding. A school shooting... I don't know if I can do this. High schoolers... potentially a massacre... the airplane crash flashed in front of my eyes. The death toll rising with each passing moment. I snapped back into this moment, and I pushed the pedal of my car a little faster.

I parked two blocks away and ran as fast as I could toward the school. Parents were swarming around the front of the school, and sirens wailed in the distance. Police had cordoned off the front, but they were still trying to calm parents and keep them behind the lines, push the press back, and come up with a plan to enter the building. You can tell that even with a policy in place for school shootings they don't ever really encompass everything – nor does it help them with all the unexpected factors.

I circled around the side, ducking behind dumpsters and hedges until I found an open classroom window. I climbed through, landing hard on the tile floor. My knees ached. The air smelled of gunpowder and a thick metallic scent. *Blood.*

I crouched low, listening.

The hallway was dim, fluorescent lights flickering

overhead, it looked like gun fire had broken through them. Lockers lined the walls, some dented, some streaked with blood. I heard gunshots echo from the far wing—sharp and hollow.

I moved slowly, keeping close to the walls, stepping over dropped backpacks and scattered papers. A fire alarm light pulsed red overhead, casting eerie shadows.

In the science lab, I found her—curled beneath a desk, clutching her stomach. Her sweatshirt was soaked in blood. Her lips trembled as she whispered, "Please." I knelt beside her, placed my hand on her shoulder, and prayed. The mark ignited. The pain ignited, but I had to ignore it and press on… adrenaline pushing me through. I instructed her to keep quiet and stay in the room. Once I leave, she needs to barricade the door until the police enter. She lifted her sweatshirt, and the gunshot wound was gone. She started crying hysterically.
"You have to keep it together, just for now. I need you to follow me to the door and do as I instructed."
She nodded.

I slipped back into the hallway, and the science door shut behind me. A door creaked open down the corridor. I ducked into a janitor's closet, waited until the sound passed, then crept toward the gym.

He lay near the bleachers, shot in the leg and chest. His breathing was shallow. I touched his hand and prayed. Another mark ignited across my back… erasing. His eyes fluttered open. "Am I dead?" he asked.
"No," I said softly. "You're going to be okay, but I need you to stay low, and hide under the bleachers until you hear the police come in. When you hear them come out slowly."
He nodded and crawled towards the back of the bleachers.

I moved through the locker room, stepping over shattered glass and a trail of blood. Room 204 was next in the hallway – the door was ajar, and I slipped inside. A teacher had been shielding

152

two students when the shooter entered. A bullet grazed her neck and shattered her collarbone. She was conscious but fading. The two students were okay and huddled together near their teacher. I placed my hand on her back and prayed. Another mark gone. She sobbed as the pain ebbed. "I didn't think anyone would come." "The police are coming... you have to stay here until they clear the building. Close the door and hunker down, block the door however you can until you hear the police."

I went back into the hallway and then I heard footsteps echoing from the stairwell and ducked into the band room. The instruments were scattered, chairs overturned. Behind the timpani drums, a boy lay bleeding from his side. I touched his arm and prayed. Another mark disappeared from my back. He blinked at me. "I heard music," he said. "I thought I was dreaming." "You're not dreaming, and you are still very much in danger. Stay here and hide until you hear the police."

I slipped through a side door into the library. Shelves loomed like sentinels. A girl had tried to run and was shot in the thigh. She dragged herself behind a shelf of biographies. Blood was everywhere around her. I knelt beside her, placed my hand on her leg, and prayed. The mark ignited off my back. She clutched my wrist. "I want my mom," she whispered. "You'll see her soon," I promised, "but for now you need to hide in the library until you hear police officers."

Near the stairwell, I found him - the shooter. Slumped against a wall, a failed suicide attempt left him gasping and stunned. His hand still held the weapon, but his eyes were vacant. I knelt beside him, placed my hand on his arm, and prayed. The mark burned. He sobbed, shaking. "I didn't want to die," he whispered.
"I understand... you need to stay here. You need to stay here until the police come. They will help you. They will get you the help you need." I removed the gun from him. I left him... hoping he would stay put. I looked over my shoulder and saw him curled up bawling. I went down the hallway and tossed the gun into a

trashcan. I knew the police would find it.

I heard a faint whimper from the custodian's closet as I passed by. I opened the door slowly. A boy had been shot in the shoulder and crawled into the dark to hide. He lay by the mop sink, barely conscious. I touched his forehead and prayed. Another mark scorched across my back. He stirred, blinking. "Is it over?"

"Almost," I said.

As I travelled down the hallways, I saw three others who were already gone. There was a young girl in a stairwell. I bent down and checked for a pulse, but she was already gone. I closed her eyes and placed her arms over her chest.

There was a boy in the cafeteria. He was lying on his side, and he had a sketchbook that had fallen next to him, his hand still wrapped around the edge. I gently rolled him onto his back, closed his eyes and placed his hands across his chest. I opened his sketchbook and found an amazing drawing of a cross, clutched in what appeared to be an older woman's hands – maybe a grandmother. I opened the sketchbook to that page and placed it in his hands.

There was a teacher that looked like she had tried to push her classroom door closed but was shot before she could. I did the same as the others and laid her respectfully.

I whispered prayers over each, but the marks did not respond.

As I crept back toward the classroom window, I heard voices outside—shouting commands, radios cracking. The police had been holding their positions, trying to talk to the shooter through the doors. They hadn't entered yet, fearing more gunfire. But now, they were preparing to breach.

I climbed back through the window just as they made entry.

I crouched behind a row of hedges, heart racing, body trembling. I waited until the pain passed, until the sirens faded into background noise.

I didn't speak to anyone. I didn't stay.
I drove to a hotel to recover. The pain was only subdued by the warm bath. I took a couple days in the hotel to recover, to the point that I could at least function.

Back home, Eli ran into my arms, asking if I'd brought him anything from Kansas City. I gave him a keychain shaped like a book. He smiled and clipped it to his backpack.

I was grateful I could be there for them. Grateful I could help. I also knew that this was one of those moments that would be difficult to recover from. It would be difficult to mentally not see the images flash across my eyes. For dreams to not repeat these moments in time.

I realize as I do more and more of these that although I know I'm doing good, it hurts to write about. As I progress in this journey, I am unsure of how much detail I will be able to continue with, but I will do what I can.

*Souls 43–49: Wyandotte High School. Kansas City, KS. April 12, 2012. Gunfire. Survival. Saved.*

# 19.

October 15, 2012. It was two days until Eli's 11th birthday! The air had turned. Leaves scattered across the sidewalks like forgotten letters. Eli was in fifth grade now, and the mornings were brisk enough for his red hoodie—the one with the frayed sleeves and the pencil shavings in the pocket. He left for school with a grin and a backpack full of spelling words.

It was such a beautiful day that I decided to take a walk – enjoy the beautiful crisp autumn air. I passed the bakery – the smell of coffee and fresh pastries filled the air. I kept walking past the post office and the park with the rusted swings. The trees were gold and rust colored, the sky pale gray. I turned down a street with older homes and cracked sidewalks. I always wanted to live in one of the old Victorians on this road. The street hadn't been redone and was still a brick paved road. Old streetlamps lined the road with fall trees. It was like a step back in time.

I took in the quiet beauty and enjoyed looking at each home, each one grander as I went. Then I saw my favorite house on the lane – it wasn't overly grand anymore, but I could just imagine all the stories it held. It was an aging Victorian with weathered clapboard siding and a steeply pitched roof that

156

creaked in the wind. Its silhouette was unmistakable: a turret rising like a watchful eye, ornate gables etched with gingerbread trim, and a wraparound porch that sagged slightly at the corners, as if tired from holding so many stories.

The paint, once a proud shade of deep burgundy, had faded to a muted rust, peeling in places to reveal the gray bones beneath. Tall, narrow windows lined the front, their glass mottled with age, some still dressed in lace curtains yellowed by time. A stained-glass panel above the door cast fractured light across the porch when the sun hit just right—an amber rose, a cobalt star, a flicker of green like moss.

Ivy crept along the foundation, curling around the stone like fingers unwilling to let go. I could just imagine the inside, the air would smell of old wood, dust, and something faintly floral—perhaps lavender from a sachet tucked in a forgotten drawer. It was the kind of house that held echoes. Of lullabies sung in upstairs bedrooms, of forgotten arguments muffled behind parlor doors. Of someone waiting by the window, long after the world had moved on.

As I traced my eyes over the home and walked closer, I saw him. A man, maybe mid-thirties, extremely heavyset collapsed on the front steps of the house. His shirt was soaked with sweat. His face was pale, lips tinged blue. One hand clutched his chest. The other trying to dig in his pants pocket – probably to locate his phone.

I ran to him.

His eyes fluttered open. "Help," he rasped. "Can't... breathe..."

I knelt beside him, placed my hand on his chest, and prayed. I prayed for his heart to remember its rhythm, for the blood to flow clean and strong. I prayed for the breath to return, for the body to fight. I prayed for the years he still had, for the people

157

who still needed him, for the chance to begin again.

The mark ignited across my back. My own breath vanished. My vision blurred. The pain ruptured through my chest and down my arms.

He gasped and began gulping in big breaths of air.

I staggered back, trembling.

He blinked at me. "What happened?"
"I believe you were or are having a heart attack, sir." I knew his heart was okay now, the heart attack was gone, but I didn't want him to know what I had done. "Where is your cell phone?"
He dug in his pocket and found it.
"You collapsed and were holding your chest. It is probably a good idea to be checked out just to be safe."
"Yes, that would be a good idea." He laid his head back. "My doctor told me that if I didn't start losing the weight this could happen, and I have been working hard to exercise more and eat better. I just didn't realize how bad I had become – what I was doing to myself. I didn't answer. I stood slowly, steadying myself against the porch rail.

I helped him to sit up on the steps and then helped him dial 911. I waited with him until I heard the sirens, I made sure he was okay, and then I wished him the best and went on my way. I didn't want to stay for the paramedics in my own town. A lot of them already know me, small town, and for other reasons. I didn't need to have this in their heads especially if another soul would be saved in my own town.

I walked home slowly, each step aching. I collapsed onto the couch and tried to sleep until Eli came home, but rest was fitful at best. My chest kept pounding and aching. Tightening like someone was gripping my heart. I slept between episodes of pain. It seemed like the further into the journey the less time I had between when the episodes would begin.

☼☼☼☼☼

October 17, 2012. Two days later, the house filled with laughter and the scent of chocolate cake. Eli turned eleven today, and we celebrated quietly at home. My parents, Alma and Dale, came early to help decorate, stringing paper lanterns across the dining room. Larry and Phyllis brought Eli's favorite lemon bars and a stack of books wrapped in tissue paper. We ate together, played board games, and watched Eli blow out his candles with a grin that lit up the room. I didn't ask what he wished for. I just held the moment close.

That night at bedtime we snuggled up on his bed and read one of his new books together. It was perfect. Although I know these moments are fleeting, I plan to embrace them all.

My 50th soul was one that hit closer than most. It was quick. There wasn't a lot of travel or trying to figure out how to plan and go about it. The pain lasted a few more days, but few and far between comparatively. Yet, this one symbolized so much. Halfway through my journey, halfway to the end, halfway to the future.

*Soul 50: Unnamed man. Heart attack. October 2012. Found on a walk. Saved.*

# 20.

July 4, 2013. The town came alive for the Fourth of July. Flags hung from porch railings, kids darted through sprinklers, and the scent of grilled hot dogs and kettle corn drifted through the air.

Eli had been counting down for weeks. He wore his blue polo shirt and khaki shorts, his hair still damp from the splash pad near the park. He carried a small notebook in his back pocket—his "music log," where he jotted down rhythms and melodies he wanted to try on the piano at home. He had been taking piano lessons for a few years now but has really started to get into it more now that he was a percussionist in the school band.

We laid out a blanket near the outdoor pavilion, where the town band was set up beneath strings of red, white, and blue lights. The crowd was cheerful, buzzing with anticipation. Eli tapped rhythms on his knees, listening to chord changes, naming instruments as they warmed up.

"That's an alto sax," he said, pointing. "I like how it bends the notes. It sounds like someone telling a secret."
The man playing it was older—mid-fifties, lean, with silver

at his temples and a posture that spoke of discipline. He wore a black button-down and black pants, his saxophone gleaming under the stage lights. His fingers moved with precision, but something was wrong. He kept pausing, pressing his palms to his ears. The music faltered. He tried again. Then again. Finally, he stopped altogether, clutching his head and slipping out the back of the pavilion unnoticed.

Eli frowned. "He looked like he was hurting."
"Maybe we should go check on him." I said.

We found him near the playground, sitting alone on a bench behind the swings. He sat hunched on the bench, elbows on his knees, head in his hands. His saxophone case rested unopened at his feet. Eli spotted a few friends from school and ran off to join them, leaving me to approach the man slowly.

The fireworks hadn't started yet, but the crowd's noise carried – laughter, music, the occasional pop of a firecracker, and the band still playing in the background.
"Are you alright?" I asked.
He didn't look up. "No," he said. "Not even close."
I sat on the far end of the bench, giving him space.
"I'm Dalene," I said trying to coax more out of him.
"I'm Steve."
"I saw you playing earlier," I said gently. "You were good."
He gave a dry laugh. "Was. I used to be. Now I can barely get through a verse without my skull splitting open."
He rubbed his temples, eyes squeezed shut. "It's like a siren inside my head. Constant. High-pitched. Like feedback from a mic that never shuts off."
"Tinnitus?" I asked.
He nodded. "Severe. Years of field work—FBI surveillance vans, gunfire, flashbangs. I thought I could outrun it. I even retired early. After retirement I needed a hobby, so I picked up my sax again. I was hoping music could be my way back to myself."
He looked at me then, eyes bloodshot and raw. "But tonight, I couldn't even finish the set. I had to walk off stage in front of

161

everyone. I've never felt so... humiliated."

I let the silence stretch between us. The cicadas buzzed in the trees. Children's laughter echoed from the swings.
"I'm sorry," I said. "That sounds unbearable."
He nodded slowly. "It is. I haven't slept more than two hours a night in months. I've tried everything—white noise machines, meds, acupuncture. Nothing touches it."
He pressed his palms to his ears again, wincing. "I just want quiet. Just for a minute. Sorry I don't know why I'm telling you all of this."
"It's okay." I put my hand on his, "I'm sorry you're going through this. I know a sorry doesn't help, but... I am sorry."

While my hand remained on his I closed my eyes and prayed for the ringing to soften, for the silence to return. I prayed for the years of noise and violence to loosen their grip. I prayed for the music to flow again—not as escape, but as healing. I prayed for the man beneath the badge, beneath the pain, beneath the sound.

The mark ignited. My ears filled with static, high-pitched whine that pierced through bone. I gasped, nearly collapsing, but held my hand steady.
He inhaled sharply. His hands dropped from his ears.
He blinked. "Wait..."
He turned his head slowly, as if testing the air.
"It's gone," he whispered. "The ringing. It's... gone."
"Wow! Really?" I tried to say without wincing.
"Ya... I ... haven't heard silence in so many years."
He got up and grabbed his saxophone case. He looked at me and smiled. "Thank you for listening to me. I can't believe this. I hope whatever just happened lasts."

I nodded and then I turned and walked back toward the swings, where Eli was laughing with his friends, unaware that anything had changed.

162

✵✵✵✵✵

It took another week for my ears to stop hurting, and another week after that before I could start listening to Eli's music again. I told Eli that I must have a sinus infection and that is why my ears hurt so badly. I know over time he will grow to not believe me, but I want to protect him from this as much as I can. Maybe that isn't the right answer, but I don't want him to worry about me.

*Soul 51: Steve. Saxophone Player. Tinnitus. July 2013. Music and silence. Saved.*

# 21.

January 14, 2014. The cold in January was sharp enough to bite. The sidewalks glittered with salt and frost, and the air carried that brittle silence that only winter could hold. Eli had just turned twelve. He was taller now, more serious, and had begun composing his own piano pieces—moody, searching, full of minor chords and unresolved endings. I listened from the kitchen as he played, the music echoing through the house like a question I couldn't quite answer.

One day after Eli was off to school I went to the grocery store, and that is where I saw her. She stood near the entrance, bundled in a torn coat that didn't close, her face hollow and jittery. Her cardboard sign read *"Anything helps"*. Most people passed without looking. I gave her a few dollars and a granola bar from my purse. She didn't speak, just nodded and turned away, eyes darting toward the parking lot like she was waiting for someone who never came.

I thought about her that night while folding laundry. There was something in her eyes—panic, maybe. Or the kind of emptiness that comes after too many years of surviving.

✿✿✿✿✿

Two days later, I was on my way to the bank. I took the
back lot to avoid traffic, cutting behind the hardware store where
the alley ran between two buildings. It was quiet there—just
dumpsters, broken pallets, and the hum of a distant HVAC unit,
and that's where I found her, the same woman from the grocery
store.

She had collapsed against the brick wall, barely breathing.
Her skin was pale, lips cracked, arms marked with the
unmistakable signs of drug use. A torn plastic bag lay beside her,
its contents scattered—cotton balls, a bent spoon, a lighter.

Her breath came in shallow gasps. Her eyes fluttered open
when she heard my footsteps.

"Didn't mean to…" she rasped. "Too much…"

I knelt beside her, heart pounding. The air smelled of rust
and rot, and her body was trembling beneath the layers of her
coat.
"I'm here," I said softly. "You're not alone."
She tried to speak again, but her voice broke. Her fingers
twitched, reaching for something invisible.

I placed my hand on her chest and prayed. I prayed for her
body to release the poison, for her heart to remember its rhythm. I
prayed for the fog to lift, for the pain to loosen its grip. I prayed
for the girl she used to be, for the woman she could still become. I
prayed for the chance to choose life.

The mark ignited. My own chest tightened, lungs burning. I
laid back against the cold brick wall, shaking and coughing. My
veins felt like they were on fire, like poison flowed through them,
and I was all the sudden very itchy. It passed slowly, and I was
finally able to get to my feet.

The woman was gulping air next to me. She sat up and looked around.

"Are you okay?" I asked her.

"I … I think so."

I stood slowly, steadying myself against the wall.

"I'm going to call for help," I said. "Please, please ask them for help. Tell them you want to get help."

She hesitated but eventually nodded.

I stayed with her until I heard the sirens, and then I got back into my car and parked a little way down, right near the bank. I had told her it was okay to get help. That everyone needs help sometimes. I waited and looked in my rear-view mirror. She talked to the paramedics, to the police, and then she climbed into the back of the ambulance with her belongings. I prayed that meant she was going to go get the help she needed.

I walked the rest of the way to the bank in silence, my body aching.

I went home after the bank, and I started feeling the effects again. I was dizzy, disoriented, nauseous, and I had a massive headache starting. I went to my room and lied down.

I kept waking up with chills. I couldn't see, because I was so dizzy. Disoriented, foggy, nauseous, and a headache pounded. My body ached; I felt the poison running through my veins.

Eli came home and I told him I must have gotten the flu. I warmed up some dinner for him, and thankfully he was old enough now to put himself to bed. So, I went to lie down again.

Sleep was fitful, the same symptoms on a broken record. Tossing and turning all night. I finally got up around four in the morning and ran a bath. I sank in letting the water absorb me. Hoping that the water would remove the toxins from me.

I stayed in that bathtub until morning – refreshing the water once. When I stepped out, I felt dizzy still, weak… hungover, but like the toxins were finally leaving.

January 2016. I thought about that girl often. I never knew what happened to her until I came across a news article with a picture of a girl standing in front of a building. It was the girl I saw two years ago. She was beautiful.

*"Former meth addict launches youth outreach program to combat addiction and offer creative alternatives. 'I nearly died in an alley,' she said. 'Someone saved me. I don't know who. But I decided to make it count.' The program offers education, counseling, and activities like sewing, art, and sports to help teens find purpose and support."*

I pressed the clipping into the ledger.

*Soul 52: Unnamed woman. Meth overdose. January 2014. Found in alley. Saved.*

# 22.

June 10, 2014. The tornado outbreak around Topeka had left the region raw - homes splintered, families displaced, and grief hanging in the air like smoke. I decided during Sunday service, when Pastor Jim asked for volunteers to help with recovery efforts, that I would go.

My parents, Alma and Dale, came to stay with Eli. "We've got him," her mother said, folding his laundry. "I think it's wonderful that you are going to help."

Eli hugged her tightly. "Bring me something cool," he said. "I will." I chuckled. "I'm going to call and see how your piano lesson went this week."
"Okay ma. Love you."
"I love you too, Love Bug."

Three days into my week-long trip, I had settled into the rhythm of service. I was stationed at a shelter and food pantry in Topeka, helping to sort donations, serve meals, and comfort families who had lost everything.

That afternoon, the pantry was quiet. Volunteers moved slowly, re-stocking shelves. A child colored at the corner table. The hum of the refrigerator was the loudest sound.

Then the radio crackled: *"Tornado warning issued for Silver Lake, Kansas. Rotation confirmed. All residents advised to take shelter immediately."*

The room froze. A woman dropped a tray of cornbread. Someone gasped. The child stopped coloring.

I stood still, my heart pounding, and then before I could overthink – I moved. I grabbed my coat and ran toward the storm.

Silver Lake was twenty minutes west. The sky was bruised and boiling, clouds swirling like smoke. Sirens wailed. The road was littered with branches, insulation, and shards of roofing. I passed homes with rooftops torn off, shattered windows, and a pickup truck wrapped around a tree. I parked my car off to the side of the road, flashers going. I got out and began walking towards the center of town.

The smell hit me first—wet wood, scorched plastic, the sharp tang of insulation. The air was thick with dust and something metallic, like blood and rain. The silence was eerie, broken only by distant cries and the crunch of debris beneath my boots. Trees were stripped bare. Power lines hung like torn thread. The school's roof had peeled back like paper.

I walked into the aftermath with no plan, only the certainty that someone needed me before it was too late.

1. **A man trapped beneath a collapsed porch**, his ribs were crushed, and his breath was shallow. I found him by the splintered remains of a front stoop; his body was twisted

169

beneath a beam that had once held up a swing. His lips were pale, and his eyes were fluttering. I knelt in the mud, bracing my shoulder against the weight, and slid my hand beneath his back. His pulse was fading. I whispered the prayer. The mark surged through me like fire in my lungs. He gasped once, then again—sharp, ragged, alive. I called for people in the streets to come to help me lift the boards to release him.

2. **A child under the wreckage of a trailer**; her leg was broken. She was buried beneath insulation and shattered glass; her small hand had been trying to reach through a gap in the debris. I crawled in on my belly, the air thick with fiberglass and fear. Her leg was bent unnatural, and her skin was cold. I pressed my palm to her chest and felt nothing. I closed my eyes and begged—*not this one, not her*. The mark raged across my back as it erased. Her chest rose, and she whimpered. I sobbed. I found two men racing around checking on people, and they helped unbury her from the rubble.

3. **A woman pinned inside a car,** her abdomen was bleeding, her voice was barely audible. The car had flipped and landed against a tree; the roof was crushed inward. She was trapped between the dashboard and the passenger seat, and blood was soaking into her blouse. I climbed through the broken window and glass sliced my forearm. She looked at me, eyes wide, lips trembling. "Please," she whispered. I pressed my hand to her side and prayed for the bleeding to stop, for the body to hold. Her breathing steadied. Her hand gripped mine. I told her I'd be back soon, and I found a firefighter and sent them her way.

4. **A teenager with a head wound**, unconscious in a ditch. I nearly missed him—his body was half-submerged in the runoff, and his face was caked with mud. I slid down the embankment, my knees scraping against gravel. His skull was split and blood was pooling beneath him. I touched

his temple and felt the mark light up as it erased. My vision blurred. He coughed and then groaned. I got him to sit up, and I helped him up the embankment. He ran off to find his family.

5. **A baby in a crib**, untouched but silent, eyes closed. The house was gone, but the nursery had been towards the middle of the home and remained almost intact in the yard. The crib was sitting upright and was surrounded by rubble. I climbed over the wreckage, my heart was pounding from fear. The baby didn't move, and I lifted him gently—his breath was weak, and staggered, and he made no sound. I pressed my hand to his chest and prayed with everything I had. The mark erased as sharp as his single cry pierced the silence, and he continued to cry. I collapsed to my knees, clutching him to my chest. I searched the area and found the baby's parents trapped beneath their roof. They are untouched but trapped. The mother is screaming for her baby. I rush towards them and tell them I have him. He is safe. He is okay. I tell them I'm going to find help, and rescuers come to help me release them from their imprisonment. The mother climbs out first and rushes to grab her child. Sobbing.

6. **A man struck by debris,** bleeding from his scalp; disoriented. I was walking near where the man was crouched beside a collapsed shed, he was trying to dig out a dog that was trapped beneath the wreckage. A huge gust of wind kicked up and knocked a sheet of plywood off the shed—it caught him across the head with a sickening crack. He staggered, blood pouring down his temple, then he dropped to his knees. I ran to him, slipping in the mud, catching him just before he fell forward. "You're okay," I said, though I knew that was a lie. His eyes were glassy, unfocused. I pressed my hand to the side of his head, fingers slick with blood, and prayed for clarity, for balance, for the bleeding to stop. The mark erased and

171

rattled me like a bell struck too hard. He blinked, then winced. "Is she out?" he asked, pointing toward the rubble. "Not yet, but close." I got him into a sitting position, and I went to the hole that the man had started digging. I dug my nails and fingertips into the mud. It was hard to gain traction with the slickness of blood on my fingertips. About ten minutes later the dog was able to get up far enough to help scratch away at the hole, and then a beautiful German Shepherd emerged from the shed. She was caked in mud, and had a small laceration on her snout, but otherwise looked okay. She ran to the man and began licking his face. He gave her a huge hug and said, "Good girl Ember."

7. & 8. **An elderly couple huddled beneath a sagging beam**, their hands were clasped together, but their bodies laid still. I found them in the remains of a living room, the ceiling was bowed above them, and it groaned with the weight of rubble and water. They lay on the floor next to each other, the woman's head was on his shoulder, their fingers intertwined. The beam above them cracked as I stepped in. "Don't move," I said, crawling low, not knowing if they could even hear me. I wedged a broken chair beneath the beam, just enough to buy us some time. Her breathing was shallow, and his was worse. I touched them both, one hand on each chest, and prayed for strength, for rhythm, for time. The marks split through me like lightning, my body ached and groaned like the beam above us. They stirred and she whispered, "We stayed together." I nodded, tears in my throat. "You still are. We need to get out of here before this roof collapses." I showed them the path and helped them to their knees so they could crawl out. The man went first guiding the way and helped his wife out of the house. I followed.

9. **A boy with a punctured lung** was gasping, his lips were turning blue. He was lying beside a broken fence, and he was clutching his side, his eyes were wide with panic. I

172

dropped beside him, pressing my hand to his ribs. "You're okay," I said. The mark surged. His chest expanded. He coughed violently, then sobbed. I held him until I could wave down the paramedics.

10. **A mother clutching her infant,** both in shock, the child unresponsive. She was rocking back and forth in the middle of the street; her baby was limp in her arms. "He won't wake up," she kept saying not to anyone, but just out of pure shock. It was like she was in a state of paralysis that she couldn't physically do anything, but her mind and heart knew she needed to do something. I knelt beside her, placed my hand between them, and whispered the prayer. The mark burned through me. The baby stirred. She screamed—not in fear, but in joy.

Each time, the mark burned, my body would tremble, and my breath would vanish. I staggered between rescues, each one carving something out of me.

By the tenth soul, I could barely stand.

I turned toward the school. Emergency crews were gathering near the gymnasium. Children were being led out in blankets, their faces pale and stunned. There was a torn sign out front advertising a summer program for kids to be at while parents worked, and that's when I saw him. The grandfather from the spring of 2008, Anthony Lead. He was kneeling under the bleachers; his arms wrapped tightly around a small girl - his granddaughter. The world swirled around me, and I was taken back to the vision I had in the library so many years ago:

*I saw a dirt road split by wind. I saw a playground swallowed by leaves. Swings flipping and tossing in the wind. A funnel cloud twisted in the distance, ripping shingles from rooftops and flinging branches like arrows. A little girl screamed, her voice swallowed by the roar. Anthony turned toward her, his leg dragging, his breath ragged. He ran—not fast, not smooth, but with everything he had. He couldn't reach her...a sharp scream impaled my ears...*

I came back to the dampness, the clouds, the wind, the stench of blood and rain. I saw her face was streaked with dirt, her hands were trembling, but she was alive. Her clothes were torn, and her shoes were missing. He held her like he'd never let go.

Her parents came running from the far end of the lot, tears streaming down their faces.
"Dad!" the woman cried. "You found her?"
"I shielded her," he said, voice breaking. "Under the bleachers. I didn't think we'd make it."
They collapsed into a hug, all four of them tangled in relief.
The grandfather looked up and saw me. When recognition struck his mouth came open, but he didn't speak. He just nodded slowly; grateful. He must have put it together, because I never told him.

I nodded back.

I went inside the school to see if I could help. I found her just outside the music room and she had collapsed against the lockers. One of her shoes was askew and her blouse torn on the shoulder. Papers were scattered all around her—lesson plans, sheet music, a roll sheet with names I couldn't read. The teacher's pulse was faint, a bruise bloomed across her temple, and her breathing was shallow and erratic.

I knelt beside her, brushing debris from her face. She stirred but didn't speak. I pressed my hand to her chest and prayed. The mark surged again. My vision was blurry, my body was exhausted, heavy from the weight of the day. My knees buckled.

The teacher woke up and right away asked about the kids. I told her I wasn't sure about all of them, but that the rescue teams were here clearing the building. She stood up shakily, smiled, and walked quickly towards the doors.

I leaned back against the lockers, my body trembling, the hallway spinning. That's when I saw her—LeAnn. She stood at the end of the corridor, her nursing badge clipped to her collar, her sons safe beside her. Her eyes met mine, wide and wet, and she didn't speak. She knew. She was one of the only ones who knew.
"You're still doing it," she said softly.
I nodded, unable to speak.
She reached out, placed her hand on mine.
Her boys stood behind her, clutching each other's hands. One of them had a scrape on his cheek. The other was holding a stuffed bear, its ear torn. LeAnn glanced back at them, then turned to me.
"They were in the gym when it hit," she said. "I was at the hospital. I couldn't get here fast enough. I thought—I thought I'd lose them."
Her voice cracked. I didn't interrupt.
"I got here just after the funnel lifted. They were okay. Shaken, but okay. I don't know how. I just know I needed to see them with my own eyes."
I nodded. "That's why I came too."
She helped me to my feet and gave me a hug. We didn't say goodbye. We didn't need to.

Outside, the sun was sinking low. The air was thick with dust and relief. Volunteers moved slowly, gathering supplies, comforting the wounded.

I had to tell the volunteers that I needed to head home, because I wasn't feeling well, but I couldn't actually head home so I spent the rest of the four days I was supposed to be away at a hotel recuperating. I knew that wouldn't be enough time, but it would at least get me over the hump. I knew I had a long few months ahead of me.

Back home, Eli ran into my arms, asking if I'd brought him anything from Kansas. I gave him a small wooden cross carved from storm debris that the church had been handing out. He held it gently, then placed it on his piano.

Later that night, I clipped the article from the paper:
*"Tornado in Silver Lake leaves 8 dead, 11 critically injured. One woman stated, "We didn't have time... the sirens went off, and the next thing we knew our town was collapsing." Local meteorologists stated, "we had a tornado watch out, but we have had one out for almost the entire state for a week. Salt Lake was a huge misfortune as we thought the storm was going to break apart. Everything lined up for it to break apart, and then instead, well, the opposite occurred and by the time we caught on, and the sirens went off it was too late for people to seek shelter." Volunteers from across the region respond. Survivors credit fast action and medical support for saving lives."*

I pressed the clipping into the ledger.

*Souls 53–63: Silver Lake, Kansas. Tornado. June 2014.*

# 23.

April 9, 2015. I hadn't planned to go. It was all over the news for the last few days. The Ozarks had been flooding due to all the rain. The church had emailed out another mission project to help the flood victims, but I didn't feel the pull this time to go. Not like with the tornadoes.

Azariah had different plans though and that night I had a dream. It wasn't vivid, not like some of the dreams I've had.

*Water was rushing and was rising quickly. Then I heard what sounded like a boy yelling for help.*

That was it. No more details. No explanation. Nothing. I knew that I had to go though.

I checked the map, and it was almost a six-hour drive to Eminence, Missouri where they expected the next big floods to occur.

I packed quietly. It was four in the morning, and Eli was still asleep, curled up with his sketchbook and a half-eaten granola bar. He was thirteen now. I left a note on the fridge: *I'll be back on Sunday. Be kind to Grandma Phyllis. No piano until homework's done. I love you so much!*

I got in the car and started driving. I called Grandma Phyllis on the way. She was always up early to do something. She answered right away and said she would be over to stay with him before he even woke up. They don't know what I'm doing, but they know that I have a strong call to serve. I explained that I was going to help with the flooding, and she completely understood.

The rain had been falling for three days straight. Not the gentle kind that softened the earth, but the kind that carved through it—fast, cold, and relentless. By the time I arrived in Eminence, the river had already swallowed half the town. Volunteers were setting up sandbags near the church, and I went inside to check in. They had assigned me to a clean-up crew clearing debris from the trails so that emergency vehicles and sandbag crews could pass through if needed.

Friday afternoon I was beginning to think I would need to call Grandma Phyllis and Eli and tell them I would be later than expected. I was walking the ridge above the ravine, checking for downed trees. The air was thick with mist and the smell of wet cedar. My boots sank into the mud with every step. Somewhere below, I heard shouting—sharp and panicking, then cut off.

I froze straining my ears to listen again for which way the yell had come from. It felt like it was forever, but then I finally heard it again. It was coming from down the ravine behind me. I ran.

The ravine was steep, slick with moss and shale. I slid halfway down before I saw him—a teenage boy, maybe fifteen, wedged between two boulders in the water. His leg was bent at an unnatural angle. One arm clung to a root. The current was rising fast. His face kept going under the water which was cutting off

178

his cries for help.

I shouted at him, but he went back under right when I did.
There was no time to wait for rescue. I climbed down, hands
scraping against stone, boots filling with icy water that had
puddled along the ravine ridges. I braced myself against the rocks
and reached for him. He came up from the water, coughing, and
that is when we locked eyes. He looked at me with desperation.
I reached again for him my hand digging into the rocks below me,
tearing my skin with the ragged edges.

I grabbed his arm, and his skin was ice cold. His lips were
blue, and he had a sickly pallor. I had to get him out of immediate
danger now.
"I'm so sorry this is going to probably hurt a lot, but I need you to
try and get your foot unstuck. Do you think you can reach if I
help lift you up?"
"I can try." I grabbed his arm tighter, and I dug my feet in harder,
my hand gripping tighter on the rocks. I lifted him up as much as
I could so he could reach against the current.

After several desperate attempts he finally was able to get
his foot undone from the rocks. He let out a terrible scream,
agonizing. That is when he blacked out – from shock or pain I'm
not sure, maybe a combination. I still had a good grip, but the
current was so strong, and he now was limp. I held onto him and
got him pulled closer to me. I sat down on the rock I had been
bracing on and dug my heels in. I got him up enough so that I
could get my other hand under his other arm. I pulled him up
enough that he landed on top of me. I rolled onto my side and
stood up to be able to drag him further up the ravine. We needed
to get out of here quickly.

I pressed my hand to his chest and prayed—not just for
breath, but for the body to hold against the cold, for the bones to
remember how to stay whole, for the fear to loosen its grip.
The mark surged through me like a flood of its own. My breath
felt constricted like I was drowning. I had to sit down as I lost

179

feeling in my legs.

He jolted upright, scrambling backwards up the ravine.
Panicked that he was still drowning.
"It's okay, you're safe." I said.
"Wha-what happened?"
"You were drowning. I helped pull you out, but we need to get up
this ravine and quickly. The water is rising too fast and if we stay
here, we will get swept back in."
We helped each other back up the ravine. Sliding, mud
splattering our clothes and faces. Knees banged against the ravine
walls, blood trickling down our hands, knees and faces from
rocks and tree branches pulling at us.

We finally made it back up the ravine, and we just laid there
on our backs for several minutes. Staring up into the depths of the
trees, rain splattering our faces. Then we stood up and walked
back to the church.

I found out later that he was part of a boy scout troop that
was in the area helping. His troop went back for help, and some
of them were trying to keep up with him, but the water was too
fast.

I took a job in the food pantry for Saturday, before heading
back home on Sunday. My left leg was in excruciating pain, I was
chilled to the bone, and my breath was ragged, but I wanted to
keep helping while I was there.

☼☼☼☼☼

Thankfully it was my left leg, so I was able to drive home
okay, but the entire way home I had the heat blasting, a blanket
on my lap, my winter coat on, and my hat and gloves on. I
worked on deep breathing the whole way home since my breath
still felt ragged.

Back home, Eli and Grandma Phyllis were waiting with a bowl of popcorn, and they had a movie all queued up and ready to go. I went to change quickly and then I snuggled up on the couch. They asked me about my trip.

"It was sad, but I felt like I helped, although I think I caught a cold."

*Soul 64: Eminence, Missouri. Flash flood. Teenage boy. Leg broken, hypothermic. Found in ravine. April 10, 2015. Saved.*

# 24.

December 12th, 2015. Eli had just gotten his learner's permit in October. He was fourteen and we'd spent the last two months driving loops around the neighborhood, practicing turns, parking, and merging. He was cautious—almost too cautious—but I didn't mind. I liked watching him learn the rhythm of the road.

Eli and I had settled into a quiet routine—school, piano, dinner, homework. He was growing fast, asking bigger questions, but still content to sit beside me on the couch and sketch while I read.

The cold came early that year. By December, the nights were sharp and silent. Eli had started sleeping with his sketchbook tucked under his pillow. I'd started waking at odd hours, unsure why.

That night, we made cocoa and watched a rerun of *MythBusters*, and then we went to sleep like any other night.

The dream came just after midnight. This time it was in the form of a newspaper article, scrolling behind my eyelids like ticker tape—black text on white, crisp and cold.

*FAMILY OF FIVE SUCCUMBS TO CARBON MONOXIDE
POISONING Kirkville, Iowa – December 13th, 2015, Authorities
responded to a call late Saturday morning after neighbors
reported a strange smell and no signs of activity. The family of
five—two adults and three children—were found unconscious in
their home. All were transported to a local hospital, but none
survived. Investigators believe a faulty furnace was to blame.*
Then I saw the photo: a modest ranch house with a beautiful
wrap-around porch and a frost-covered car in the drive. The
address was listed in the caption. I read it twice. The date was for
tomorrow which meant they were going to die today.

Alma was in Lincoln for the weekend. Eli was asleep. I
couldn't take him with me, and he was old enough to be alone for
a while. I left a note on the counter in case he woke up: "I'll be
back soon. Please stay home and no driving!"

I didn't pack; I just had to go. I knew that if I didn't, if I
called the police, that the dream would play out. Azariah was
sending me.

The drive to Kirkville was only ten minutes, but it felt
longer. The roads were slick with black ice, the sky low and
colorless. I passed shuttered gas stations and frostbitten fields.

I found the house just as in the dream—porch light on, car
in the driveway, no movement inside. I knocked. No answer.
I tried the door, and it was locked tight. I went around the side of
the house and tried the windows. None of them budged. The back
door had a big glass window, and it left me with only one choice.
I wrapped my hand in my hat and punched the window open. I
reached in and unlocked the door.

When I got inside, the air was warm, it felt… off. Stale. The family was in the living room - two adults and three children, all unconscious. The youngest, a toddler, lay on the couch, lips tinged blue. The parents were slumped in chairs. A teenager was slumped on the floor. It looked like they had been having a movie night. Popcorn littered the floor.

I quickly ran and opened windows and turned off the furnace. Then I knelt beside the toddler, I pressed my hand to his little chest and prayed. I prayed for his lungs to fill, for the article to be wrong. For strength and life. The mark surged through me like fire in a sealed room. He gasped. I moved to the others—one by one, I prayed. I prayed for them to live again. For their lives to be restored.

Once the family was healed, I told them what had happened and got them to the porch. I called 911, made sure they were alright, and then I left. They stood on their porch hugging each other as tight as they could.

✧✧✧✧✧

I drove home through the ice, through the cold, through the darkness. Thinking about that tiny little toddler, thinking about how Eli used to be that small. Thinking about how this was becoming harder and harder. Harder to write, harder to find the mental and emotional capacity to thrive, but I knew that I had to continue. I said *'yes',* I said I would do this until all 100 tally marks had faded.

I left home around 9:00 p.m. I had no idea how long it would take, but it was only 9:47 p.m.

When I got home the note was untouched. Eli was still sound asleep. That night I began the symptoms. I felt dizzy, nauseous, I kept having hot and cold flashes, and my vision kept blurring around the edges. I felt like I had severe flu symptoms. I took a bath, closing my eyes, letting the water absorb into my pores.

184

When I decided to finally crawl into my bed it was hard to sleep, not just because of the ongoing symptoms, but because I kept worrying that the same fate could happen to us. I kept going to Eli's room and checking on him. We had a carbon monoxide detector, and I made sure the light was on – and I even changed the back up batteries in it just to be safe. First thing tomorrow I was going to call a furnace company to come do some preventative maintenance.

*Souls 65–69: Kirkville, Iowa. Carbon monoxide poisoning. Family of five.*

# 25.

October 3, 2016. Eli came home today carrying his drumsticks but not his usual energy. He dropped his book bag and drumsticks by the door and sat at the kitchen table without a word. His face was pale, his eyes rimmed red.

When he saw me, Eli came over and gave me a hug, and explained that Mr. Harlan, his band director, had returned to school after a long absence. The students had whispered for weeks—illness, surgery, maybe retirement—but no one knew. Today he stood before them, thinner, slower, his voice steady but fragile. He told them the truth: stage 4 cancer, a tumor in his brain. He would not be able to continue teaching.

He said the room fell silent. Eli said even the cymbals seemed to echo the words. Mr. Harlan had been more than a teacher, he was the one who pushed Eli to lead the percussion section, who believed he could keep tempo when others faltered, who taught him that rhythm was not just sound but responsibility. Eli learned that leadership wasn't about being the loudest—it was about holding the rhythm steady when others lost their place. He carried that lesson home, practicing until his wrists ached, determined not to let the section down. I saw how proud he was when the younger percussionists began looking to him for cues, trusting his timing. That confidence was Mr. Harlan's gift.

And Eli wasn't the only one. I remember hearing about a shy clarinet player who nearly quit after her first year. Mr. Harlan sat with her after class, teaching her how to breathe through the nerves, reminding her that music was more than notes—it was courage. She stayed, and by senior year she was leading solos.

There was also the trumpet player who struggled with discipline, always late, always distracted. Mr. Harlan didn't give up on him. He made him section leader, forced him to show up for others, and in the process taught him responsibility. Even the quiet tuba player, who never spoke above a whisper, found his place because Mr. Harlan believed every sound mattered, no matter how deep or low.

Mr. Harlan had a way of seeing what each student needed—not just musically, but personally. He gave them more than instruction. He gave them belief. And that belief carried them further than they thought possible.

☼☼☼☼☼

October 4, 2016. This afternoon, I went to the high school. The band office was dim, the blinds half-drawn, dust floating in the light like notes suspended in air. Boxes lined the walls, some already taped shut, others half-filled with sheet music, trophies, and photographs of concerts past. The room smelled faintly of brass polish and old paper; the scent of years of rehearsals and performances now being packed away.

Mr. Harlan sat at his desk, thinner than I remembered, his shoulders hunched as if the weight of the boxes were pressing down on him. His daughter was beside him, carefully folding programs into a crate. Her hands trembled, and every so often she stopped, staring at the cover of a concert program as if trying to hold onto the memory inside it.

187

I knocked softly on the doorframe. He looked up, startled, then smiled faintly. "Dalene," he said, his voice weak but warm. "I didn't expect anyone."

I stayed in the doorway, "I wanted to thank you," I said. "For what you've given Eli. For what you've given all your students."
He leaned back in his chair, eyes glistening. "They gave me more than I gave them," he whispered.

We stayed together in silence. He packed another box slowly, pausing to trace his fingers over a framed photo of the marching band at state competition. His daughter tucked it carefully into the crate, her hands lingering on the frame as if reluctant to let go.

I told him about Eli—and the others that he inspired and helped along his way. His daughter's eyes filled with tears, "That's what he always wanted—to make them believe they mattered."
I sat down next to him, and I placed my hand lightly on his arm. His skin was cool; his eyes clouded with exhaustion. I prayed. Prayed for his body to heal, for him to be able to teach again, for him to be able to continue inspiring those around him. The mark surged through me like fire breaking open a sealed room.

Mr. Harlan's breath caught, then steadied. His shoulders lifted, his eyes cleared, and for the first time in months, color returned to his face. He blinked at me, bewildered.

I squeezed his hand. "I'm so glad I got to see you again. I'll be praying for you."

They both sat in silence, staring at me as I walked out the door.

Eli came home the next day absolutely floating with excitement and joy. "Mom! Mom! Mr. Harlan… I don't know how it happened, but he is okay! He doesn't have the tumor anymore. He said it just went away, and when he went to his doctor for an emergency appointment yesterday, they couldn't explain it. He doesn't have to retire!"
"That is so wonderful!"

The next few days my body broke in two. My blood felt thin, my veins sore. My head burned, throbbed, and my eyes would blur from the pressure I felt. My joints and muscles felt like that of a 100-year-old. The bathtub was my friend, and I soaked in it every moment Eli was gone to not concern him. When he was home, I pushed through the best I could, but I could tell he noticed I wasn't feeling well.

*Soul 70: Eddyville, Iowa. October 3, 2016. Band director, mentor to Eli. Stage 4 cancer with brain tumor. Breath restored. Time rewritten. Saved.*

Some rescues are not about holding space when the rhythm stops. Some are about giving the rhythm back.

# 26.

February 16, 2017. I was only running errands. Nothing unusual. The day was quiet, the kind of February cold that settles into your bones. But halfway down the highway, something shifted. My vision blurred, my hands tightened on the wheel, and it was as if I was being pulled forward by a force I couldn't resist.

The trance was heavy, like driving underwater. I don't remember the turns I took. I don't remember the miles. When it broke, I had no clue where I was at. Nothing looked familiar. I turned around in my seat and looked out of my windows. I couldn't tell where I was. I pulled up my phone to check the maps – I put in my home address to find that I was nearly thirty minutes away from my house. My heart was pounding.

*How in the world did this happen? What was I doing?*

I looked through my side mirrors about to leave when I saw them. Tire marks, sharp and erratic, carved into the dirt and rock. The hair at the nape of my neck rose, and I got chills. What was I about to find.

I got out. The air was cold, biting against my face. I followed the marks to the edge of the road and looked down.

The ravine was steep, dropping into a river lined with bare trees. At the bottom, nose down in the water, was a yellow school bus. Its back end tilted upward, the river slowly rising into the windows. My hands started to shake but not from the cold this time. I had to get down there.

I slid down the ravine, mud and rock tearing at my hands, my breath ragged. The water was icy, rushing against the bus. I pulled at the emergency hatch at the back; my boots were sliding in the mud. The door stuck, and I had to try several times to gain traction, but finally it gave way with a groan.

Inside, the air was heavy with panic and silence. The driver was slumped forward at the wheel, the river already lapping at his chest. His face was white; his eyes were closed. I climbed over the seats, bracing myself against the rising water, and pressed my hand to his shoulder where he sat. As I did I was washed into a different moment in time: *the driver. He was looking in the rearview mirror watching the kids laughing and talking amongst each other. He smiled. They took the country road heading towards a small town that didn't have their own school and consolidated with the larger town nearby. The bus driver suddenly grabbed his chest, the vision was fading in and out, he couldn't keep consciousness, the bus swerved...* and I was thrown back into reality. A medical emergency; heart related. That is what caused this accident.

I kept my hand on his shoulder and I prayed. The mark surged through my back as it erased. My chest raged, my breath taken away, my vision blurred. The driver's body shuddered, his chest seized, and then a violent cough tore through him. He was breathing steadily again. I regained my composure, pushing through and I left him to gain more consciousness to begin helping the children.

The children were scattered across the bus—some sprawled in the aisle, others slumped against windows, their faces pale and lips slack. A few moaned faintly, but most were still. I pulled the smallest girl first, her hair plastered to her face, her body limp in my arms. She gasped when I touched her, coughing weakly, and I prayed. Another mark sending shooting ripples through my skin as it erased. I carried her to the back of the bus near the hatch.

The driver had gotten up and started checking on children. "Sir, can you please crawl out this back hatch and help the children out? They can head up the ravine and some of them can climb in my car to get out of the cold."
"Yes, I can do that."
"I'll start helping them out the hatch to you."

The water was climbing fast now, swirling around my knees, soaking the seats. I dragged a boy free from where his leg was pinned, his head lolling back. His chest rose sharply when I prayed over him, and he groaned, clutching his leg. Another mark ignited. I fell forward but braced myself on the seat by me. I lifted him toward the opening, telling him to head towards the emergency hatch, my muscles screaming.

Two sisters were slumped together, heads against the glass, water licking at their shoulders. I pulled them both close to me and I prayed for them. This time two marks burned my skin as they erased. Their little bodies perked up, skin turning a normal color. I carried one in each arm, my knees buckling under their weight. I helped them to the emergency hatch and helped get them to the driver.

The older children were heavier, harder to move. One boy's forehead was split open, blood mixing with river water. Another girl's arm hung limp, broken. I carried them as best I could out of the water, each step a battle against the rising current. Each time I prayed another mark raged as it erased from my skin. My body was taking a toll, but I had to keep going.

The bus was filling quickly now, the front nearly submerged. I waded through the freezing water, pulling bodies from seats, lifting them toward the hatch, urging them to climb, to move. My arms burned, my legs shook, my back on fire from the marks erasing, but I didn't stop.

192

Seventeen children. One driver. Eighteen souls.

☼☼☼☼☼

The sound of sirens cut through the air. Fire trucks, voices shouting, ropes thrown down the ravine. I turned, breathless, mud streaked across my arms, and that's when I saw him.

Kevin VanderLeest.

The firefighter from January 2011. Soul 39. The man I had once stood over in a hospital bed, praying for his body to wake up, for his body to remember how to live. He had never seen me, never knew, but I knew him instantly.

He moved with urgency, sliding down the embankment, shouting orders to the crew above. His shoulders were broad, his stride steady, his face alive with focus. He didn't look at me with recognition — only as another civilian caught in the chaos.

"Ma'am, are you hurt?" he asked quickly, before turning to the children. I shook my head, unable to speak. My throat burned with the weight of the moment. Six years ago, I had saved him in silence. And now, here he was, saving eighteen more lives without ever knowing the thread that bound us.
To see the ripple effect of what I was doing, to see those souls in action, helping others, spreading hope – it made me realize how incredibly purposeful this mission really was. Even if it didn't spread far or wide… it made an impact.

Together, we lifted the children that hadn't made it up the ravine yet, passing them up to waiting arms. Kevin steadied the driver, helping to pull him up the ravine. His voice was calm, commanding, the voice of a man who had returned to his calling.

When the last child was safe, Kevin helped both of us climb back up the ravine, mud streaked across his gear, me soaking wet and muddy from head to toe. At the top the cold air hit like a wall. My body shook. The paramedics came over to me quickly and gave me a blanket to wrap up in and gave me a check over.

"Are you sure you don't want to come to the hospital for tests ma'am?"
I replied, "No, I just want to get home to my son."

The next few days were the worst… I thought I could tough it out and still take care of Eli through this, but after the first day I called my mom and asked if she could come to help.

The pain never really subsided, and I found my state of consciousness going in and out. I would shake violently, different parts of me would ache, throb, and scream in pain. The bathtub was my solace, my refuge in the thick of it.

Eli would come into my room and check on me when he woke up, before he left for the school day, when he got home from school, before dinner, before bed… I'm so blessed to have such an amazing son looking over me.

It took a full week for it to become even somewhat manageable, but I was so glad to be out and back to a somewhat normal routine. I knew this would be a long recovery full of bumps along the way. It didn't matter though… it was worth it knowing seventeen kids and a driver who cared for those kids daily were safe.

*Souls 71–88: February 14, 2017. School bus accident. Seventeen children and one driver. All unconscious or severely injured. Kevin VanderLeest returned, firefighter, soul from January 2011. Saved.*

# 27.

November 21, 2018. It has been almost two years since the bus accident. My body has not been the same. The toll of pulling eighteen souls from the river left me hollow for months. The mark has been quiet, almost mercifully so. I have lived in solace, enjoying letting Eli grow into his own rhythm, watching him step into his junior year of high school. He is seventeen now, full of life and joy, and continuing to explore what he might want to do outside of high school.

This morning, I was sipping my Kona coffee when a post appeared on my Facebook feed. It was one of those warnings' parents share, urging others to protect their children from the latest social media challenge. The headline read: *"Prevent Your Teens from Trying the Choking Challenge."*

I almost scrolled past. But then I saw the name.

*Noel Lincoln.*

The article went on to describe Noel had participated in the choking challenge and that she had developed Unresponsive Wakefulness Syndrome (UWS) according to the doctors at the

Owatonna Hospital in Minnesota. She lives near the southern border of Minnesota, and she was seventeen years old. She is a senior in high school and has just been accepted into Berklee College of Music for cello. The doctors never expect her to survive without being on life support.

I stared at her photo. A girl with long auburn hair, a cello resting against her shoulder, her eyes bright with the kind of hope only youth carry.

I knew what I had to do.

☼☼☼☼☼

Thanksgiving was the next day, so I wanted to get there and back by tonight. This year my mom was hosting Thanksgiving, so Eli and I were heading over the next morning to help set up. I called mom quickly and asked if I could drop Eli off today instead and then I'd be there tonight. She said that it was fine, and Eli was happy to go help his grandma with prepping food. Not that he needed a sitter anymore by any means, but for us all being together and not knowing exactly how long this would take – well it just seemed like the best solution.

By late morning, I was driving north. The roads stretched endlessly, the November sky heavy with gray clouds. My hands trembled on the wheel, from anxiousness of never knowing how saving this soul would go. I've had plenty of practice, but every time is so different and going into an unknown situation is always nerve-racking.

I arrived at Owatonna Hospital in Owatonna, Minnesota and needless to say the visiting rules were the same as any hospital, but thankfully her parents had allowed visitors to her room so her classmates and teachers could come visit. The sweet older woman at the information desk gave me her room number and gave me directions to the nearest elevator. Room 412.

I made my way along the corridors to Noel's room. When I got there the door was closed, but there were no signs saying that you needed special permission to enter, etc. I also didn't see any family members in the room, but it was right about lunch time.

Noel lay motionless, machines humming beside her. Her skin was pale, her lips parted slightly, her chest rising only because of the ventilator. Tubes and wires surrounded her, a fragile metaphorical orchestra keeping her alive.

I stepped closer, my breath catching. I thought of her cello, of the music she had dreamed of playing, of the acceptance letter she must have held with trembling hands. I thought of her parents, sitting vigil, praying for a miracle.

I placed my hand gently on her arm, and I prayed for her to wake, prayed for her body to heal, prayed for her to realize this was a mistake; to help urge others to not meet the same fate. I prayed for her to go on and spread music and joy to those around her. The surge was immediate, violent. My knees buckled, my lungs seized, and I gripped the bedrail to keep from collapsing. The mark burned across my back.

Minutes passed like hours. Then her fingers twitched. Her eyelids fluttered. A faint sound escaped her throat, not from the machine but from her own breath.

The monitors shifted, alarms sounding, nurses began rushing in. I stepped back, trembling, my body hollowed out by the effort. I walked out into the hallway, and I saw a pair of middle-aged people rushing down the hall as they saw the red alarm above what I assumed was their daughter's door. I can only imagine the fear washing over them right now, but I know soon that the fear will turn into inexplicable joy.

I quietly drove the almost four hours to my parents' home. I

197

knew that tonight would be restless. I couldn't help but think about the music I might one day hear from this beautiful soul.

I arrived just in time to watch my parents and Eli finish their game of Greed. I joined them for another round. We rolled dice, laughed, told stories, and enjoyed our time together. I knew the next few days might be difficult – so I wanted to soak up the moment as much as I could. Grateful for everything I've been given.

**Geneva Daily Chronicle**

**November 25, 2018**

**Local Teen Survives Dangerous Social Media Challenge, Now Advocates for Awareness**

*By Sarah Jensen, Staff Writer*

GENEVA, MN — Just days ago, 17-year-old Noel Lincoln lay in a hospital bed in Owatonna on life support after attempting a viral social media challenge known as the "choking game." Doctors warned her family that the oxygen deprivation had caused severe brain damage and that recovery was unlikely.

Today, Noel is breathing on her own, speaking, and determined to use her second chance to warn others. "I don't want anyone else to go through what I did," Noel said in a statement released by her family. "I gave in to peer pressure, a moment I thought might help me relax, to take some of the stress off my plate. It didn't do that. It's not worth the risk. I almost lost everything — my music, my future, my life."

Noel, a senior at Geneva High School, had recently been accepted into Berklee College of Music in Boston, where she planned to study cello performance. Her accident shocked classmates and teachers, many of whom described her as a gifted musician and a role model.

Her recovery has been described by medical staff as "remarkable." Noel has already begun speaking with local schools and youth groups about the dangers of social media challenges.

"She's turning her pain into purpose," said Principal Karen Meyers of Geneva High. "Students listen to her because she's one of them. She knows how quickly a moment of curiosity can turn into tragedy."

Noel's parents, who spent days at her bedside, say they are grateful for the community's support and hope her story will prevent other families from experiencing the same fear.

The Lincoln family has partnered with local organizations to launch a campaign called "Breathe Free", aimed at educating teens about the risks of oxygen deprivation games and encouraging parents to talk openly with their children about online trends.

Noel plans to continue her advocacy even after leaving for college. "Music is my passion," she said, "but awareness is my mission now."

*Soul 89: November 21, 2018. Owatonna, Minnesota. Noel Lincoln, social media challenge. Permanent brain damage. Life support. Saved.*

# 28.

April 12, 2019. The air smelled of rain and fresh plants, the kind of spring day when the ground still remembers winter. Eli had borrowed the car for school and rehearsals, and I knew it was overdue for an oil change. That morning, I dropped him off at school, and I drove to a small garage on the edge of town, the kind with faded signage and a row of dented toolboxes lined against the wall.

The waiting area was cramped, with a single counter and a coffee pot that had burned itself into bitterness. I sat down, listening to the clatter of wrenches and the hiss of compressed air from the bays. That's when I noticed him.

A man walked in from the shop floor, his hands wrapped thickly in gauze, the bandages stained faintly at the edges. He moved stiffly, his shoulders rounded, his jaw clenched as though every step carried weight. The other mechanics glanced at him; their eyes filled with something between respect and sorrow. I caught fragments of their conversation. *"Mike… crushed both hands… saving the kid."*

While my car was being worked on, I asked the receptionist quietly what had happened to him. She told me there was a new technician that had been working under a transmission lift, securing bolts that should have been locked in place. Something slipped. The heavy casing lurched forward. Mike saw it happening and shoved the young man clear and took the weight himself. His hands were caught between steel and concrete. The sound of bones breaking echoed through the shop. By the time they pulled him free, his palms were mangled, his fingers bent at unnatural angles. The new tech came away unharmed, but Mike's hands were ruined.

"He just got out of the hospital for the third time. He has had too many surgeries to count. He wanted to come say 'hi' to everyone. They said he has a lot of physical therapy left, and that even with it he'll never be able to pick up a wrench again. I think what hurts him the most is that he loved to teach new techs all about the job... give them a love for it, ya know?"

"Ya... I understand." I replied.

I watched him talking with some of his coworkers. His friends. He was gently smiling, but his eyes were hollow, the eyes of a man who had built his life on work he could no longer do.

✺✺✺✺✺

I waited for an opportunity, and he came over to say goodbye to the receptionist and then headed out the front door, the chime dinging overhead. I got up and I followed him outside, my voice low. "You saved him," I said.

He turned, startled, as if he hadn't expected anyone to speak.

"Excuse me, ma'am?" he replied.

"You saved that tech."

"...um... yes, I suppose I did."

"I'm so sorry about your hands."

He looked down at his hands, "I'm just glad the boy is alright."

I reached out, resting my hand lightly on his shoulder, as if I were reassuring or comforting. I prayed for his bones to knit, for

201

his tendons to remember, for his hands to reclaim their strength. For him to go back to being able to mentor young technicians and to inspire. The mark flared across my back as it was erased. My hands seared, pain shot up my arms and into my neck. A tear fell from my eye. I staggered for a moment.

"Are you okay, ma'am."

I shook my head to try and shake away the pain. "Oh my gosh, yes," I played it off, chuckling a little. "Sorry, just an inner ear infection or something making my equilibrium a little off today." The chimes of the door rang out again. "Dalene, we have your car all ready for ya," the receptionist hollered from the door.

I looked back at Mike. He was flexing his hands. "I wish you all the best Mike. You deserve it." I walked towards the door. Mike stood there staring at his hands, and then he began unwrapping the bandages…

The next few days my hands were on fire, immobile from pain. I could hardly do anything with them. I kept soaking them in warm water trying to wash away the pain. It helped them to feel better, but after so long of being out of water the pain would return.

Eli asked what happened. I had to lie to him, which I don't like doing, and told him I must be getting some arthritis. I told him I would schedule an appointment with a doctor to have it checked out, which I plan on doing regardless. If nothing else to always uphold the promise to my son.

*Soul 90: April 12, 2019. Auto mechanic. Hands crushed saving a new tech. Saved.*

# 29.

October 27, 2019. The air carried the sharp bite of late October, the kind that makes every breath feel thinner, edged with smoke from neighbors burning leaves. Eli is eighteen now and will be graduating in May of 2020. He talks often about Iowa State in Ames — mechanical engineering, the possibility of continuing his music there with the marching band and their programs. His eyes light up when he describes the labs, the campus, the percussion program. I smile when he talks, though inside I ache. Ames feels far away. Too far. But I know it would be best for him. He needs space to grow, to test himself, to find his own rhythm.

This summer was heavy. Larry Byrnes — Eli's grandpa, my late husband's father — passed away. His absence has left a hollow place in all of us. Phyllis has been restless since then. Their house feels too big, too quiet, too full of memories. She's been visiting senior living communities nearby, places with activities and companionship, places where she wouldn't feel so alone.

On one of her visits, she came home with a story. A friend had told her about a man named Mr. Wayne.

*Katie Espinoza*

Mr. Wayne was a custodian at her friend's granddaughter's school, but he was more than a custodian. He worked at West Carroll Primary and High School in Savanna, Illinois. He wasn't just the man who swept the halls or fixed the lights. He was the one who showed up at every game, every concert, every play. He cheered for the kids as if they were his own. He knew their names, their stories, their struggles. Teachers said he was a friend to the faculty, a steady presence in the background of their days.

He wasn't supposed to retire for another five years. He didn't want to, but rheumatoid arthritis had taken its toll. His joints were swollen, his hands stiff, his knees refusing to carry him through the long hours of work. The doctors told him he couldn't continue. The pain was too severe. He would be retiring right before Thanksgiving.

The children cried when they heard. The faculty grieved. He had become part of the fabric of the school, and now he was being pulled away by a disease that showed no mercy.

I thought about him for days after Phyllis told me. I imagined him sitting at home, his hands and knees wrapped in heat packs, his body aching, his heart heavier than his bones. I imagined the silence of the school without him, the empty space in the bleachers where he used to sit, the quiet hallways missing his laughter.

I knew what I had to do.

November 1, 2019. I woke up early and drove to Savanna. The town was small; the streets were lined with brick buildings and fading storefronts. The school sat at the edge of town, its

204

windows glowing faintly in the autumn light.

I walked into the office and a middle-aged secretary sat behind the desk. Her face was rounded and her dirty blonde hair surrounded it. She had beautiful brown eyes that lit up when she spoke.

"How can I help you?" she asked.

"Do you know where I could find Mr. Wayne? Or could you ask if he could come to the office?"

"Sure thing. Is he expecting you?"

"Um… not exactly."

She looked at me, her brown eyes filling with confusion, but after a moment she reached for the phone and the loudspeaker crackled overhead: *"Mr. Wayne, please report to the office."*

I waited in a nearby chair. Minutes later, he appeared in the doorway. His steps were slow, his posture weary, his hands swollen and stiff. He looked surprised to see someone waiting for him.

"Mr. Wayne?" I said softly.

"Yes," he answered, his voice was rough. "Can I help you?"

"I heard your story from my Mother-in-law," I said. "How much you've meant to the school. How much the children love you. I wanted to meet you."

He gave a tired smile, the kind that carried both pride and sorrow. "They're good kids. I wish I could stay. But my body… it won't let me anymore." He lifted his hands slightly, the joints swollen, the fingers bent. "I can't even hold a broom without pain."

I asked if we could step outside. He looked puzzled but agreed. Together we walked through the office doors into the crisp October air. The parking lot was quiet other than the autumn wind rustling the leaves.

We stood near the edge of the lot. He rubbed his hands slowly, wincing. "Where are you from?" He asked.

"I live in a small town in Iowa."

"My silly 'ol arthritis story made it to Iowa huh? And you drove

205

all this way to meet me?"

"I think you have more of an impact than you know."

He smiled gently. "I don't know what I'll do now," he admitted. "This school was my life."

I reached out, and took his hands in mine, reassuring, and as I did, I prayed for his joints to loosen, for his hands to remember, for his body to release the pain that had bound him. For him to be able to continue being a shining light, and a person that students and faculty could always count on. For him to be able to decide when his time to retire was.

I winced and my body contorted, but I tried to hide it as much as I could. The burning sensation fired to life as the mark erased off my back. My joints felt tight, stiff, and painful. Then it all released and the pressure wore down, my heart rate steadied, and the pain subsided. I knew it would return, but for now things were better.

"I'm sorry that this is happening to you. I just wanted you to know that your dedication to this school, to the students, the faculty is an inspiration to so many. I just needed to let you know that there are so many supporting you."

As I was speaking Mr. Wayne began to stretch out his shoulders and back. He began to shift his feet. I let go of his hands and he stretched his fingers and rolled his wrists. "It was so wonderful to meet you in person Mr. Wayne. I wish nothing but the best for you in the future." I quickly touched his arm and then turned and walked back to my car, watching him in my rear-view mirror as I drove away. He looked up, tears streaming down his eyes. He waved.

☼☼☼☼☼

Around midnight the pain began. My joints began to ache, every part of me was stiff. My knees, wrists, and fingers felt swollen. I slowly got up and out of bed, creeping into the bathroom. I ran the hot water in the tub and lowered myself in.

The water felt amazing. I let it surround me.

    I reflected on my journey thus far, and the years that had passed. The people I had encountered and how fast Eli was growing up. I had eight unknown souls left, and then this journey was done.

*Soul 91: October 27, 2019. Savanna, Illinois. Mr. Wayne, custodian. Rheumatoid arthritis. Forced retirement. Beloved by students and faculty. Saved.*

# 30.

April 14, 2020. The world feels different now. Streets are quiet, churches closed, schools empty. Masks cover faces, and fear lingers in every conversation. COVID-19 has changed everything.

Eli is finishing his senior year online. His teachers send assignments through email and video calls, but it isn't the same. He sits at the kitchen table with his laptop, headphones on, tapping his pencil against the wood as if he were back in class. He should be walking the halls with his friends, rehearsing for concerts, planning senior pranks. Instead, he studies alone.

Graduation will not be like normal. The school announced they will arrange an outdoor ceremony for anyone who wants to come — a stage set up in the football field, chairs spaced apart, families watching from a distance. Eli says he wants to go. He wants to cross that stage, even if the bleachers are half-empty and the applause muffled behind masks. I ache for him, for all the seniors who lost the ending they deserved. But I know he will carry with him this year, a reminder of resilience.

✿✿✿✿✿

Our church has been gathering donations — masks, gloves, hand sanitizers, even homemade meals for staff who barely have time to eat. Today I volunteered to deliver supplies to the hospital in Oskaloosa. The building itself looked weary, its windows glowing faintly against the gray spring sky. Signs at the entrance warned of restricted access. I carried boxes of donations and headed towards the main doors.

Inside, the atmosphere was tense. The front desk staff thanked me quickly, their voices muffled behind masks. They pointed me down the hall for donation drop-offs. The halls smelled of disinfectant, sharp and sterile. I could hear the hum of machines, the shuffle of hurried footsteps, the muffled coughs from behind closed doors.

As I turned down a corridor near the ICU, it happened. A young respiratory therapist, no older than thirty, staggered against the wall. Her mask slipped as she coughed, her body collapsing from exhaustion and fever. She had been working nonstop, intubating patients, monitoring ventilators, carrying the weight of too many lives. Just feet away, a middle-aged man in his forties sat slumped in a wheelchair, his chest heaving, his lips tinged a greyish color. He had been waiting for a bed, alone, no family allowed inside. His eyes were pointed towards the ground, but wide with panic – he couldn't get air but was too weak to call for help. Too weak to even reach for his throat.

I dropped the box and rushed forward. I ran to the man first, dropped to my knees and placed my hand on his arm and prayed. Prayed for immediate relief, for his lungs to fill, his fever to fade, his strength to return. The mark erased with a burning sensation, and my chest heaved in pain. A tight burning feeling rushed through it and went into my head. It felt like it was on fire like I had a fever. And then it washed down my body and morphed into chills that ran down my body.

As soon as it passed, I got to my feet shakily and half crawled and half walked to the nurse. I got to her and fell to my knees and placed my hand on her arm. I prayed for her strength to

209

return, for her hope and faith to be restored, for her body to heal, the exhaustion to vanish and the fever to dissipate. Another mark surged across my back as it erased. The immediate rush of exhaustion came over me; the fever came back and then faded again. I sat there for a moment and then slowly rose to my feet.

I grabbed the donation box and quickly continued down the hall; checking over my shoulder as I went. I saw them both sitting up looking at each other. Then the nurse got up and ran over to the man helping him sit back up in the wheelchair.

On my drive home I was thinking about if Azariah or God meant for me to save those two souls. I don't believe in coincidences though, and I have to think I was there at that time for a reason. At this point I truly believed that Azariah trusted who I chose.

Over the next couple weeks I struggled to breath properly, I felt feverish non-stop, and I was exhausted. I pushed through for Eli. We were closing in on his graduation on May 23rd. His graduation party will be on the same day. Outdoors at a park so that family and friends can come and be with him.

*Soul 92: April 14, 2020. Oskaloosa, Iowa. Respiratory therapist. Collapsed from exhaustion and infection. Saved.*

*Soul 93: April 14, 2020. Oskaloosa, Iowa. Middle-aged man. Severe respiratory distress. Saved.*

# 31.

October 10, 2020. The leaves have turned, and the air carries the sharp scent of harvest. Cornfields stretch golden across the highways, and every roadside stand seems to overflow with pumpkins and gourds. Eli will be nineteen in just seven days. He calls from Ames when he can, his voice bright with excitement about mechanical engineering classes, though I can hear the fatigue too. He talks about labs, about equations, about the hum of campus life. He says he misses home, but he is where he belongs. I think about his birthday often — how different it feels to celebrate with him away at college, beginning his own life.

I drove northeast today, nearly three hours, to Dubuque. The church had asked for volunteers to work unloading food boxes and helping restock the local food and clothing pantry and helping organize all the new donations of clothes. It was right on the Mississippi River and had a beautiful view, but the Mississippi looked restless, its surface rippling under the autumn wind. Barges moved slowly, their engines humming, ropes creaking against the docks. The air smelled of diesel and river water, sharp and metallic.

As I carried boxes toward a small warehouse, something

drew my attention over to a nearby barge. It was docking. I saw a man reaching over the barge trying to help secure it. He was in his forties, broad-shouldered, the kind of worker whose life had been shaped by the river.

My body began to tense as I watched. I subconsciously set the box I was carrying down. I began walking towards where the barge was. Then it happened. He slipped. The barge was swaying with the river, and he was trapped between the heavy vessel and the pier. Thankfully, not smashing him against the pier completely, but pinning him. His coworkers pulled frantically, their boots scraping against the dock as they tried to free him. His face was pale, his eyes wide with terror, his lips already darkening. I ran.

"Get him out!" one shouted, voice breaking. Another crossed himself quickly, the look of panic was etched across his features. They managed to loosen the ropes enough to drag him onto the dock, but his breathing was ragged, fading. His coworkers hovered, helpless, their hands trembling. Another was on the phone with the police.

I made it over to him, sliding on the wet dock as I came to a halt by him. I knelt down next to him. I pretended to put my head to his chest as if I were listening, and at the same moment I put my hand on his arm and I prayed. I prayed for his body to be restored, for his breath to return, for his chest to expand, for his body to be healed. The mark ignited up my back as it erased. My body heaved with agony. My chest felt as though it was collapsing. My whole body felt as if it were being crushed.

Minutes stretched. The river's humming seemed to fade, the shouting dulled to silence. Then his chest lifted, steady, his breath deepened, his eyes fluttered open. His coworkers gasped. One knelt beside him, tears streaming down his face. Another whispered, "It's a miracle."

The man blinked, confused, then coughed, his voice hoarse but alive. He reached for the dock with trembling hands, as if to anchor himself back to the world.

As everyone checked on him and the police arrived, I backed away slowly. I walked back to where I had left my box. Picked it up and carried on.

The church had us staying in a church in Dubuque. They had cots set up for us, but I knew that I wouldn't be able to stay there. I drove home that night instead. There was more work to be done the next day, but I explained that I wasn't feeling well and wanted to be better before Eli's birthday. I was going to drive to Ames on the 17th and have dinner with him.

The drive home was long, the fields rolling past in silence. I thought of Eli, of his birthday just days away, of the wonderful man he was turning into. Life is such a mystery… a beautiful mystery.

*Soul 94: October 10, 2020. Dubuque, Iowa. Riverboat worker. Crushed against pier. Saved.*

# 32.

May 3, 2021. Spring has returned to Iowa. The fields are waking, tractors rumbling across the soil, and the air carries the scent of rain mixed with fertilizer. Eli is nineteen now, deep into his second semester at Iowa State. He calls when he can, his voice bright with talk of mechanical engineering projects — systems that withstand pressure, equations that hold structures together. I think of him often when I drive past barns and silos, wondering if he notices them differently now, through the lens of design.

The house feels emptier without him. His laughter, his music, even the sound of his footsteps, all gone. I have decided to volunteer more frequently now, filling the silence with purpose. The church always has needs — deliveries, food drives, outreach — and I find myself saying yes to nearly everything. It keeps me moving, keeps me from dwelling too long on the quiet.

Today I traveled northeast, nearly three hours, to Cedar Rapids. The church had asked for volunteers to deliver supplies to a farming family recovering from a rough season. The roads wound past endless fields, the horizon broken by the tall silhouettes of silos.

When I arrived, the farmyard was buzzing. Tractors were moving, farmers and farmhands were moving equipment and beginning to unload corn. I took the supplies up to the farmhouse and handed the supplies over to the wife and children inside. As I was getting ready to leave, shouts carried across the yard. Dust hung in the air, thick and choking.

A grain silo had partially collapsed during unloading. Corn poured out like a flood, burying men waist-deep, beams splintering, dust rising in suffocating clouds. Three workers were trapped inside.

The foreman, a man in his fifties, was pinned against the wall, his chest compressed, his breath shallow. A young farmhand lay unconscious, his face gray from dust inhalation, his body limp. A truck driver, caught under a fallen beam, gasped in pain, his legs trapped, his voice fading.

The air was thick with panic. "Push! Lift!" the workers shouted, their voices hoarse. Together they strained, shifting the beam inch by inch, shoveling grain away until at last the men were dragged free. But their bodies were still, their breaths fading. I ran towards the three men. I knelt down next to them, and I did the same thing I did at the dock. I pressed my ear against the foreman's chest pretending to listen to his heartbeat. I pressed my hand on his chest and I prayed. I prayed for his body to expand, to heal, for his breath to be restored. The mark raced up my back as it erased. My body jolted with pain, but I had to keep going.

I moved over to the farmhand; he was wheezing and couldn't get his breath right. His face was ashen. I pressed my hand to his chest and I prayed. I prayed for the dust to lift out of his body, for his breath to be restored, for his lungs to open. The mark burned as it was erased. My chest and throat felt tight, and my lungs felt like they were collapsing in. I moved on to the driver.

The drivers' legs were crushed, his eyes were rolling back, and he was clearly in shock. His breathing was ragged at best. I

215

placed my hand on his chest, and I prayed for his legs to be restored, for his body to calm, for his mind to be clear again. The mark raged as it erased and my legs felt like they were flattening. My breath was short. I fell back and sat on the ground. The mother and children were outside helping prop the men up and getting them water. The police and emergency management showed up.

As the emergency crew began checking on the men I again backed away, got in my car, and left. The silo loomed behind me, broken and spilling, a reminder of how quickly strength can collapse.

*Soul 95: May 3, 2021. Cedar Rapids, Iowa. Foreman. Chest crushed in silo collapse. Saved.*
*Soul 96: Young farmhand. Dust inhalation, unconscious. Saved.*
*Soul 97: Truck driver. Trapped under beam. Saved.*

# 33.

January 9, 2022. Winter has settled deep across Iowa. The fields lie bare, the rivers edged with ice, and the air carries a sharpness that cuts through every breath. Eli is twenty now, back in Ames for his second year at Iowa State. He speaks with excitement about mechanical engineering, about projects that challenge him, about the independence of living away from home. I am proud of him, though the house feels emptier than ever. His absence echoes in every room, and I continue to volunteer to help fill the void.

I had agreed to deliver supplies westward, toward the edge of Nebraska, where the church partners with a small outreach group near the interstate. The sky was heavy with snow clouds, the kind that promise trouble. As I drove, I thought of Eli — of how quickly he has grown, of how his life is unfolding beyond my reach.

By late afternoon, the storm whipped up suddenly. Wind howled across the highway, snow slashed sideways, and the pavement turned slick with black ice. Cars slowed, hazard lights flashing, but visibility was poor. I took my exit and travelled down a few miles and that's when I saw them.

A silver sedan sat buried in a snowbank, its hazard lights blinking weakly through the snow. That is about all I could see, and honestly, I was surprised to even be able to see that much. All four doors were packed around with snow, just the back lights were visible. The trunk was even covered with snow. Probably from when the car hit snow it came over the top of the car.

I pulled over, turned my hazard lights on, and I checked my phone for a signal – none. I had no choice; I stepped into the storm. The wind whipped around my body, the sleet stinging my face. The temperature had plummeted to negatives, and with the wind chill it had to be more. There was no exhaust coming out, which told me they either ran out of gas or the car stopped running when they crashed. My boots sunk into the drift as I approached the car.

I couldn't see inside the car. The snow drift came up to my upper thigh. I went to the back driver's side door and wiped as hard as I could to get the snow off the window. It was hard packed and heavy, but I finally got it cleared off enough to see inside. I pressed my face close to the glass, squinting through the frost. Two figures sat motionless inside. The driver's head was slumped forward against the air bag, his shoulders rigid. The passenger lay tilted against the seat, her face pale. It looked like she had a head wound. There was no air bag on her side that had deployed.

My heart pounded. I clawed at the door handle, but the snow was packed tight against it. I dug with my gloves, scooping handfuls of icy crust until my fingers were numb, but I could finally wedge the door open just enough to slip inside. The cold air rushed out, sharper even than the storm outside.

The cabin was silent. No hum of the engine, no warmth from the vents. Their breaths were shallow. I leaned across the driver, pressing one hand to his chest, the other to the woman's arm. I prayed for their bodies to warm, for their lungs to fill, for their bodies to heal, and for their happiness to continue. The two marks emblazoned across my back as they erased. My body felt frozen solid, like my soul itself had been sucked out of me.

Seconds stretched into eternity. The wind howled, sleet rattled against the windows, and the world blurred into haze. Then — The man coughed, his chest lifting, his eyes wide with shock. The woman gasped, her face regaining color, her forehead wound healing and leaving nothing but some dried blood. They looked at each other, looked back at me, and then they clung to each other, tears streaming, whispering words of disbelief. "It's okay," I said. "Are you both able to crawl back here and get out this back door? I can drive you to a nearby hotel for the evening. You can call for help there."

They nodded their heads and we climbed through the door and to my car. They grabbed her purse, a small suitcase in the back seat and a bouquet of flowers wilted from the cold.

The heater in my car blasted warmth as we drove slowly through the storm toward the nearest hotel. The road was treacherous, black ice glistening beneath the headlights, snow swirling in sheets across the windshield. My hands gripped the wheel tightly, every mile a battle against the storm.

In the back seat, they held each other close, whispering softly. When their voices grew steadier, they told me their names were Doug and Josie, and they told me their story. They had been married only days ago. Their rings still gleamed, new and un-scuffed, catching the faint glow of the dashboard lights. They were heading west to Colorado for their honeymoon, eager to see the mountains, to begin their life together with adventure. The storm had caught them by surprise, the black ice sending them into the snowbank. With no phone service, they had waited, growing weaker, believing no one would come.

"Thank you so much for stopping to help us. You saved us."
I smiled.

## Katie Espinoza

☼☼☼☼☼

At last, the hotel lights appeared through the storm. I pulled into the lot, the tires crunching against packed snow. Inside, warmth and safety waited. I watched them check in, their hands clasped tightly together, their voices soft with gratitude.

Before disappearing into the lobby, the wife turned to me. She thanked me profusely before leaving to go to their room for the night.

☼☼☼☼☼

I decided it was best for me to check in for the night as well. I'd leave in the morning to finish the delivery. I walked to my room. I knew what was coming. Cold, soul consuming frigidness would be consuming my body soon. So, I did what I always did. I took a bath. I immersed myself in the hot water, washing away the pain. The day. Then I began crying softly to myself...

These are the last two souls before my final save. One last mark on my back. Ninety-nine souls I've saved, and it all comes down to the inevitable. What I knew from the beginning would be the ending. What Azriah told me the very first day. The ending I always knew would happen. The ending I agreed to, but now... it just seems so real. It is here.

*Days away?... Weeks?... Months?*

I didn't know. I didn't have a timeline. I just new it was coming... approaching.

Please understand that these tears do not mean that I regret my decision. I don't regret choosing to say *yes*. I don't regret this journey I've been on.

The weight of the unknown was still there though. Eli's life

220

is just beginning, but mine feels as though it is moving toward something inevitable.

*Soul 98-99: January 9, 2022. Western Iowa highway. Newlyweds. Black ice accident, trapped in snowbank. Saved.*

# 34.

# Flashback

I opened the door to the Cozy Cafe and the door chime jangled above our heads. I walked in confidently but then realized I had no clue what I was walking in to. The worry, anxiety, fear coursed back through my body. I stood frozen in the doorway a minute, gazing around looking for a middle-aged man. There was an elderly couple in the corner booth drinking coffee, a mother and young daughter peering at the doughnut selection in the glass display, and what appeared to be a businesswoman sitting at the table by the front window drinking a smoothie, typing frantically on a laptop. I grabbed a highchair from the wall, and we sat down at a booth on the opposite wall of the elderly couple. Eli sat in the highchair and played with a toy I had brought on the table. I glanced up at the clock on the wall: *8:55am.*

The time seemed to stand still. Every second seemed to take minutes. A man walked in at 9:00am exactly, but he didn't even look around. He walked straight up to the counter and ordered a coffee and a breakfast sandwich. He paid and then walked to a table in the center of the Cafe and sat down. I studied him for quite some time, watching his movements. He was probably in his late thirties, wavy brown hair, slight bags under his eyes, black square-rimmed glasses, and blue flannel button up under his heavy winter jacket. He pulled a newspaper out from his inner jacket, removed his jacket, and slung it over the back of the chair. He pushed up his glasses on his nose and unfolded his paper to begin reading the front page. The edges of his mouth twitched while he read. The waitress brought over his coffee and breakfast sandwich, he looked up, smiled, and thanked her. I turned back towards Eli who was busy trying to chase around his toy on the table. I poured out a few Cheerios for him onto a napkin. I looked back up and the man appeared to be frozen. He held his coffee cup midair as if he were about to take a drink but was lost in thought; or about to have a stroke. His eyes looked dull and didn't shine anymore; lifeless. I was about to stand up and go see if he was okay when he suddenly shivered like a chill ran down his spine. His eyes lit up again and he set his coffee cup back on the table, setting his paper down. The man stood up and turned and walked towards Eli and me. He sat down in the booth across from me.

I stared at the man across from me. Now that he sat in front of me, he seemed older than his thirties, maybe early forties would be more accurate. Crow's feet around his eyes, and now up close he had speckles of gray across his brown hair. He brought his hand up to his glasses and removed them from his face, rubbing his eyes with the other hand.
"I do not know how this man sees out of these."
I stared at him, mouth agape. There it was, the deep, calm, smooth voice. "Azariah?" I questioned.
"Yes, hello. My apologies as I adjust to this body a moment," he shook his head a bit and rotated his neck. "Alright, I don't have much time in this body, so I need you to listen closely," he said in a very low serious voice.
I nodded my head in agreement. An impulse at that moment.
"None of which I am telling you will be repeated to anyone, and if you don't agree with something I say please let me know and your life will go back to normal immediately and you won't remember any of this."

I sat up in my seat and leaned on the table a little more, "okay."
"The world is in a bad place. It lacks hope, faith, and humanity.
God sees this and feels that something needs to be done before
the world crumbles. He has chosen twenty people across the
world to help restore faith in humanity. These are people who
have lost significantly, people that want only the best for others
and that will put others first always. People like you. This journey
comes with rewards and disadvantages along the way. The 100
marks on your back represent lives of others. God is trusting you
to choose who you save, but He will give you suggestions and
choices along the way as needed. This journey will take several
years to complete. When you find someone that you feel needs a
second chance you simply place your hands on them and in your
heart and mind pray for them to be cured. You cannot bring
anyone back from the dead. The disadvantages of this will be that
whatever they were going through..." he paused, "you will too."
"What do you mean?" I asked.
"I mean if someone has cancer, and you decide to cure them you
will feel the effects of the cancer. You won't have cancer, but you
will feel sick as if you did. This could go on for days depending
on the severity of the condition in which the person you save is
in. That is why this journey will take you so many years to
complete. Your body will need to rest along the way, before
saving others. The advantages of this journey are clear. You will
be able to help restore humanity and faith to those around you and
help others as you so much enjoy doing. You will be taken care of
and provided for. You will not have to worry about your home,
food, etc. At the very end of your journey, when the last mark on
your back is left, we will reward you with something that you
have wanted for so long. Something you have dreamed of, prayed
for, but it too will come with a cost. You will be able to save your
own son. You will be able to cure his Hypoplastic Left Heart
Syndrome. He will be able to live a full life free of heart issues,
but it must be the last soul you save. This journey will result in
your death. After you save Eli, you will pass away. I can't tell
you about his or your future. I can't tell you if Eli will live
without you saving him. Regardless, of whoever you save for
your 100th soul this journey will end the same way. Everlasting

peace for your soul. God is choosing twenty people based on their lives, who have experienced great loss as I said, but also with someone they wish more than anything to save. I know this is a lot to process. Do you have any questions so far?"

"Uh... sorry this is just a lot... I..I don't think so."

"I unfortunately need to know now if you are willing to do this journey or not."

"What if I have questions after you leave?" I asked.

"You pray. You pray about your question, and we will answer."

I stared at him for a moment. I looked at Eli and he looked up at me and smiled. He was so sweet and innocent. What would his mom being sick all the time do to him? Would he understand in the end?

"Dalene... I apologize for the shortness of this chat, and my 'to the point' directions, but I really do need an answer," he stated, "I do apologize, I understand this is a monumental decision, but I can't keep this man's body forever, and the longer you think the more time I will need to erase if you choose not to do this journey."

I went with my gut and ended up blurting out, "Yes. Yes, I will do the journey," more loudly than I anticipated.

"That is wonderful news," he smiled. He stood up, "thank you for doing this. You will do wonderful." He walked back towards the table where the man had sat prior, returning the glasses to the man's face that he had removed, and sat back down. The man froze again for several moments and then he blinked a few times. He sat there for a moment contemplating, shrugged, and returned to his paper and coffee.

# 35.

October 19, 2022. The leaves have turned, and autumn has settled across Iowa. Eli turned twenty-one just three days ago. We celebrated quietly, a small gathering at home, his smile faint but still present. He is slowing down now. His body cannot keep pace with his mind. Hypoplastic Left Heart Syndrome has caught up with him, and though he has fought bravely, the strain is visible in every step, every breath.

Classes at Iowa State have become harder for him to attend. He misses more lectures than he makes, his energy drained by appointments in Omaha and Des Moines. The cardiology clinic knows him by name; the hospital staff greet him like family. He is on the transplant list, waiting, hoping, but the wait feels endless.
I knew this day would come. Azariah told me long ago, in that café, when Eli was still a toddler chasing Cheerios across the table. He told me the journey would end with my son. He told me the cost.

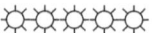

I drove Eli to Omaha for his appointment. The sky was

gray, the air sharp with the bite of fall. We didn't speak much on the way — he stared out the window, headphones in, lost in thought. I kept my hands tight on the wheel, praying silently for strength.

The exam room was quiet except for the hum of the fluorescent lights. Eli sat on the table, his shoulders slumped, his face pale. I sat beside him, clutching my purse tightly, waiting for the doctor to speak.

Dr. Reynolds entered, his expression serious but kind. He pulled up a chair and sat across from us, folding his hands. "Eli," he began gently, "we've been monitoring your heart closely. The latest tests show that your left ventricle is deteriorating faster than we expected," Eli looked down at his hands, silent.

Dr. Reynolds continued, his voice steady. "You've been on the transplant list for some time, but now it's critical. You need a new heart as soon as possible. Without it, your body won't be able to keep up much longer."
Eli swallowed hard. "So... what does that mean? Weeks? Months?"
The doctor shook his head. "It's hard to predict. But I want you to understand — this isn't something we can wait on anymore. We'll be pushing your case forward, making sure you're prioritized. You'll need to limit your activity even more, and we'll schedule you for closer monitoring here and in Des Moines."
I reached for Eli's hand, squeezing it. His fingers trembled in mine.
Eli finally spoke, his voice quiet. "I thought I had more time."
Dr. Reynolds leaned forward. "I know this is overwhelming. But you're strong, Eli. And we're going to do everything we can to get you back on your feet. You're not alone in this."
Eli nodded slowly, his jaw tight. "Okay. I'll... I'll do whatever I have to."

227

The doctor gave a small, reassuring smile. "That's all we ask. We'll walk this with you."

The drive back to Ames was the same as the drive to Omaha, silent and full of thought. When we reached his dorm, I parked and walked with him to the front of his building. Before he went upstairs, I pulled him into a hug — tighter than I had in years. He stiffened at first, then melted into it, his arms wrapping around me.

"I love you, Mom," he whispered.

I closed my eyes, holding him close, and prayed. I prayed for his strength, for his future, for his heart to be made whole. I prayed silently, knowing this was the moment Azariah had told me about so long ago. The mark didn't burn this time. It didn't ignite… it merely disappeared – fading into an abyss. There was no pain.

"I love you too, Eli."

Before I went to bed I wrote a letter to Eli. I put it in a manila envelope and addressed it to Ray Montgomery, and I put it into the mailbox. I then sent an email to Ray Montgomery. He was now living a full life, and he started the program *Second Chance 4 Veterans*. I didn't want Eli to find me, and I knew that Ray would understand better than anyone. He would call someone, and when he received my letter to Eli, he would mail it back. He would delete my email to make sure no one knows my secret.

October 20, 2022. The next morning, I would not wake. At home, in my bed, the journey would end. My body would be still, but my soul would be at peace.

Eli's heart is now whole. He would live.

*Soul 100: October 19, 2022. Omaha, Nebraska. Eli, my son. Hypoplastic Left Heart Syndrome. Saved.*

# 36.

## Eli

I closed the journal slowly, my hands trembling as the final words blurred through my tears. The leather cover felt heavier than it should, as if it carried not just her handwriting but the weight of every soul she had saved.

Mom.

All those years, all those moments when she disappeared for hours, came home exhausted, or seemed to carry pain she never explained — they weren't just random. They were the journey. The marks. The lives she gave back.

And me. I was the last.

I pressed the journal against my chest, my heartbeat steady, strong, whole. For the first time in my life, I could feel it without strain. No pounding, no gasping, no fear. She had given me this. She had given me life.

But the cost...

She knew. She knew from the beginning that this journey meant her inevitable death. And still, she chose it. She carried that knowledge for all those years.

I remember the hug. October 19th. She held me tighter than she ever had before. I thought it was just because of the doctor's words, the transplant news. I didn't know it was goodbye. I didn't know she was praying over me, finishing her journey at that moment.

Her words echo in me: *"Live your life, Eli. Live it fully."* I don't know how to do that without her. But I know I have to try. She didn't save ninety-nine souls just to give me a chance at life for me to waste it. She didn't endure the pain of every sickness, every injury, every collapse just for me to sit in grief. It was time to take that *Tour de Overseas* trip. I know that is what my mom would have wanted.

I set the journal down and looked out the window. The autumn leaves swirled in the wind, golden and fleeting. For the first time, I felt the air fill my lungs without struggle.

For the first time, I felt alive.

And I whispered into the silence, "Thank you, Mom.

# 37.

## Eli

Florence was alive with winter light. The streets glowed with strings of lamps, the air carried the scent of roasted chestnuts, and the chatter of Italian voices echoed through the narrow alleys. I ducked into a café to escape the chill, the warmth wrapping around me like a blanket.

Mom and I had planned this trip for years — Italy, then onward to other countries. We traced routes together, circled cities on maps, dreamed about the food, the art, the history. Now I was here alone, carrying her memory with me.

I ordered a coffee and sat near the window. The cup warmed my hands, but my chest still felt hollow. I thought of her journal, of the words that had changed everything. *100 Souls.* Her journey had ended, but mine was only beginning.

The door opened. A man walked in — mid-forties, brown hair streaked with gray, glasses slipping down his nose. He ordered a cappuccino, thanked the barista, sat down, and then froze mid-movement, cup in hand.

My breath caught. I waited… it felt like déjà vu. I knew this moment. I had read about it.

He shivered, blinked, and turned. His eyes locked on mine. He walked straight to my table, sat down, removed his glasses, rubbed his eyes. The voice was unmistakable. Deep. Calm. Smooth.
"Eli," he said.
"Azariah," I whispered.

✡✡✡✡✡✡

He leaned forward, his gaze steady. "I'm here to tell you more about your mother's journey. It is complete, and she is at peace, but there are things you must understand about her journey. Things that might help explain that journal she wrote a little bit better. Make things clearer."
I swallowed hard, my fingers tightening around the cup. "Tell me."
Azariah nodded. "Her name, Dalene, carries echoes of Magdalene. Mary Magdalene was a follower of Jesus, a woman from Magdala. Your mother's name tied her to that lineage — a woman of devotion, of sacrifice, chosen to walk closely with God's work."
I felt my throat burn. "She always said names mattered."
"That is probably why she named you Elijah. Elijah is a name that carries weight. It means 'the Lord is my God.' It comes from a prophet who stood unshaken in his faith, who called down rain when the skies were dry, who raised the dead when hope was gone, and who defied false gods on the mountain to prove God's power. Even his departure was extraordinary — carried to heaven in a chariot of fire. Your mother chose that name because it speaks of strength, of devotion, of a life meant to remind others that God is real and present. She believed you would carry that truth in your own way."
I sat there trying to soak everything Azariah was saying in. Not aware of anything but his words.

233

"She passed on October 20th," Azariah continued. "The number twenty often marks a waiting period, a season of struggle before release. Her life was a long waiting, a patient endurance, until the day came when she gave her last gift — you."
He paused, eyes steady
Azariah's voice softened. "She was born in March, the third month. She died on the twentieth. Ephesians 3:20 reminds us that God can do immeasurably more than all we ask or imagine. Her life was proof of that — she asked for all their lives back, and God gave more than she could have dreamed."
He leaned back, folding his hands. "And the numbers — the tenth, the day of her birth, and the twentieth, the day of her death. Matthew 10:20 says it is not you who speak, but the Spirit of your Father who speaks in you." He paused, "Eli, her words, her prayers, her touch — they were not hers alone. They were God's Spirit working through her."
I wiped my eyes, my voice breaking. "She carried all of that… and never told me."
Azariah nodded. "She carried it so you could live free of it. That was her gift."

I didn't know what to say. How to react, other than to continue crying softly. Azariah continued.
"And water — you saw it in her journey. It wasn't only about healing or refreshment, Eli. Water has always been the sign of new life. In baptism, it washes away the old and marks the beginning of the new. It cleanses, it renews, it declares that someone belongs to God. Your mother's touch was like that — not just easing pain, but offering renewal, a kind of rebirth. Every soul she saved carried the mark of being made new, just as baptism reminds us that we are raised into life again. And when the burden of another soul nearly broke her, water was often what restored her — usually in the form of a bath. It gave her strength to rise again, to keep going, to continue the mission she had been given."
I sat in silence, the weight of his words pressing into me, yet strangely lifting me at the same time.

Azariah reached into his jacket and pulled out a book. He slid it across the table. The cover was deep blue leather, the title gleaming in gold: *Eli's Awakening*.
I froze. I knew that handwriting. It was hers.
"This isn't mine," Azariah said softly. "It's your mother's. She wrote it for you — about you. About the journey she saw unfolding in your life. She wanted you to have it when the time was right."

My hands trembled as I touched the cover. Another journal. Another piece of her voice reaching across the silence.

Azariah stood, placing the man's glasses back on his face. "Her journey ended, Eli. Yours is beginning. This journal is her gift to guide you."

He turned, walked back to where the man had been sitting, and sat down. For a moment he froze, then blinked, shrugged, and returned to his cappuccino as if nothing had happened.

✿✿✿✿✿

I sat alone at the table, the book before me, the café buzzing around me. I opened the cover, my heart pounding. In her beautiful script, the first page read simply:

*This is not the end. It is the beginning.*

*Katie Espinoza*

# Author's Note

    This book is kind of a mix of my life. It has names of important people in my life. It has my mother, who was an angel on this earth. She passed away in 2020 from Cancer. She was forgiving of everyone, always helping, and always doing God's work. It has my own son who has Hypoplastic Left Heart Syndrome. There is no cure. This book kind of fell into my mind, coincidentally while I was having a particular rough week and I was taking a long hot shower. I'm not sure why it was put into my mind, but it has taken me almost three years to finish due to life, hesitation that it would be accepted amongst all the other incredible authors in this world, and my own personal emotional and mental journey as I wrote the words.

*Katie Espinoza*

# Acknowledgements

I want to take this time to thank my children. I want to thank them for always going with my crazy ideas. I'm always trying new things, whether it is trying a new recipe, buying a cow, or writing a book. They are always supportive of everything I do. I love you all.

I want to thank my mom and dad for always supporting me in my dreams growing up. Even when they failed miserably and I came running back home lost in life. From joining the military to purchasing a small business and writing books. You've always supported my ideas even if you didn't think they'd pan out. I love you.

To my grandparents who always loved me, showed me how to bake, made me a card shark, and ignited my creative spirit. I appreciate your love, your support, your kindness, your expanding my mind and helping me grow up. I love you all.

To my crazy neighbors who love me in my worst and best times. Who always encourages me and shows me love and support. From listening to me vent, giving me hugs, loving my children like your own, for volunteering for things you don't always want to do, but doing anyway to support me. I love you all. Thank you.

To my communities of support from my church family, the parents that fill the heart warrior and angel groups, my neighbors, families that I grew up with, and friends, I appreciate each one of you supporting me and helping me grow into myself.

And most importantly to my husband. Without you by my side and being my biggest supporter I don't know if I ever would have finished this book or published it. I can't thank you enough for being my partner in chaos, for loving me through all the ups and downs, and for loving life with me. Thank you for accepting me as I am – even if it throws chaos into your life. I love you with all I am.

# About the Author

Katie lives on a farm in Iowa with her husband and six beautiful children, three cows, two turkeys, and a peacock in a mulberry tree. Multitudes of chickens and barn cats. She loves traveling, photography, working out with her neighbor, and spending time with her family.